THE HEART OF IT

Also by Barry Hines

THE BLINDER

A KESTREL FOR A KNAVE

FIRST SIGNS

THE GAMEKEEPER

THE PRICE OF COAL

LOOKS AND SMILES

UNFINISHED BUSINESS

THE HEART OF IT

Barry Hines

MICHAEL JOSEPH
LONDON

MICHAEL JOSEPH LTD

Published by the Penguin Group
Penguin Books Ltd, 27 Wrights Lane, London W8 5TZ
Viking Penguin Inc., 375 Hudson Street, New York, New York 10014, USA
Penguin Books Australia Ltd, Ringwood, Victoria, Australia
Penguin Books Canada Ltd, 10 Alcorn Avenue, Toronto, Ontario, Canada M4V 3B2
Penguin Books (NZ) Ltd, 182–190 Wairau Road, Auckland 10, New Zealand

Penguin Books Ltd, Registered Offices: Harmondsworth, Middlesex, England

First published in Great Britain 1994

Typeset in 12/13 pt Baskerville by
Datix International Limited, Bungay, Suffolk
Printed in England by Clays Ltd, St Ives plc

ISBN 0 7181 3640 3

For My

Mother and Father

The house had been damp[illegible] advertised [illegible] where the people who [illegible] the top. Number one [illegible] [illegible] the way. Nu[illegible] its two dogs [illegible] [illegible] Monty [illegible] [illegible]

The houses had been demolished. A peeling hoarding advertised FACTORY UNITS TO LET, but Cal remembered the people who used to live there. He started at the top. Number one: Mr and Mrs Betts who had once fallen through the chemist's shop window on their way home from the pub. Number three: old Mr Curtis and his two dogs Monty and Patch. They used to work as a team. Monty ran at you barking while Patch sneaked up from behind and bit your ankle. Number five: Mrs Ellis whose husband had been killed down the pit . . . And so on, down the row to number seventeen where Cal had lived as a boy until the family had moved to the new council estate on the edge of the village.

Across the road, the rec. was still there, with a row of swings and roundabouts at one end and the football pitch taking up the rest of the park. Cal started the car. It was many years since he had played on that pitch, but as he drove through the village on to the council estate, all the ancient insults he had suffered from the other boys flared up inside him and made him blush.

He turned down Attlee Way. When he had left home and gone to university in London, he hadn't even known the people who lived in the same house. He had loved it. The freedom. He had been so pleased to escape.

He stopped outside his parents' house and got out of the car. A gang of youths, sitting on a wall opposite, were throwing bricks at a bottle in the road. They stopped throwing and stared at him and Cal wondered if they were going to start throwing at him instead. But they were distracted by the appearance of a cat in the next garden and Cal turned away and walked down the path towards the house, relieved that the car he was driving was hired and not his. He went round the back and opened the kitchen door. The only time he could remember the front door being opened was once when they'd had a new sofa delivered and the men couldn't manoeuvre it through the kitchen into the living-room. He recalled how different the room had seemed with the door open: lighter and noisier as if it was part of the street.

Hello!

It was his mother from the living-room.

Karl?

Yes, it was. Well, technically at least. But only his family called him that now.

He walked through into the living-room and met his mother coming out to meet him. She hugged him. She started to cry and her tears stained the lapel of his pale cotton jacket.

Thank goodness you're here. I thought you weren't coming.

Cal looked over her shoulder at the bed against the wall where his father was lying, then walked across the room and looked down at him. He was shocked by his appearance. His hair had turned white and the stroke had twisted his face into a leering grin. He looked like a reflection in the Hall of Mirrors.

Dad . . .?

His father made no response. He didn't even blink. He just stared through Cal as if he was invisible.

Cal turned round to his mother. Can he hear me?

She crossed the room and stood beside him. He can hear you. It's speaking that's the problem.

Shouldn't he be in hospital?

There's no point. They say he's out of danger now and the nurse comes every day to wash him and feed him. Anyway, he's better off at home with me looking after him.

She wiped a trickle of spittle from his chin.

Pitiful, isn't it? A man of his stature reduced to this. Mind you, he's made a marvellous recovery. He was in a coma for two days. He'll be up and about in no time, won't you, Harry?

Again there was no response, and looking at his father's tortured features Cal found it difficult to believe that he could understand the question, let alone reply. Seeing his father in such a helpless state depressed him. The house depressed him. The place depressed him. He had been back for only a few hours and he wanted to leave already.

Has our Joe been over to see him?

Of course he has. There was an edge to her voice. He's been nearly every day.

Is he still living in Leeds?

Manchester. He hasn't lived in Leeds for years.

Cal walked across to the window and watched the gang of youths running up the bonnet of his car and launching themselves off the back. A man walked by without a second glance as if this was a normal pastime in these parts.

Are you stopping for your tea?

No thanks. I'd better get back to town. I'm expecting some phone calls.

You could have stopped here, you know. It's ridiculous stopping in a hotel. Especially the George. It must cost a fortune.

The thought of sleeping in the cold back bedroom which he used to share with his younger brother Joe depressed him even further. Outside, one of the boys on top of the car saw him and waved. Cal waved back. He didn't know whether to laugh or cry.

Cal drove the two miles back into town. The George, to which his mother had referred, had been renovated since the last time he had been home. The stone façade had been cleaned. A striped canopy decorated the entrance and the name had been changed to the Rio.

There were two messages for him at the desk: one from Hélène and one from his agent. He went up to his room and phoned Hélène. He glanced at his watch while he listened to the dialling tone. Five o'clock – six o'clock in France. He could see the telephone on his desk, the jug of dried lavender and the picture on the wall above it.

Hello. He smiled at the sound of Hélène's voice. Yes, I thought you might be. That's why I let it ring . . . It's hard to say. He looks terrible. His face is all twisted. He looks as if he's been struck by lightning . . . Pleased to see me! I wasn't even sure if he knew I was there. And even if he did, I doubt if he'd have said anything . . . He laughed at Hélène's protests. You don't know him. We've hardly spoken for years . . . I'm not sure. I'll have to stay for a few days at least. It'd look a bit callous if I came back straight away. He looked at his luggage which lay on the bed unpacked. I wish I was leaving tomorrow. It's a right dump, the whole place is on its last legs . . . Cal laughed again. Last legs? It means dying, finished, *fin*. He sat down on the bed and took off his shoes while Hélène told him the day's news and how much she was missing him already . . . Cal smiled. Yes . . . Yes! . . . Don't worry. I'll be home soon . . . OK . . . Love you too. Bye . . . Suddenly, he felt desperately homesick even though he had only been away for a few hours. Hélène! But he was too late. She had already hung up.

Cal phoned his agent. He was in a meeting. His secretary said he would ring back. Cal stared at the print of *The Haywain* on the wall. Now what? Take a bath? Do some work on the script? He switched on the television and watched a story on the local news about plans for a new shopping complex on the old Foxmoor colliery site being under threat, because the developers had doubts about possible subsidence. Cal imagined it: huge cracks suddenly appearing in the floor of Tesco's and shoppers being swallowed up still clutching their trolleys. He had included a similar scene in an earthquake film he had once written called *Quake Rattle and Roll*.

He wondered if his father was watching the programme. He hoped not. Even though the stroke hadn't killed him, the prospect of a shopping centre replacing the pit, where he had worked all his life, might.

The following morning, Cal went to see his father again. His mother was helping the nurse to dress him. Cal couldn't bear to watch. It was embarrassing to see an adult, especially his own father, in such a helpless state.

Put your arm through, Mr Rickards . . . That's it . . . Good boy. Now then, where do you want to sit?

They helped him to the armchair by the fire and carefully sat him down. This was his appointed place and had been for as long as Cal could remember. Anybody sitting there when they heard the back door open, including his mother and the dogs they had kept over the years, immediately got up and went to sit somewhere else. Cal could see him now, bending over and unfastening his shoes as he pursued an argument started earlier at a union meeting, at work or in the pub. A formidable figure in his time, difficult to recognize in the stricken creature before him, helplessly staring into the fire.

When the nurse had left, Cal crouched down by the side of the armchair and touched his father's arm.

How are you feeling, Dad? Are you any better?

He did not respond.

Go in front of him, Karl. So he can see your face. And you've no need to shout, he's not deaf.

Cal moved round to the front of the chair and faced his father. He could feel the heat of the fire down his side. Mr Rickards slowly turned his head and stared at him. Cal smiled.

Hello, Dad . . .

Before he could say any more, his father opened his mouth and started to make gasping, choking sounds. Cal thought he was having a fit or something and looked round at his mother in alarm, but she was smiling at her husband and nodding at him encouragingly. He persevered; it was painful to watch him, but eventually he found his voice and the words stumbled out:

W-w-when-are-you-going-to-write-something-that-matters?

He flopped back, exhausted by the effort.

Cal stared at him in disbelief then turned furiously to his mother. Did you hear that?

She was smiling. I know. Isn't it marvellous?

Marvellous?

She nodded. She had tears in her eyes. It's the first proper sentence he's said since his stroke.

Yes, he's probably been saving it up until I got back. He never lets up, does he? I travel all the way from France to see him and that's what I get.

What did you expect? You know what he's like.

It's nothing to do with him what I write.

He's disappointed in you, Karl.

It's none of his business! What does he want – *War and Peace*?

I don't know. But it's done him the world of good seeing you.

Good! Well, in that case I can go back to France now then, can't I?

He turned quickly and left the room.

Karl!

But she was too late. The back door slammed, shaking the house, and moments later she watched him through the living-room window striding furiously up the path and out of the gate. As Cal was unlocking the car door, he noticed that the gang of youths were sitting on the wall again across the road.

And you lot (pointing over the top of the car)! Touch this fucking car again and I'll kill you!

He got in and drove away. Right! That's them sorted out! And my dad can go to hell as far as I'm concerned. He was considering whether to fly back to France today or tomorrow when the brick shattered the back window. He hunched his shoulders instinctively at the impact and momentarily lost control. There was laughing and cheering behind him and through the rear-view mirror he could see the youths jumping up and down in the road. As he accelerated out of range, the back of his neck was burning with shame. He had never been convincing as a hard man.

Cal drove around for a while to calm down, then returned to the hotel and went into the bar. A ceiling fan revolved above empty tables and the only customers in the room were two businessmen sitting on high stools at the bar. Cal ordered a beer. He watched the barman filling the glass. He had big scarred hands and his shirt cuffs were turned back revealing a pair of shapely legs tattooed on his forearm. Cal thought he recognized him. The barman turned round and caught him staring. Cal looked away. Perhaps the barman thought he was gay. It could be a dangerous tendency in a town like this. He felt compelled to say something when the barman brought his beer.

Excuse me, don't I know you from somewhere?

Then, for an instant, the boy eclipsed the man and yes, he was right.

It's Charlie Thomas, isn't it?

The barman looked surprised. Cal didn't look like anybody he would know.

Cal . . . Karl Rickards.

The barman gave him a long, hard look. Well, bugger me! So it is.

As they shook hands across the bar, Charlie's sleeve rode up, undressing the nude tattooed on his forearm.

What you doing here? I haven't seen you for donkey's years.

Cal told him about his father's stroke. Charlie had already heard about it and hoped he would soon get better.

He was brilliant during the strike, your dad. It wasn't his fault we went back, I can tell you. He'd have stopped out for ever. And your Joe. I haven't seen him for a long time either. Not since he split up with Christine.

He lives in Manchester now.

We worked together for years, me and your Joe.

You were always good friends, weren't you?

We were in the same year at school together. Started at the pit together. It's closed down now, Foxmoor.

Yes, I know.

There's millions of tons of coal still down there, you know. It's criminal. Excuse me a minute . . .

One of the businessmen had attracted his attention and he walked along the bar and refilled their glasses. When he returned Cal said:

It must be a big change, working behind a bar after the pit.

You've to take what's going, haven't you? I've got four jobs on the go just now.

Four! Cal found it hard not to laugh.

Charlie counted them off on his fingers. This job. Window-cleaning. Gardening. And I'm a bouncer at the Roxy. And I'll tell you something else, Karl. The money from all four jobs put together doesn't add up to a living wage.

He produced a dish from behind the bar and filled it with peanuts from a big bag.

Remember them games of football we used to have in the rec?

Cal smiled and took a peanut. Yes. Mind you, I can't say I was much good. I was always last choice and shoved out on the wing somewhere.

You didn't have to be any good, did you? You were clever. It didn't matter to you.

It did then.

It mattered desperately. He was the odd man out in his school blazer. How he had wanted to be like the others.

Charlie pulled himself a glass of bitter. They were right games them. We used to come home from school and play through till dark (Cal didn't. He was usually doing his homework), and on Saturdays, they'd go on all day. Players coming and going . . . Charlie smiled at the memory of those marathon games with teams rising to twenty or more at some times of the day, falling to four or five at mealtimes. Finally, when they had played themselves to a standstill and it was time to go home, the result would be more like a cricket score.

What are you doing now then, Karl? What kind of work are you in?

Cal paused, chewed a peanut. I'm a writer.

What do you mean, a reporter, that kind of thing?

No. I write film and television scripts.

Anything I might have seen?

I don't know. I did four episodes of the Agatha Christie series that has just been on television.

Charlie shook his head. No. I don't like that sort of thing. There's no action. I like American detectives best.

I did a couple of episodes of *Miami Vice*. Did you ever watch that?

Yes. That was great stuff.

Charlie was impressed. He refilled the bowl of peanuts. And do you write under your own name then?

Cal hesitated, then nodded. It was near enough his own name, and there was no point in complicating matters. Sometimes he wished he had used a pseudonym when he considered some of his credits. There was the undertaker film for a start, *Over My Dead Body* . . .

Mind you, you never notice who writes a film, do you? I mean it's not like writing a book, is it?

It was a question for a film festival debate. Cal gave him the short answer. I suppose not.

Charlie pointed at Cal's empty glass. Same again?

No thanks.

The beer had gone straight to his head. The peanuts had given him heartburn. He missed Hélène. He wanted to go home. But as much as he hated his father, he owed it to his mother to stay for at least a few more days.

Charlie offered him a cigarette. Capstan Full Strength. Cal refused.

You wouldn't believe some of the things that happened during the strike, Karl. You should write a story about that.

Cal went up to his room and phoned Hélène. He felt better after they had spoken. She was missing him too, but she agreed that he should stay a little longer for his parents' sake. Abscess makes the heart grow fonder, she said. It was an intriguing diagnosis, and he was still smiling when he sat down at his word processor. But then, his French wasn't perfect either.

He was writing a script about an American brat who is turned into a dog by a crazy professor, after the boy plays one cruel trick too many on the professor's pet dog. It was called *It's a Dog's Life*. Cal read the last scene he had typed before he left France.

INT. PROFESSOR KNUTT'S LABORATORY. NIGHT.

PROFESSOR KNUTT is angrily dragging TOBY across the room towards the 'Transformation Chamber' which resembles a diving bell and is fitted out with wires and tubes and flashing lights etc.

PROFESSOR KNUTT

That's the last time you'll ill-treat
my dog! I'll teach you a lesson
you'll never forget!

TOBY

Help! Mom! Pop! Save me!

PROFESSOR KNUTT

You can scream and yell as much as you like! Nobody'll hear you here!

PROFESSOR KNUTT opens the door of the Transformation Chamber and pushes TOBY inside, locking the door behind him. TOBY bangs and yells to be let out as PROFESSOR KNUTT makes final preparations, checking various dials and switches on the operating machine. Finally, he is ready.

PROFESSOR KNUTT

OK boy! Are you ready?

PROFESSOR KNUTT throws a switch. The Transformation Chamber begins to rumble. Lights flash; the chamber is enveloped in smoke. The lights stop flashing and the smoke gradually clears. There is no sound from inside the Transformation Chamber. Pause. Then PROFESSOR KNUTT crosses the room and unlocks the door. Pause. Then a dog runs out. TOBY, the boy, has been transformed into TOBY, the dog. It stands there, a nondescript mongrel, looking round bewildered.

TOBY

(Voice Over)

Help! What's happening?

But when he starts to speak, the words come out as barks.

PROFESSOR KNUTT
(grinning)
Perfect!
(He opens the laboratory door)
OK, hop it. Let's see how you get
on out there.

TOBY rushes out of the laboratory, barking furiously.

When Cal went to see his father the following day, Joe was at the house. They shook hands.

Hello, Karl. Sorry, it's Cal now, isn't it? Cal ignored the question. Nice tan you've got. Still, I suppose you get a lot of sun in the south of France. Mrs Rickards handed Cal a cup of tea. Don't start, Joe.

Cal added some more milk but it was still too strong. It would have matched a burnt umber paint sample. He took a sip, then looked round for the old aspidistra which was the usual dumping ground for leftovers and unwanted drinks, but it was no longer in the room.

How's my dad? He walked across to the bed where his father lay asleep. I think he looks a bit better.

He was lying. He looked worse with his eyes closed, like a damned soul suffering purgatory. Cal turned away and had another sip of tea. He looked as if he was taking medicine.

Joe poured himself another cup and lit a cigarette. My mother says he seemed pleased to see you.

Cal wasn't sure whether he meant it ironically or not. I wouldn't have interpreted it that way myself.

Mrs Rickards fetched Joe an ashtray. The picture on the transfer had been worn beyond recognition but Cal knew that it was Tower Bridge. He had bought it for his father on a school trip to London. He had considered buying one with a picture of Buckingham Palace on it, but he doubted if his father would have seen the joke. It was his first trip to London, and after that visit he dreamt of living there.

Well, at least he showed a bit of life, Karl, that's something.

I'm not surprised. He was always the golden boy, our Karl.

Don't be silly, Joe. He treated you exactly alike.

Cal felt annoyed. They were talking about him as if he wasn't there. He tried to change the subject. I saw Charlie Thomas yesterday. He's working in the bar at the hotel.

I told him, Joe. It's ridiculous stopping in a hotel when we've a spare bedroom here. It'll cost a bob or two there, I can tell you.

She was right. It did. Almost as much as the hotel near Grasse where Cal and Hélène had met Ronnie Bax, the American producer, to discuss *It's a Dog's Life*. But what a difference! Ronnie had reserved a table on the terrace with a view across the wooded hills towards Cannes. The waiters recognized Hélène and fussed over her, telling her how much they enjoyed her films and asking what was she working on next. As they crossed the terrace towards their table, people paused and looked at her. It was always the same. Ronnie was enchanted by her. Who wasn't? Men felt important and expansive in her presence. They made fools of themselves trying to impress her. She was good to have around when deals were being struck, and anyone observing their conversation that evening would have thought that Ronnie was doing business with Hélène.

They watched the sun slide behind the hills, and as the light softened and faded into night, the sky glowed softly in the distance over Cannes . . .

Joe stubbed out his cigarette in the ashtray, obliterating the remains of Tower Bridge. What do you expect? You don't think a famous writer's going to stop in a council house, do you?

It's nothing to do with that. It's more convenient to stay in a hotel, that's all.

It's a wonder there isn't a plaque on the wall outside saying, Karl Rickards lived here.

Mrs Rickards shook her head.

If there's going to be a plaque outside this house it'll not be our Karl's name that'll be on it, it'll be his.

She pointed at the bed. Cal and Joe turned round and looked at their father, who was awake, watching them. They didn't know if he had been listening or not, but his silent stare reduced them to boys again and immediately ended the argument.

Cal gave Joe a lift into town. Cal was relieved he wasn't driving his Merc.

My van's off the road. It needs taxing.

What are you doing now?

A bit of this and that. Anything that's going.

As they passed the rec., Joe smiled. It was the first time he had looked relaxed all day. We had some right matches in there . . .

A pack of dogs ran between the goalposts. The lead dog had something in its mouth. A fight broke out near the swings.

Cal drove Joe to the railway station. They sat in silence for a few moments in the car park looking through the windscreen at a vacant office block across the road.

The strike knocked the stuffing out of this place, Karl. Destroyed it. It was like a police state round here. The government were determined to win at all cost. They already had the police and the army out against us. They'd have brought the navy and the air force out if necessary. When you try to tell people what it was like, they don't believe you.

Cal was in Los Angeles during the strike, working on a new adaptation of *Jack the Ripper*. One evening he was having a drink in a bar with Eva, a production assistant he had met at the studio. She had visited England: London, Oxford and Stratford. Real cute, she said. There was more to England than that, Cal said. Next time she was over there, he'd like to show her round. Yeah! I'll bet! she said. They laughed. They were getting along fine. Cal was drawn to a news item about the miners' strike on television. There was footage of a picket line followed by an interview with the NUM president, Arthur Scargill. The man sitting on the stool next to Cal raised his middle finger at the screen.

Commie bastard!

Cal let it pass. He was a big guy.

It's about time those lazy bastards got back to work.

Cal thought about his father and Joe. He was incensed! He couldn't let him get away with that! But he did: and it was Eva who intervened.

Why don't you button it, mister?

You talking to me, lady?

Yeah. I'm talking to you.

They were talking across Cal. He leaned back to get out of their way.

You a Commie too?

It's nothing to do with Communism. Those guys are just fighting for their jobs.

Bullshit! It's a Commie plot to bring down the government.

Yeah. They probably took lessons from the CIA.

What's that supposed to mean?

Chile, Nicaragua, Panama. Nobody does it better than us.

Hey! Careful what you're saying, lady. That's the United States government you're talking about.

So what? Asshole!

She threw her drink in his face. Cal was knocked off his stool as the man jumped up. The barman and some of the other customers cooled things down and Cal and Eva left the bar.

Later, when Cal told the story at parties, he always played Eva's part.

Joe looked up at the station clock. I'd better be going or I'll miss my train. He opened the car door but remained in his seat. They say the pen is mightier than the sword, Karl, but I know which I'd sooner have been holding when I was arrested during the strike.

Cal couldn't argue with that.

It's been good seeing you, Karl.

Yeah. Look after yourself, Joe.

When are you going back?

I'm not sure. I'll be here a few more days.

Go round and see Christine before you leave. She'll be pleased to see you.

Yes. I will.

Joe got out of the car then ducked down at the open door. Try and make it up with my dad, Karl. I know he's been a bastard, but he's an old man now. You'll never forgive yourself if you don't.

He slammed the door and crossed the station concourse with his shoulders hunched and his hands in his jacket pockets, pulling it tight across his back and stretching the seams of the cheap material. When he reached the ticket barrier, he turned to wave but Cal had already left and was on his way back to the hotel.

He phoned Hélène straight away. He was missing her. She was missing him. His dog Bruno was missing him too. He was just mopping around, Hélène said. Cal grinned. That'll save Annette a job then. Hélène didn't get it. He won't eat his dinner and he's missing his walks. Cal was missing his walks too . . . Up through the dark pine wood at the back of the house, with Bruno ahead of him seeking fresh scents. Then out of the trees into the blinding heat, and the steep climb over rocky ground to the top of the mountain. He rested there and sometimes watched eagles riding the thermals in the shimmering sky above the valley . . .

After he had spoken to Hélène, Cal poured himself a whisky from the mini-bar then stretched out on the bed and thought about the strike, and what a profound effect it had had on his family. He thought about the occasion four? five? years ago when he had flown back from France for his parents' ruby wedding anniversary. They had had a meal in one of the reception rooms downstairs – it was still called the George then – and in the bar afterwards, expansive and boastful after several pints, his father told him about when the first scab went back to work.

We'd been out for months but the strike was still solid. Not a single man had gone back at our pit. Then one morning we were on picket duty, six of us, all legal like, when three police vans came down the lane. They drove straight past us into the pit yard and stopped outside the offices. Then somebody jumped out of one of the vans with his coat over his face and ran inside. We realized what had happened then. They'd driven a scab in. We were bloody furious. The word went round like lightning and next day hundreds turned up. We built a barricade but it made no difference: they just smashed through it and got him in again. There was a right battle. Dozens of our lads got arrested. They didn't half get some stick!

Of course it was in all the papers next day. Miner goes back to work, strike crumbling, that sort of thing. It didn't say that it had taken a bloody army to get him back in, though. There was a massive propaganda war going on, and once they got a man back, they made sure he stopped back. From the outside it looked as if we were losing heart and men were breaking ranks and drifting back. They just made things up. If the pit cat caught a mouse they classed it as a working miner.

I went in to see McLintock the manager. I knew him well. He'd been at the pit a long time. He was getting ready for retiring, like me. So he says to me,

Now then, Harry, what can I do for you? I said I've come to see about that scab who's gone in. There's this copper in the office as well. Inspector Tolson they called him. He was a right bastard, he was. They'd got video equipment set up in the office so they could monitor the picket line, and there was a chart up on the wall showing where everybody who worked at the pit lived. They'd turned the manager's office into a bloody police station! So Tolson says to me, Don't you mean working miner? I said no, I mean scab.

Cal's father had a drink of beer and licked his lips, anticipating the memory of the confrontation. Cal looked round the bar. Family friends and relatives were sitting around in raucous groups. Somebody had started singing. There was a fair chance of a fight before closing time. Cal was thinking about the French actress he had just met at the première of a film directed by a friend of his. She had been cast as a small-town librarian, and when they were introduced before the screening, he thought she looked too attractive, too special, for the part. But when he saw the film he soon changed his mind. She was totally convincing, and if he had gone to borrow a book, he wouldn't have given her a second glance. He congratulated her on her performance at the party afterwards. They spent most of the evening together, and arranged to meet again when he returned from England.

. . . McLintock says, Anyway, what about him, Harry? I could see that he didn't like Tolson either. He'd taken over, it was obvious. I said, I'd like to know if he's in our branch or not. For all we know, he might not even work at this pit. He could be a ringer you've brought in so the press can say somebody's gone back to work. Tolson says, We're disclosing no names of working miners for fear of intimidation. So I said to him, Intimidation! Don't talk to me about intimidation. We've got the government against us. The Coal Board against us. The law against us. The media against us. And the police against us. You can't get much more intimidated than that. Tolson says, We're not against you. I just looked at him. I thought he was taking the piss! You what? Not much you're not. Why have you got two hundred men out there then, just to get one scab back to work? It's obvious whose side you're on. We're on nobody's side; we're here to keep the peace, he said. I said to him, I'll tell you the best way to keep the peace. Tell that scab to stop at home. There'll be no trouble then. I could see that McLintock wasn't very happy at what was going on. I think if it had been left to us, we'd have been able to sort it out between us. But it was out of his hands now. It had turned into a police operation. He said, Look, Harry, we've got to break this deadlock somehow. We've got to get this industry back to work. I said, There's nothing we'd like better. Our members have gone skint, gone without food and gone into debt, fighting for their jobs. If this pit closes down, what do you think we're going to do? There's no work round here and no prospects of any either. Now then, are you going to give me that scab's name? Or have we to find out who he is ourselves? McLintock shook his head. He doesn't want to talk to you. I said, You mean you've told him not to talk to us. Tolson comes up to me then, threatening like. He was eating Polos. I could smell them on his breath. He said, Listen, Rickards, we know all about you. You're nothing but a troublemaker. We know you're a Communist. We know you're an agitator. And if you get arrested like you did during the last strike, you'll not get away with a fine this time, I can tell you . . . Well, I was a bit shocked at that, Karl, I must admit, knowing they'd got a file on me. It was like being in . . . He paused. Cal looked at him sharply. Surely he wasn't going to renounce . . . But no, his party loyalty swiftly reasserted itself . . . I said to him, What's your fucking name, J. Edgar Hoover?

*

As he was driving past the rec. the following day, Cal thought about the boys he had played football with and wondered what had happened to them. There was Bob Markham, who ran past players as if they weren't there. Jack Lacey, who could head a ball further than Karl could kick it. And little Ronnie Harrison, who never took his coat and cap off and wore braces on his teeth.

Suddenly, he thought about something else and got an erection . . . He was playing in goal. Somebody shot wide and the ball ran down the steep bank into the bushes. He ran after it but he couldn't find it among the undergrowth. He could hear the others shouting from the pitch for him to hurry up. Then he spotted it under an elder bush, and as he pushed aside the branches and picked it up, he revealed Jack Collins and Mary Hanson lying in the grass. Jack was leaning back on his elbows with his trousers open, watching Mary suck his cock. When they heard the leaves rustling, they looked up, startled. Karl just stood there with the football in his hand, transfixed. Mary was still holding Jack's cock. Her jumper and bra had been pulled up and Karl stared at her tits. They were bigger than his mother's and she was only a girl! When they saw the little boy standing in the leafy shadows, they laughed and relaxed. Looking straight at him, Mary slowly raised her skirt and opened her legs. Karl blushed and went hot all over. Mary flicked out her tongue and beckoned him with a wagging finger. Karl turned and fled back up the bank to the football pitch. The others shouted at him and wanted to know what had taken him so long. If he had told them, they would have been down the bank in a flash, the match forgotten.

He let in three quick goals after that (his mind was on other things) and his team were forced into choosing a new goalkeeper. He was banished out on to the wing where he never received a pass for the rest of the game. He was like a linesman: he stayed level with the play but never touched the ball.

Cal was still thinking about Mary and Jack when he reached his parents' house. He looked down at his crotch as he walked down the path and tried to think about something else. He thought about the burnt-out car he had passed at the end of the street, and wondered if it was meant as a warning.

His mother was standing at the table trimming a bunch of roses when he walked in. She was alone in the room, and for a brief, irrational moment, triggered off by the sight of the flowers, Cal thought that his father had died.

Where's my dad?

He's in the toilet.

Cal was relieved to hear it, but more for his mother's sake than his own.

She held up a rose. I love roses. Get that vase out from under the sink, Karl, while I go and see if your dad's all right.

She left the room and went to the lavatory which led off the hall. Cal could hear her talking to his father. Her tone was cajoling and flattering, as if she was attending a child. He went into the kitchen and opened the cupboard door under the sink. As he took out the glass vase, he noticed the goldfish bowl at the back of the shelf. It all came back to him: the two goldfish called Khrushchev and Bulganin which Joe had won at the fair. His father had named them that. He named all the pets that came into the house. There was the budgie called Jack after Jack London, the dogs Fidel and Fred; even his two sons, he chose their names too. His mother objected bitterly to him being called Karl. It was too soon after the war for him to be given a German name, she said. Did he expect the other children to know the difference between Karl Marx and the other Karls their fathers had fought against during the war? He should have known. He'd been in the war himself. But she was overruled as usual and Karl it was. She was right, of course, and he suffered many a playground beating for his father's political convictions.

Joe had it easier; his was a common name with no German associations, but there were political ramifications nevertheless. He was born in 1956 when many Communist Party members tore up their membership cards in protest against the brutal Russian invasion of Hungary. Harry Rickards remained loyal, though, and he named his second son Joe, as an act of defiance and sheer bloodymindedness in the face of outraged public opinion against Stalin.

Cal filled the vase with water, then carried it back into the living-room and placed the roses in it, one by one. Hélène loved roses. He had sent her a bunch after the location party at the end of the film. She phoned later to thank him . . . He imagined the scene at the airport when he arrived home. Hélène and Bruno would be waiting for him in the passenger lounge. The dog would be tense and whining softly with his tail wagging in anticipation, as he watched the passengers coming through the gate. Then they would see him! And Bruno would pull Hélène into his arms, and she would be tearful and the dog would be up on his hind legs barking to be fussed . . . It was like the end of a film. He could hear the swelling music as the screen faded to black and the minor credits came up. He arranged the roses carefully and ran the scene through again.

It was interrupted by his mother helping his father back into the room. He had his arm across her shoulder and she was supporting all his weight. If she had let go of him, he would have gone down like a sack of potatoes. Cal was unsure whether to help his mother or not, then decided against it. It would have been intrusive. There was something intimate and moving about watching them work their way painfully across the room towards the bed. Seeing his father in such an enfeebled state, Cal found it difficult to believe that he had been such a despot and, briefly, he softened towards him and forgave him his bullying past. He even forgave him the name that had been forced on him and which he had always loathed. After all, it could have been worse. He might have been called Vladimir Ilich Ulyanov, after Lenin. Imagine going to school with names like that!

Cal ate at the hotel again that evening. Except for fast-food places, there didn't seem to be any other restaurants in town. Cal grinned as Charlie Thomas approached his table.

Have you got five jobs now?

Charlie handed him the menu. He was wearing a bow tie and the sleeves of his shirt were rolled down to hide his tattoo.

One of the waiters hasn't turned up, so the manager's sent me in here. It's quiet in the bar anyway.

Cal glanced round. I wouldn't say it's throbbing with life in here.

Only two other tables were occupied: a party of four and the two businessmen from the bar. They were still studying business reports.

Cal closed the mock-leather menu and handed it back. I'll have the sole. No starter.

Do you know the history of the Dover sole?

Cal looked up at him and laughed. I'm hoping the one on my plate doesn't have much of a history.

When they sunk the first pits, the men who worked in the shaft putting supports in were called dovers and they used to heat the soles of their boots to get a better grip.

Sounds like a fishy story to me. You should be a writer, you'd have six jobs then.

Would you like anything to drink?

Yes. I'll have a bottle of Chablis.

If I was you I'd have the house wine. It's half the price and just as good.

Cal looked up at him doubtfully. He would have trusted Charlie's judgement of beer without question. But wine? That was a different matter.

Honestly. It's delivered straight from the grower. It's brilliant.

Cal was still dubious, but not wishing to hurt Charlie's feelings, he ordered a bottle. Will you bring it straight away, Charlie?

He felt lonely. He stared at the undisturbed place setting and folded napkin across the table and wished that he had insisted on the Chablis. It would have kept him company. It was Hélène's favourite wine.

Charlie returned from the kitchen and showed him the label. Cal nodded, glumly. It was too late to change his mind now. Charlie opened the bottle and held it over Cal's glass.

Would you like to taste it?

No, fill it up. And pour yourself a glass while you're at it.

Cal reached across the table and picked up the other wine glass.

Charlie glanced round the room. I shouldn't really. I'll be getting the sack.

He filled both glasses nevertheless and they raised them together.

Cheers!

Charlie waited for Cal's verdict.

Cal kept him waiting. Then he laughed. Delicious!

What did I tell you? I've saved you a fiver there.

As Charlie crossed the dining-room back to the kitchen, one of the businessmen raised his arm and snapped his fingers a couple of times to attract his attention. Cal smiled. Charlie wouldn't be saving him a fiver if he could help it.

Cal refilled his glass and thought about his visit to his parents that afternoon and how much it had depressed him. Every time he entered the house it brought back unhappy childhood memories of his father's bullying arrogance and political rigidity. It applied to everything. He had no sense of proportion. The naming of his sons and the household pets was bad enough. But what about the time he made them get rid of the white mice, because they reminded him of the traitorous White army which nearly overthrew the Bolshevik government in 1919? . . . It was difficult to believe now, and Cal was still shaking his head at the absurdity of it all when Charlie returned with his dinner. He looked at the fish on his plate and thought about his favourite fish restaurant in the flower market in Nice. They would go there again as soon as he got back and he would think about tonight and tell Hélène how much he had missed her.

Charlie topped up Cal's glass, then stepped back from the table. *Bon appétit.*

Cal looked up at him in surprise. Thank you. Have another glass.

No thanks. I'd better not. He nodded towards the businessmen across the room. See them two? They've just paid twelve quid for a bottle of claret and it's like fucking vinegar.

Cal laughed and watched him walk away. It had been a row with his father concerning a bottle of wine which finally brought matters to a head and established his independence.

It happened when he was home from university on vacation. He called in at the local Co-op for a bottle of wine. He didn't know anything about wine then; he was just showing off, trying to prove how sophisticated he had become. There wasn't much choice anyway. So he just picked up a bottle off the shelf at random. It was called Bull's Blood.

His father knew even less about wine than he did, although he would have been reluctant to admit it. So when he picked up the bottle and shook his head at the label, Karl thought he was playing the expert as usual.

I'm having no Hungarian wine in this house.

He replaced the bottle decisively on the table. Karl was amazed. No Hungarian wine! Why not? Did it have a bad reputation or something? Had his father become a wine buff while he had been away? Then it dawned on him . . . But surely not!

Go on, pour it down the sink.

Don't be ridiculous.

You'll have to drink it outside then, because you're not drinking it in here.

Why, because of the Hungarian uprising?

He didn't answer. He didn't have to. Karl rehearsed a crack about Château Stalin 1956, but thought better of it in case his father hit him with the bottle.

They were traitors. They had to be crushed.

What do you mean, traitors? They were Hungarians. It was their country. They didn't want to be a Soviet state, that's all.

But you've got to look at the times. It was the height of the Cold War. Russia had to maintain a strong buffer against the advance of Western Imperialism.

Cal had heard it all before. But he had never dared oppose it so openly. His new-found freedom had given him confidence.

What do you mean? It was Russia that was advancing. They'd advanced into Czechoslovakia, Poland and Hungary.

They had to! They'd no choice. They were protecting the gains of the Revolution against World Capitalism. He stabbed out his cigarette in the Tower Bridge ashtray. Haven't you learned anything? I can see I've been wasting my bloody time with you!

He wasn't used to opposition, and this counter-revolution from his brilliant son and political heir-apparent was intolerable. Karl stepped back a few paces before replying.

But they wanted their freedom! Can't you understand that? Nobody wants to be a satellite state. They want to make their own decisions. They want to lead their own lives.

As their voices grew louder, his mother came out of the kitchen to see what they were shouting about. She stayed out of the argument, but neutrality was no defence in her husband's eyes, and when he denounced Karl as a turncoat, a revisionist and a bourgeois opportunist, he hurled the insults in her direction, as if in some way she was to blame for their son's betrayal.

When it was all over, and his father went up to bed shaken and unusually subdued, Karl decided to celebrate his survival with a glass of wine. His mother went into the kitchen to fetch the corkscrew, but when she returned, she said she couldn't find it. Karl realized that it would be diplomatic not to pursue the matter, and the bottle remained unopened on the table.

Cal couldn't remember what happened to it after that. As Charlie removed his plate, he said:

Christine's in the bar.

Christine who?

Your Joe's ex-wife.

Cal tried to work out the last time he had seen her. She hadn't been at his parents' ruby wedding anniversary, because they were already divorced by then. He was amazed to realize that it was ten years ago, during the strike, just before he had flown to Los Angeles to work on *Jack the Ripper*. He finished his coffee and went into the bar.

Christine was sitting with another woman at the back of the room. There was a photograph of Humphrey Bogart on the wall above them and the smoke from their cigarettes was drifting up into his face. Cal's entrance had been screened by customers standing around the bar and Christine hadn't seen him come in. He ordered a Scotch then stood with his back to the room wondering what to do next. What if he introduced himself and she was unfriendly towards him? It sometimes happened that the injured party in a divorce took against the rest of the family, as if somehow they were all guilty by association. Anyhow, he would soon find out. He turned round and crossed the room towards the two women. Christine's friend noticed him first. She stopped talking and Christine turned round to see who she was looking at. She didn't recognize him immediately. It wasn't that he'd changed out of all recognition in the intervening years; it was her sheer surprise at seeing him that delayed her reaction.

Karl! She stood up. What are you doing here?

Cal held her arms and kissed her on both cheeks. Afterwards, he realized that his greeting could have been seen as presumptuous, but the spontaneity of the gesture overcame any initial embarrassment between them and Christine responded with a hug. Christine's friend was deeply impressed by Cal's Gallic flamboyance. There's not many like that down our street, she told Christine later.

This is Karl. You know, Joe's brother. Karl, this is Mary.

Mary would have liked a hug too, but as they were strangers – or so she thought – a smile across the table seemed more appropriate.

Would you like a drink?

They looked at their glasses, then at each other.

Christine replied for them both. Yes please.

While he was at the bar, Mary quizzed Christine about Cal's past.

I didn't know him all that well. He was at university when I met Joe . . . I don't know. He brought a girl home once or twice but I don't know what happened . . . He worked on a newspaper but he's a writer now. He lives in France, I think, but I haven't heard much about him since Joe and me split up.

Cal returned with the drinks. He found a chair and sat down. Cheers!

They raised their glasses. Cal relaxed for the first time since he had arrived back.

What are you doing here, then? Have you come to visit your parents?

My dad's had a stroke.

Oh dear . . .

Christine couldn't have looked more concerned if the news had been about her own father.

How is he? Is he going to be all right?

He's not going to die, that's the main thing. He's in a bad way, though. He's paralysed down one side and he can hardly speak. My mother has to do everything for him.

Christine shook her head slowly. She had tears in her eyes. It's hard to imagine your dad in that state, after what he's been like.

I thought you might have known already.

No. We've completely lost touch. I haven't spoken to Joe for ages now.

She turned to Mary. Did you know Joe's dad, Mary?

I knew of him. My dad used to work with him at the pit. He said he missed his way. He said he should have been a lawyer.

Cal and Christine, both past victims of his rhetoric, looked at each other and laughed. But in spite of the resentment Cal still bore towards his father, he couldn't help but feel pride in Mary's remark. Christine touched his arm.

Have they still got that picture on the wall?

What picture?

You know. That portrait over the sideboard . . .

She frowned and closed her eyes in concentration. Cal watched her lips. He could see the cracks in her lipstick. He wanted to lean forward and kiss her.

Harry! Harry whatsisname?

Harry Pollitt.

That's it! Harry Pollitt!

She laughed and squeezed Cal's arm.

Mary was feeling left out of it. Who's he?

That's what I said. It was the first time I'd been to Joe's house and I was trying to be polite and that. So I said to Joe's mother, Who's that? I thought it was a relation or somebody. Anyway Joe's dad looked at me as if I was a complete idiot. As if everybody in the world knew who Harry Pollitt was.

Tell me, then. Who is he?

Christine still hadn't answered Mary's question. Cal answered it for her.

He was the secretary of the British Communist Party. He made his name just after the First World War, when he organized a campaign on London docks not to ship out armaments against the Soviet Union . . .

You sound like your dad. Then Christine remembered something else. And that statuette! That statuette on the sideboard. Is that still there?

Cal thought about it. He wasn't sure. He was so used to it being there that he hadn't even noticed. He tried to picture the sideboard and what was on it now, but all he could see was the bronze group flanked by the biscuit barrel and fruit bowl.

Christine was describing it to Mary. Cal played his father's role and mentally supplied the analysis as she went along.

It was three men sitting in a carriage. There was a fat bloke wearing a top hat and smoking a cigar in the middle (the capitalist oppressor). There was a vicar on one side of him (bishop actually, the Church). And a general or somebody at the other side (the military). And they were being pulled along like in a rickshaw, by a man in rags (the proletariat).

Cal could see the bent figure as if it was on the table in front of him: his strained face, his tattered shirt and trousers, his bare feet . . .

Christine was still describing the tableau. It was horrible! I'd have thrown it in the bin!

She crossed her legs. Cal looked at her knees and followed the line of her thighs under her tight skirt . . . . He thought, not in our house you wouldn't. You wouldn't have dared lay a finger on it. He recalled his father's wrath when his mother accidentally snapped the capitalist's cigar while she was dusting it. Karl suggested that it symbolized the imminent victory of the working class now that the capitalist had been reduced to smoking butts. But the class struggle was no joking matter to his father and he glued the cigar back on to restore the integrity of the piece.

Cal was ready for another drink. He found the memory oppressive.

I'll go, Christine said.

She stood up directly in front of him. He could smell her perfume. If he had leaned forward he could have kissed her breasts.

While Christine was at the bar, Mary asked him what he was writing. He told her he was working on a script about a dog which rescues a poor urchin from the clutches of a wicked tyrant who has kidnapped him and is using him as slave labour.

Mary nodded approvingly. Sounds interesting. Plenty of slave labour round here, with too many people chasing too few jobs. Cal wasn't listening. He was wondering why he had told her such a bare-faced lie. He blamed it on the drink: a gin and tonic, a bottle of wine and a whisky so far. He was just being fanciful, trying to impress her by making the story more significant, that was all. But he was kidding himself. The memory of the statuette, linked to his father's disapproval of his work, had forced him into a more ideologically correct reply.

But the drink had made him randy, though. He looked at Mary. She was older than Christine. Probably older than him, too. So what? She was still sexy. He glanced round the bar. All the women were sexy.

Porn queens every one of them. What would Mary say if he asked her to go up to his room? What would Christine say? What would they say if he asked them both? He imagined the scene. He would sit on the bed and watch them undress down to their underclothes. Then they would undress him and feel him and ask him what he would like. Perhaps they would make love to each other first . . .

Mary said, Did you used to wear glasses when you were young?

She was lowering herself on to his . . . What? Cal blinked. They were back in the bar.

I said, did you wear glasses? I'm just trying to place you, that's all.

I did when I was at school.

You lived on the new estate, didn't you?

Cal nodded. He was looking at Mary's tits, still wishing they were upstairs in his room.

We lived in the village just past the rec. Then we moved into town just after I left school.

Suddenly, Cal realized something. He stared at her. Was it her? Was it *really* her? He wasn't sure. She didn't have blonde hair then. And she was slim. She was so slim that her tits had seemed too big for her body. But it was her. Yes! Definitely! And the young mocking face materialized through her make-up. It was the girl in the bushes with Jack Collins.

Mary shook her head. No, I can't remember you.

What if she had remembered him and said, I remember you? You were that little lad with the football who surprised me and Jack Collins that day.

And what if he said, Yes, you were sucking his prick, then you opened your legs and showed me your knickers.

And what if she said, Have I to open my legs and show you my knickers now?

Instead she said, What are you staring at?

Cal blushed, embarrassed. He didn't know what to

say. Then he said, I was just thinking how attractive you are.

She laughed and slapped him on the arm. You're drunk.

You're still attractive, though.

I'm married, you know.

Lucky feller.

When Cal went to bed, he had a wank. But he wasn't fucking Hélène. Or Christine. Or Mary. Or both of them together. He pictured a little boy in glasses, watching Mary Hanson sucking Jack Collins' cock.

The following morning Cal had a hangover. He sipped a cup of coffee in his room then went for a walk round town to try to clear his head. It made him feel worse. Most of the shops which hadn't already closed down had sales. SALE! SALE! SALE! The fluorescent signs hurt Cal's eyes and he felt for his Ray-Bans. But they weren't there; they were in France. He wished he was with them. He wished he was in Albania, Romania, Bosnia! He wished he was anywhere but here. It was like the Third World. The Fourth World if there was such a place. His delicate condition heightened the squalor around him. He winced at a clatter of drink cans blowing by. A polystyrene burger box skidding across the pavement set his teeth on edge. And he had to place his hand over his mouth and turn away at the sight of a tramp eating cold chips smeared with ketchup from a discarded tray.

He couldn't wait to get back to the hotel and up to his room, where the full-length net curtains obscured the view.

He rang room service and ordered a pot of coffee, then sat down at his word processor. Perhaps working on the script might help him to forget his headache. But even if it didn't, it might help him to forget the horror outside.

EXT. SUBURBAN STREET. NIGHT.

TOBY is running home. He dashes across the road and is almost run over by a car. He races along the sidewalk and almost knocks an old couple over. The old man angrily waves his walking stick after the dog.

OLD MAN

Pesky critter!

EXT. SUBURBAN STREET. NIGHT.

TOBY arrives home. He lives in a large, comfortable house with a neat front lawn and an expensive car in the drive. He can't get in, of course, so he stands outside the front door barking frantically. Eventually, MR DUNCAN, Toby's father, opens the door.

MR DUNCAN

What the hell's going on here?

TOBY dashes past him into the house.

MR DUNCAN

Hey! Come back here!

INT. LIVING ROOM. TOBY'S HOUSE. NIGHT.

TOBY dashes into the living-room. MRS DUNCAN is sitting on the sofa reading a magazine, Toby's younger sister, PATTI, is lying on the carpet watching TV and the family cat is curled up in an armchair fast asleep.

TOBY is so relieved to see them all. He jumps up on the sofa and licks MRS DUNCAN's face. Then he jumps down and fusses PATTI. He is even glad to see her. He runs across the room to say hello to the cat, who has been woken by the disturbance. But the cat is terrified and it flees across the room, past MR DUNCAN who is standing in the doorway . . .

Cal looked up from his word processor and stared at the wall. If they decided to feed Toby, would he eat like a real dog? Or would he want to use his front paws? What if they fed him in the cat's dish – would the cat get jealous and attack him? Perhaps if the film crew starved the cat for a few days, it might have a go at him then. There was no guarantee with animals, though, that was the problem . . .

The pattern on the wallpaper was making him feel sick. The recurring diamonds were expanding and contracting like an accordion and he felt as if his head was being squeezed between the folds. He decided to visit his father and finish the scene when he got back.

There was a car outside the house when he arrived. It was probably the nurse visiting his father. He decided to have a word with her before she left, and if she considered his father's condition stable, he would make immediate arrangements to go home. He was finding it difficult to work. He had written only a couple of scenes since he arrived. He couldn't blame the hotel. He'd worked in hotels before. Usually, he could work anywhere: hotels, aeroplanes, trains . . . It was the place, the circumstances. It aroused bad memories and conflicting emotions. It unsettled him.

As he walked down the path, Christine came round the corner from the back door. Cal felt better already.

What a nice surprise.

I phoned your mother up. She was pleased to see me.

She stared at Cal and laughed. You look dreadful!

Your dad's a picture of health compared to you. Then, seriously, as if regretting her levity: He looks terrible, doesn't he? It's hard to believe it's the same man.

Cal nodded and looked at the overgrown front lawn. I was still a bit scared of him, though, even in that condition.

Cal looked at her and smiled. You're not the only one.

I think your mother's marvellous, the way she's coping with it all . . .

Cal noticed the tears in her eyes, but before he could say anything, she brushed past him and hurried up the path. Cal watched her drive away, then turned round and went into the house.

His father was sitting in his chair by the fire. He had a towel round his neck like a baby's bib which made him look more helpless than ever. His mother was smoothing shaving foam onto his face.

It was nice of Christine to come. I was really sorry when her and our Joe broke up. I always liked her.

Cal watched her raise his father's chin and carefully draw the razor up his throat. The number of times he had wanted to draw a razor across it.

I'll cut the grass for you, while I'm here.

Good. It's about time you did something useful.

It sounded like something his father would have said. Perhaps she was reading his mind.

Cal enjoyed mowing the lawn. The first cut through the long grass was hard work and made him sweat. It was the same manual mower with the bleached wooden handle that he had used as a boy. But the exertion cleared his head and the simple satisfaction of the job relaxed him. The short grass, pale from lack of light, looked as if the colour had been washed out of it.

Going strong and still in the mood, he decided to complete the job by weeding the border round the lawn. When he reached the clump of irises under the window, he thought of the irises in his own garden: the baked, red clay, the splash of blue against the dazzling white wall. He heard the rasp of the cicadas in the pine trees behind the house; Hélène laughing in the pool and Bruno barking furiously at the edge as she splashed and teased him.

When he had finished, he put away the tools in the shed at the bottom of the garden and went into the house. He felt like a little boy again when his mother looked out of the window and said how nice the garden looked.

I'll go and make some tea. You must be ready for it after all that work.

I'll come and help you.

I don't need any help. You've done enough for one day.

But he insisted and followed her into the kitchen. He wondered if she realized that he didn't want to be left alone with his father. He was ashamed of himself for admitting it. His own father, a broken old man! But he couldn't help it. His animosity ran deep.

He placed the teapot and two mugs on the tray.

There's three of us, his mother said.

Cal blushed and completed the set, then carried the tray through to the living-room and placed it on the coffee table in front of the sofa. He sat down next to his mother and poured the tea.

Put plenty of milk in your dad's. I don't want to burn his throat.

There's so much fire come out of it, it's probably heatproof anyway.

Cal didn't dare say that, but it was what he thought.

His mother tested the tea herself, then carried the mug across to her husband. Cal watched him drink. There was something bird-like about the way he raised his head after each sip. There was something bird-like about his remaining good eye too, but it wasn't benign like a budgie's, it was fierce like a falcon's and it unnerved him. Or perhaps he was just imagining it and his father glared at everyone like that.

Maisie Rickards sat down again on the sofa and asked Cal what he was writing. He hesitated and glanced at his father. If she had asked him in the kitchen, he would have told her the truth. But not here, not with his father in the room. If his father had been deaf, dumb and blind he still would not have told her. It would have made no difference if his father had been dead, and all that remained of him was a portrait on the wall. Cal was convinced that if he told her he was writing a script about a boy who is turned into a dog by a mad professor, the portrait would crash to the floor in disgust.

So he said he was writing a script about a boy who has an argument with his parents and runs away from home. That seemed ambiguous enough to prevent a 999 call to the hospital.

This all started when he got arrested during the strike. I'm convinced of it.

Cal looked at her.

What do you mean?

Your dad. When he got beaten up by the police. That and going to prison. He was never the same again somehow.

That's a long time ago isn't it, 1984?

These things can have a delayed effect, Karl.

She picked up the teapot and refilled their mugs.

Don't forget my dad's.

She smiled.

I haven't. He's had enough now.

I suppose he saw himself as a political prisoner.

Well, he was, wasn't he?

Cal stirred his tea and wondered how many tea bags his mother had put in the pot. He decided to bring a box of Earl Grey tea bags the next time he came to the house.

What happened?

What do you mean?

When my dad got arrested.

It was a scandal. Nobody'd believe some of the things that went on during the strike. It was like a police state round here.

Cal looked at her in surprise. It was the kind of wild assertion he was used to hearing from his father.

Your dad had gone to have a word with Phil Walton. He was the scab who'd gone back. They'd found out who it was by trailing the police van when it took him home from work. It was funny really. Your dad said he was the idlest man at the pit. They called him the phantom fitter because nobody could ever find him when there was any work to be done. Your dad said the ones who went back first were usually the biggest skivers.

Rotten elements.

Maisie looked at him to see if he was being facetious. Cal remembered some of the other political terms of abuse which his father habitually used: ideologically unsound, political adventurer, class traitor . . . Cal had been called all of them (and more) at one time or another.

Anyway, because the police were driving him straight into the pit yard so the pickets couldn't get near him, your dad decided to go to his house to have a word with him. He lived on Morrison Crescent, opposite the shops. When he gets there, there's a crowd outside and SCAB painted on the wall and that, and a bobby at the gate.

Don't go in there, Harry, somebody says. You'll get contaminated. You'll have to burn your clothes when you come out.

I hope not, your dad says. These are the only ones I've got.

So he goes up to the gate to have a word with the bobby.

I'd like a word with Phil Walton. I'm the branch secretary at Foxmoor. I thought as we can't get near him on the picket line, I might be able to talk to him at home.

The bobby wouldn't let him past, though.

You can't.

Why not?

Orders. Nobody's to go near him. There's been enough intimidation already.

Yes, and most of it's come from you lot, your dad says.

The bobby didn't like that at all.

Look, don't think I agree with everything that's happened, he says. Because I don't. I live round here. My brother-in-law's a miner. I didn't join the police force to beat miners up. It's outside forces who are causing the trouble.

Your dad wasn't having any of that.

What did you think you were joining – the bloody scouts? he said. You knew what you were letting yourself in for. It's like joining the army and then complaining when you've to shoot somebody.

Look, all I'm saying is, don't tar us all with the same brush, that's all. Then he points towards the house. And if it's any consolation, I've no time at all for that idle bastard. We'd to drag him out of bed to go to work this morning.

Just then, a police van draws up outside the house and bobbies jump out and start to clear the crowd away. Your dad said they weren't asking them to leave, they were pushing them and that, and being aggressive and abusive. There was this Inspector Tolson in charge, a right nasty piece of work I understand. Your dad had had a run in with him before in the manager's office when the scab first went back.

Anyway, he's strutting about, little Hitler type, shooting his mouth off. Come on you lot! Move it or you'll be arrested! That sort of thing. Then one of the bobbies shoves a woman, Helen . . . Helen . . . She turned to her husband. What did they call that woman who got arrested with you, Harry, Helen who?

Cal couldn't even tell if his father was listening or not as he sprawled inert in his chair. But after a series of barking sounds, he managed to produce the name . . . Woofitt.

That's it. Helen Woofitt. So she says to this bobby, Hey! Keep your filthy hands to yourself. I'm not having you pushing me around. So he starts insulting her then. You know. You can imagine, can't you? I wouldn't touch you with a barge pole. Called her a filthy bitch. That kind of thing. Well, all hell breaks loose then. Helen attacks the bobby. Fights break out. The bobbies wade in and start arresting people at random – including your dad, who's trying to act as a peacemaker! They just set on him, truncheoned him, and threw him into the back of the van with the others. He'd to have five stitches in his head. She tapped the back of her own head to indicate the spot. It was a disgrace.

Cal nodded slowly and tried to look concerned, but it was more out of respect for his mother's feelings than belief in her story. It was too one-sided, too simplistic to be credible, and try as he might he could not imagine his father in the role of peacemaker. He was a protagonist and Cal wondered heretically (he would have been banished from the house for suggesting it) if his father had caused the trouble and deserved all he got.

EXT. TOBY'S HOUSE. NIGHT.

We can hear barking inside the house, then the door opens and TOBY runs out. Moments later, MR DUNCAN appears in the doorway. He is furious. His trouser leg is ripped. He throws a shoe after the retreating dog.

MR DUNCAN

Get out of here, you vicious brute!

MR DUNCAN goes back inside and slams the door. TOBY stands on the sidewalk and whines pitifully as he looks back at his comfortable home with its inviting lighted windows.

Cal read through the scene, then phoned Hélène. She was fine but she was missing him. She was working hard on the script, immersing herself in the character. She was so excited about it. It was a wonderful part.

When Cal replaced the receiver, he felt vaguely aggrieved. She didn't seem to be missing him enough somehow and she hadn't even enquired about *his* work. He stared at the screen and thought about the film that Hélène was due to begin shooting in a few weeks' time.

It was set in Berlin just after the reunification of Germany. Hélène had been cast as the wife of a discredited Stasi officer. She leaves him and moves to Berlin from a dismal, former East German town. At first she loves it: the excitement, the glamour, the attractive men she meets. She looks stunning in her fashionable new outfits, after the dowdy clothes she had worn in the first few scenes. Sexy too; especially – the scene where the corrupt industrialist buys her a new dress and she tries it on for him in the hotel bedroom. But gradually she becomes disillusioned as she realizes that capitalism isn't paradise after all and that there is more to life than materialism . . .

It was a good part. It was a good script. Cal could imagine the film at the Cannes or Venice film festivals. He could imagine Hélène receiving the Best Actress Award . . . He returned to his own script. Where would Toby go now? The most appropriate place he could think of at the moment was under a fucking bus.

Still undecided as to what to do with him, Cal phoned his agent. Had he heard anything about the gay cop idea he'd put forward to the BBC? Yes. They liked it, but they're not sure if it's the right time, what with the AIDS scare and all that. They're worried about undermining the confidence of the general public in the forces of law and order. But they're planning a new 'Biggles' series. Was he interested in that?

Cal replaced the telephone, then paused before reaching for the directory. He had been deliberating whether to phone all afternoon and he was still uncertain when he found the number and began to press the buttons.

Cal met Christine at an Italian restaurant a few miles out of town. It was in *The Good Food Guide*, she said. Cal was surprised. He hadn't anticipated Christine being a gourmet and he thought she had looked up the place in the book then reserved a table to impress him. But no, the waiters greeted her like a friend when they arrived and she recommended various dishes as they studied the menu.

This wasn't the Christine who used to visit the house when she was courting Joe. She had been the quiet, blushing type, happier clearing the table and washing up with his mother than joining in the conversation. Perhaps she was overawed by him, the clever elder brother, or by his father, the militant trade unionist.

But whatever she was like then, she was different now. Cal felt the same way about his mother. She wasn't the same woman either. Something significant had happened to both of them.

Your mother was marvellous when Joe left me.

Christine poured the wine and lit a cigarette.

I suppose she felt bad about it. Wanted to make it up to you in some way.

I know, but she didn't have to. If it had been the other way round, I can't imagine my mother having had much to do with Joe. She'd have been too embarrassed.

What did my dad say about it?

I think your dad had other things on his mind. He was in prison at the time.

The waiter brought their starters and lit the candle on the table. The ruby in Christine's ring caught fire too as she picked up her fork. Cal wasn't sure whether to continue the subject of Christine's divorce. He didn't want to ruin the evening with a morbid trawl through the past. But she was the one who had brought it up and he was interested to know if she was over it yet, and what had happened to her since.

What I don't understand is why the magistrate sent Joe to Scarborough in the first place. I mean, it's English justice at its most eccentric, sentencing somebody to the seaside.

Christine laughed loud enough to make the diners at the next table laugh too.

He didn't *sentence* him to Scarborough. What happened was, he'd been arrested at Orgreave coking plant when they tried to stop the lorries coming out. It was incredible. When I saw it on television I couldn't believe it. I've never seen so many police. There were thousands of them! You couldn't believe it was happening in this country. It was like watching something in South Africa. The miners took a terrible beating. Your dad said that it was the turning point of the strike. He said they never really recovered after that . . .

Christine went quiet. She had forgotten about Cal's question. She had forgotten about her food. Cal stopped eating too in solidarity.

Anyway . . . rallying, resuming her meal. Joe got arrested and . . . She started laughing again. You'll never believe this but it's true. He said he'd just got a sausage roll out of his bag when he was hit over the head with a truncheon. When he went to court, the copper who did it said he mistook it for a missile!

They were both laughing now.

God, can you believe it?

Christine dabbed carefully at the corners of her eyes with her napkin. Cal noticed her thick black lashes, her vivid mouth. He wanted to lean across the table and kiss her.

They charged him with breach of the peace. It was ridiculous. They charged them with anything. They just made it up. There were so many arrests that sometimes they were going before the magistrates in batches. Joe was remanded on bail but released on condition that he stayed outside the Yorkshire coalfield and away from the picket lines until the date of his trial.

Internal exile.

What?

That's what it was called in Russia.

Christine stared at him.

Sorry, I was thinking aloud.

Anyway, he'd no idea what to do, where to go. Then he remembered your Auntie Joan in Scarborough and he went to stay with her. The bail conditions were ever so strict. He had to report to the police station every day and if he broke them he'd have been arrested and remanded in custody until his trial.

Cal ate discreetly, nodding sympathetically in the appropriate places as Christine continued her story . . . How Joe found a job in an amusement park. Then he met Lisa at a disco. He felt terrible about it and Christine could tell something was wrong when she went to visit him. Sometimes he borrowed his mate's car and came home unexpectedly for the night. But he was desperate and she had to force him to go back in time to report to the police station . . .

Narrated in the present tense, it could have been a pitch for a film. A good film too, Cal thought, with human interest in spades. He wrote the beach scene:

EXT. BEACH. DAY.

JOE is sitting on the beach staring moodily out to sea. He is wearing jeans and no shirt and his feet are bare. LISA, wearing a bikini, is building a sandcastle. A wave sweeps in and destroys it. She laughs and looks at JOE. Her smile fades. She can see that he is miles away.

LISA
What's the matter?

JOE continues to stare out to sea. LISA sits beside him.

LISA
Come on, what is it?

JOE
I feel like a spare part sat here. I should be at home, helping the lads.

LISA
It's not your fault. You didn't ask to be exiled.

JOE
It's like living in Russia.

He picks up a handful of sand and lets it run through his fingers. LISA links his arm.

LISA
(pause)
That's not what's really worrying you, is it?
(JOE does not reply)
Look, I'll stop seeing you if it'll make it any easier for you.

JOE

I just feel guilty, that's all.

LISA

I'm not holding you to anything,
you know. No promises. No regrets.
Remember?
(She strokes his back)
You're getting a nice tan.

JOE

I don't want to stop seeing you
though, Lisa.

LISA

I don't want to stop seeing you
either . . .
(Then, businesslike)
Anyway, your trial'll be coming up
soon. Then you'll go back home
and we'll never see each other
again.
(She picks up a camera from a pile of clothes)
Let me take your picture.

JOE

No. Not now.

LISA

Why not?

LISA kneels in front of him and points the camera.

LISA

Say Scargill.

JOE smiled in spite of himself as LISA takes his photograph.

. . . When Joe went on trial, his solicitor destroyed the police evidence. He was brilliant. Christine moved the crumbs round on her side plate. It was too late by then, though, the damage had been done. He couldn't settle. And after a few weeks he told me what had happened and left.

Cal was still in Scarborough.

Christine reached across the table and squeezed his arm. Don't look so sad. It's a long time ago now.

Cal brought her back into focus. Sorry . . . It's always sad when couples part. You start off with such high hopes.

It could have been worse. We might have had children. At least we were able to make a clean break.

Yes. It's always more complicated when children are involved.

Cal looked at the potted geranium on the window-sill behind her. It was an old plant with a woody stem and the reflection in the dark glass doubled its meagre flowers. He thought of the geraniums on the balcony at home. He saw Hélène cross the bedroom and fold back the shutters. She stepped outside and stood naked, framed against the blue wash of the sky, her every movement, every gesture considered, as if she was on camera.

. . . It was the best thing that could have happened in the long run. For both of us.

Cal could hear the swifts squealing above the house.

. . . It made me grow up, become more independent. I'd always been the little housewife type. You know: job, marriage, mortgage. That sort of thing. Do you know, Joe was the only boyfriend I ever had before I got married?

She shook her head in disbelief as if she was talking about somebody else.

And since?

He wondered if he had gone too far, but thinking about Hélène with no clothes on had made him randy.

Christine laughed and lit another cigarette. Cal watched her fingers sliding up and down her lighter as she played with it on the table.

The strike changed Joe as well, you know. I don't mean meeting Lisa. I mean before that. He didn't want it to end. He didn't want to go down the pit again. It was a kind of freedom. Being on strike all those months gave him time to think . . .

Cal wondered what Christine would say if he put his foot up her skirt.

. . . I can remember Joe saying that before the trouble started at Orgreave, they'd all gathered in a field next to the coking plant. It was a lovely summer morning and he said he was lying on his back listening to a skylark singing. He put his hand up against the sun to try and spot it, and he said that at that moment he never wanted to go down the pit again.

Brilliant. What a brilliant opening to a film! Cal stopped speculating about Christine's underwear and imagined the first scene.

It opens with a close-up of Joe lying on his back in a field with a skylark singing somewhere overhead. It looks idyllic, as if he is alone in the middle of the countryside. He raises his arms to block out the sun so that he can see the bird. Then the camera pulls back to reveal a field full of miners sitting and standing around in groups, talking, laughing, some eating sandwiches. The atmosphere is relaxed. In the background the police lines are forming up to keep the road clear for the coke lorries leaving the plant. There are thousands of them, reinforced by mounted police and dog handlers . . . What a scene! It was like the build-up to the Battle of Agincourt in *Henry V*.

Inspired by this opening, he revised the scene between Joe and Lisa on the beach.

EXT. BEACH. DAY.

JOE is lying on his back on the beach dressed only in a pair of jeans. His position mirrors the earlier scene at Orgreave, when he lay in

> the field before the violence began. He hears a gull overhead and raises his hand to blot out the sun, exactly as he did when he tried to pinpoint the skylark at Orgreave . . .

Christine topped up their glasses. Joe said he was lying there enjoying the sun on his face and he said to your dad, I wish the strike would go on for ever. Sunshine, fresh air, you can't beat it. Your dad said, You'll get plenty of fresh air if we lose the strike, because you'll end up on the dole . . . And he was right.

Cal nodded gloomily. His father's appearance in the story was like a cloud across the sun. He usually is.

Christine thought he meant it as a compliment. She was wrong. He was annoyed at the old bastard's prescience.

Joe said it was a massacre. They were set up. They had a police cordon in front of them, dog handlers at one side of the field and mounted police at the other. When the lorries had gone through, they just charged them. It was terrible. They were out to teach them a lesson. They chased them right up into the village. Mounted police hitting them with their batons. They chased Alan Jarvis, who lived across the road from us, straight through somebody's house. Alan said the look on the woman's face when he dashed through the living-room – she couldn't believe it!

Cal couldn't help but laugh. It was pure Keystone Cops.

But Christine wasn't laughing. It was all rushing back to her, clear and strong.

I saw it on the news on the telly. It was awful. Then when Joe didn't come home, I went round to your mother's to see if he was there. Your dad had just got back. He said Joe had been arrested. He was furious. Not about Joe. I think he'd have been disappointed if a son of his hadn't been arrested. He was mad because he'd been bitten by a police dog and his trousers were all ripped.

Christine had no idea how seriously she had wounded Cal with her unwitting remark about his father's reaction to Joe's arrest. It pierced him to the heart and for the first time in his life he was jealous of his younger brother.

Your dad said they were naïve. They should have known better. They'd gone dressed as if they were going to a picnic in T-shirts and trainers and that. We should have been prepared, he said. We should have gone wearing pit boots and helmets and armed with pick handles. We'd have seen how brave the police were then!

She remembered it clearly: Joe's father astride the hearth rug jabbing his finger in the air. His mother comforting her on the sofa . . . It resembled a scene from a silent film when the girl gets pregnant and her father is about to banish her from the house.

Christine shook her head in disgust. I was pathetic, crying all over the place.

Cal placed his hand over hers on the table. He could feel her ring in his palm. It was a natural reaction, Joe having been arrested.

I can't believe it's the same person, looking back.

I'm glad you weren't. I might have been jealous.

Only might?

I definitely would.

She removed her hand and placed it over his. Let's ask for the bill.

They went back to the hotel. Christine didn't make any opening remarks about the room. They didn't use the tea-making facilities or the mini-bar. They started kissing as soon as they got inside the door; and while they were kissing they undressed each other, urgently and clumsily in their eagerness. They were trembling with lust. Cal unzipped her skirt and let it fall; then he sat on the edge of the bed and pulled down her knickers and tights together. Christine leaned over and slid her tongue into his mouth while he unfastened her bra. She stood in front of him with one foot up on the bed while he sucked her nipples and slid his fingers inside her.

Lovely cunt.

He unzipped his trousers with his free hand. Christine knelt in front of him and pulled them down with his underpants but she couldn't get them over his feet.

Lovely cock.

Suck it.

Wait.

She was growing impatient with the tangle of trousers and pants and socks. She held his cock in one hand and struggled with his clothes with the other. Cal helped her remove them before the mood turned to farce; then he sat with his legs open and watched her lower her mouth over his knob.

Oh, God . . .

She raised her head. Don't come.

Why not?

I want you to fuck me. I want you to come inside me.

You'd better get up, then, or it'll be too late.

Cal lay back on the bed and Christine knelt astride him.

Cal pushed up her. She gasped.

You fucker, she said.

He held her buttocks then ran his fingers round the rim of her arse. He wanted to shove it up but he wasn't sure if she was ready for that yet. He watched her tits bouncing as he jigged her up and down. They were so white. Her whole body was white except for her nipples and the brown V on her chest. So different from Hélène, who was evenly tanned all over.

Let me lie down, Karl. I want you on top of me.

Karl . . . So strange. A different man with a different woman.

He pulled her to him and rolled over, still inside her. He kissed her eyes, her cheeks, her mouth.

Go on, Karl, fuck me . . . Yes. Oh, yes . . . That's it. That's it, Karl. Fuck me. Fuck me hard . . .

After breakfast, Cal left the hotel and bought a small tape recorder in a CLOSING-DOWN SALE at an electrical shop on the high street. As he drove to his parents' house, he tried it out by acting the scene during the strike where his father and George Moody had identified the scab by following the NCB van from the pit.

They're here . . . Let them carry on a bit or they might spot us . . . OK, George, follow that scab.

I wonder who it is?

I don't know, but I wouldn't like to be in his shoes when we find out.

Slow down, they're stopping.

. . . Well, bugger me! Look who it is: the phantom fitter.

It's incredible. The idlest man at the pit. He's been sacked once for absenteeism.

And to think that the union fought to get a sod – (no, cunt. His father would have said cunt). And to think that the union fought to get a cunt like that his job back.

Cal switched it off, then played it back. His accent sounded stagey, like a southern actor playing a northerner. He believed the dialogue, though.

His father was asleep when he arrived at the house. His mother put a finger to her lips and took him into the kitchen.

It seems a shame to wake him up. He's only just dropped off.

How is he?

He's coming on, slowly. We'll just have to be patient, that's all.

It must be exhausting for you. Can't you get a home help or somebody in cases like this?

I don't need any help. I can manage very well on my own, thank you.

She wasn't thanking him at all. The rising inflection and sing-song final syllable suggested the opposite. She turned away and started to clatter about in a cupboard. It was a good job he hadn't offered to pay for a private nurse to help her, or she might have hit him with one of the pans she was piling up. And what would his father have said about a scab nurse? Cal had to find something else to think about to stop himself from laughing. He noticed the cat feeding in the corner near the sink.

I didn't know you'd got a cat.

We haven't. It's a stray. I feed it sometimes, poor thing. The lads throw stones at it and that. It's a wonder it survives.

The cat glanced up from the dish.

Maisie laughed. Look! She knows we're talking about her. Would you like a cup of coffee?

Who, me or the cat?

She'd drink anything you put down for her, she's that hungry.

Maisie filled the kettle. The rush of water made the cat glance up again.

You know when my dad was arrested – were there any witnesses?

Of course there were.

Can you remember who they were?

Of course I can. I might be getting old but I've still got all my faculties, you know.

And as if to prove it, she scooped two heaped spoonfuls of coffee into the mugs without spilling a speck.

You think I'm exaggerating, don't you?

What about?

The police. Your dad's arrest. What went on round here during the strike. She didn't give him time to equivocate. You've no idea what it was like: *you* weren't here.

It was the second stinging remark about his absence in less than twenty-four hours. First it was Christine over dinner and now his mother. But this one hurt most because it was intentional. He stared sulkily out of the kitchen window across the back garden. The runner-bean canes had blown down. The gutter on the greenhouse was hanging off and the vegetable plot needed hoeing.

Cal was unmoved. He didn't care if the greenhouse collapsed before his eyes, or caterpillars reduced the sprouts to barren stalks. And they could forget the privet hedge. He didn't care if it grew ten feet high. He wasn't going to lift another finger. They were so ungrateful. He was here, wasn't he? All the way from France and with a script to write, to boot. He was still furiously cancelling chores when the kettle began to boil.

Maisie made the coffee. As Cal sat down, he looked at the calendar on the wall above the table. He had sent it from France as a Christmas present. The July photograph showed a street scene in Nîmes. Cal wanted to be there. Now. This very instant. He didn't want to be here, in this council house, in this chilly kitchen, drinking disgusting coffee with his ungrateful mother and a stray cat in the corner.

He wanted to be sitting outside that café near the fountain, drinking real coffee and sharing a croissant with Hélène. *Non, rien pour moi*, she always said when he ordered. But she always managed to eat most of his when it arrived . . . *Un morceau, s'il te plaît. Mm . . . Oui, c'est bon . . .*

So what was keeping him? He had done his duty. His father wasn't going to die. All he had to do was pick up the telephone and book a flight and he would be on his way home. He looked away from the calendar and continued to stir his coffee.

If you stir it much longer, you'll wear the bottom of the mug out.

Cal glanced up at her and laughed. She used to say that to him when he was a boy. Look, I know I wasn't here, but there's nothing I can do about that now. He tapped the spoon on the rim of his mug and placed it on the table. I'd like to find out what happened.

What do you mean?

When my dad was arrested.

I've told you.

Yes. I know you have.

Don't you believe me?

Of course I do!

It doesn't sound like it to me.

It's not only that. I mean during the strike.

What's the matter – are you feeling guilty or something?

Cal wasn't sure what he was feeling, except that he was being drawn in, in spite of himself. He looked up at the photograph of Nîmes again. It looked more inviting than ever.

Maisie stood up and left the kitchen. Cal listened to her going upstairs; then he watched the cat feeding in the corner. When it had finished, it stretched by walking away from its back legs and pressing hard against the floor with its front paws.

Maisie returned, carrying an old shoe-box. Cal recognized it immediately. It was the family archive and contained an assortment of old photographs, letters and insurance policies. Maisie placed it on the table and Cal read the label on the end of the box: TAN LEATHER-BROGUE-SIZE 9. Cal remembered those shoes. His mother used to polish them until they glowed, then place them by the fireside chair ready for his father to put on.

While Maisie rummaged in the box, Cal picked out a couple of old holiday snaps. One showed him leading a donkey with Joe on its back; the other, his parents sitting in deckchairs with his father reading the *Daily Worker*. Cal couldn't read the headline, but it wouldn't be a rib-tickler, he was certain of that.

This is your dad's prison diary. You can take it and read it if you like.

She handed him a spiral notepad with *Prison Diary* printed on the front. Cal opened it at random.

> *23 JULY*
> This is the worst time, when you've just left and I might not see you for a day or two. It's funny but when you're outside, a couple of days don't seem like anything. Even a week or a month. Days just go by and you never think about them. In here every hour seems like a day and every day's as long as a week on afternoons. I always used to grumble about the afternoon shift but I wish I was on it now.
>
> *28 JULY*
> A lot of miners hate travelling in the cage because of the risk of accidents. I know which cage I'd sooner be in, though, in spite of the danger.
>
> *3 AUG.*
> It's the little things that hurt most. Unexpected things that catch you off guard. I heard a thrush singing on the roof the other day. It was singing its heart out. I've never felt as miserable in my life. I keep wondering how our Joe's going on in Scarborough and how Christine's bearing up. It'll be a bugger if we're both found guilty and finish up in the same prison together.

Cal closed the notepad and placed it on the table.

How long was my dad in Armley before his trial?

Three weeks. It took it out of him as well.

Yes, I can tell.

Even though they found him not guilty, it knocked the bottom out of him, somehow. He felt degraded.

Couldn't you have sued for wrongful arrest, or miscarriage of justice or something to clear his name?

No. You know what the law's like. It could have dragged on for years. Anyway, your dad had had enough by that time. He couldn't face any more.

Amongst the jumble of documents and snapshots in the shoe-box, Cal noticed a photograph album which he had never seen before. He took it out and turned the pages. It contained coloured photographs of his mother speaking at crowded meetings in lecture theatres and halls. Some showed her enjoying herself in cafés and restaurants, and there was a group photograph with Maisie at the centre, set against a background of Gothic buildings in what looked like a town square. Interspaced between the pages, like bookmarks, there were leaflets in German, and letters and postcards with German stamps.

That's when I went to Freiburg to raise money for the strike.

Did you go on your own?

Yes. It was marvellous. I raised over five hundred pounds.

There was pride in her voice. Turning the pages of the album, Cal found it impossible to reconcile the orator in the photographs with the skivvy of a mother he remembered from childhood. The transformation was incredible. There she was, travelling abroad for the first time in her life. Alone. And on a speaking tour at that! Cal shook his head in wonderment. It looked as if his father would be polishing his own shoes in future.

As Cal replaced the album in the shoe-box, a photograph slid out from between the pages on to the table. He picked it up and glanced at it. It was a creased, sepia picture of a farmhouse on a hillside. He turned it over but there was no information on the back.

Where's this? It looks more like Italy than Germany.

Maisie took it from him without answering and slipped it into the pocket of her pinafore.

Cal could see that she was embarrassed. What's the matter?

Nothing.

What is it?

She shook her head. Nothing. I'll tell you about it some time.

Maisie knew which road Tommy Johnson lived on, but she didn't know the number. As Cal drove across the estate to ask him about his father's arrest, he remembered Tommy from the epic football matches in the rec. Periodically, through the day-long Saturday matches, Tommy would have to go home to run errands or do chores for his mother. She didn't come and fetch him, or send one of his younger brothers or sisters: she called him in. From the back doorstep. Three streets away. The match would be at a tense stage with the score at something like 36–35, when suddenly, across the rooftops, came the dreaded call, TOM-EE!! It gathered force like an air-raid siren, then, as it died away, it was picked up by children across the estate whose mocking impersonations extended Tommy's misery. He would rage and curse and shout that he wasn't going. But he did. Every time. Accompanied by jeers and taunts from the others. He had no choice. His mother was a fearsome woman who used to beat her husband as well as the children. On one occasion, during the annual visit of the fun fair, she had responded to the barker's challenge for anybody to go three rounds with the resident bruiser in the boxing booth. Three rounds for a tenner? she said, climbing into the ring. It's money for old rope! The barker had no objection – the match had certainly drawn a crowd. But when a book was opened, and he saw which way the local money was going, he hurriedly cancelled the bout on the grounds that mixed boxing was against the law.

But they always allowed Tommy back into the

game when he returned. He had a lot to put up with and the other boys were secretly grateful that Mrs Johnson was his mother and not theirs.

Cal remembered one particular game which continued until it went dark. The street lamps were on. The moon was out. The scores were level but nobody could score the winning goal. Then Roy Barraclough (Jimmy Greaves) was clean through on his own with only Tommy (Gordon Banks) to beat in goal. Roy dribbled round him but Tommy tripped him up as he was about to tap the ball into the empty net. Penalty! No doubt about it. Roy placed the ball on the penalty spot. Tommy crouched between the posts. The moon went behind a cloud and Roy looked up and waited for it to come out again before stepping back to take the crucial kick. Then, as he ran up, a familiar cry came through the darkness: TOM-EE! TOM-EE!

It was only afterwards that Karl realized why she had called twice. Usually, one call was enough.

Everybody laughed and groaned and Tommy instinctively turned to go. But a few seconds more wouldn't make much difference, so he crouched again to face the penalty kick before running home to face his mother. Roy ran at the ball and kicked it hard and low towards the corner of the goal. It was perfectly placed just inside the post, but Tommy guessed correctly and dived across and saved it. It rescued Tommy's team from defeat and seconds later they attacked upfield and Karl, under cover of darkness, materialized to score the winning goal.

It was the climax of his career in the rec. A few months later he was transferred to the grammar school in town, while Tommy and Charlie and the other boys went to the secondary modern school on the estate. After that, they gradually drifted apart . . .

But that was in the future. All that mattered then was Tommy's decisive save, followed by Karl's winning goal. The triumphant climax to the game made

Tommy reckless enough to defy his mother and he ran across to the swings with his team-mates. He wanted to prolong his moment of glory for as long as possible, but after a few minutes his sister Linda appeared at the wall and shouted to him to come home. Tommy was in for it now. His mother would kill him. She must have sent Linda to fetch him rather than call him again, in which case people would think she was losing her authority.

Tommy leapt off his swing while it was still at a dangerous height and raced across the football pitch. The others went quiet as they anticipated his fate, and after he had disappeared over the wall, they too went home in solidarity, leaving the swings creaking in the darkness as they slowed down.

But it wasn't Tommy who got killed. It was his father, who had been crushed in a roof fall down the pit.

Cal drove slowly down Cook Avenue looking for someone who might know where Tommy lived. He wound down the window as he approached a youth wearing a leather jacket and jeans, wheeling a supermarket trolley along the pavement. As Cal drew level, he saw that the trolley contained a television set.

Excuse me!

The youth turned sharply, stared at him, then glanced up and down the road. He looked as if he was going to make a run for it.

Could you tell me where Tommy Johnson lives?

Why? What do you want him for?

I'm an old friend. I'm trying to get in touch but I don't know where he lives.

The youth was still suspicious. Cal didn't look like an old friend of Tommy's. He didn't look like a new friend either. In fact he didn't look like any kind of friend of Tommy's at all, unless he had just won the fucking football pools or something. He looked more like that flash cunt at the massage parlour. *He* had a sun-tan and wore fancy shirts as if he was on holiday in fucking Marbella or somewhere.

Are you from the massage parlour?

What? Cal started to laugh.

What's funny about that?

Cal couldn't answer for laughing.

It's a good job I didn't tell you a joke, mister, or you'd have had a fucking heart attack.

This amused Cal even more. The youth observed him solemnly.

Silly cunt. At least he's not a bailiff. Or from the council. Them cunts laugh at fuck all.

He pointed along the road.

It's down there on the right. You'll see it. There's a goat in the front garden.

Cal thanked him through tears: a blurred figure in runny clothes.

The goat was tethered to a pole. It went for Cal as soon as he opened the gate. He stepped back sharply, but the rope pulled it up short. It accompanied him up the path, sidestepping smartly and grinning up at him. Its teeth were so perfect that they looked false. Cal was relieved to leave it behind. He kept wanting to glance back to make sure the goat hadn't slipped its collar, but he didn't want it to know that he was scared of it.

He forgot all about the goat and trying not to be scared when he walked round the back of the house and an Alsatian ran out of its kennel and leapt up at him. Its chain uncurled like a striking snake, and when it pulled taut it jerked the dog backwards off its feet. As Cal knocked on the kitchen door, he wondered what was going to attack him from inside.

An old man opened the door. He ignored Cal and roared at the dog which was still up on its hind legs straining and barking.

Down, Caesar! Down!

Caesar dropped down on all fours. Its chain rattled and sagged and it stood there as silent and still as a clockwork toy with its spring run down.

Now then, what can I do for you?

Cal stared at him. He couldn't believe it. It was Tommy's dad! He was so confused that he almost asked him if Tommy was coming out to play. But it couldn't be. Mr Johnson was dead. He was killed in an accident down the pit. So who was this then? No, it couldn't be . . . Yes. Yes . . . It was! It was Tommy. Tommy had turned into his dad . . . All this in a fleeting kaleidoscope of memories and thoughts.

Hello, Tommy. It's Cal. Karl. Karl Rickards.

It was Tommy's turn to stare now.

Well, bugger me! So it is! Come in, Karl. I wouldn't have recognized you.

As Cal followed Tommy into the kitchen, he wondered if Tommy thought that he had grown up to look like his father too. Not as his father was now, old and infirm, but as he was then, when they were boys. Reluctantly, Cal had to admit that he would have taken it as a compliment.

It's a bit of a tip, Tommy said, scooping up a heap of flattened clothes covered in dog hairs and throwing them into a corner. Here, sit down.

Cal looked at the stained upholstery and sat on a stool by the table.

Would you like a cup of tea?

Without waiting for an answer, Tommy put the kettle on, then took two mugs out of a pile of dirty pots in the sink and rinsed them under the tap. Cal noticed the filthy tea towel on the hook by the sink and prayed that Tommy would leave the mugs to drain.

What a surprise, Karl. I can't remember the last time I saw you. Can you remember when we used to play football in the rec.?

Cal wondered if Tommy remembered the circumstances of his father's death, when he was fetched home by his sister Linda.

They were good times them, Karl. We had some good fun.

Judging by the state of him, any time must have been better compared with what he was going through now. The baggy seat of his trousers was shiny with wear (like the seat of the armchair) and his sweater looked as if the goat had been at it.

You went away somewhere, didn't you? Tommy asked, drying the mugs thoroughly on the tea towel. Didn't you go abroad?

Yes. I live in France now.

I don't blame you. Anywhere's better than round here.

Cal nodded seriously to stop himself from laughing. Tommy made Provence sound like a desperate alternative to Cook Avenue.

My daughter, Debbie, she works in a hotel in London. She doesn't like it down there, but she's no choice. You've to follow the work these days, haven't you?

Tommy made the tea then cleared a space on the table for the mugs.

Do you take sugar?

No thanks.

It's a good job, because I haven't got any.

He placed the mugs on the table. If Cal hadn't known otherwise, he would have sworn it was Bovril.

I've run out of milk as well, if it comes to that.

Cal stared apprehensively at the dense black brew and wished that Tommy had also run out of tea.

I'll tell you what I have got, though.

He opened the sideboard door and brought out a half bottle of Scotch.

This'll put hair on your chest.

Before Cal could refuse, Tommy topped up both mugs. He took a swig from the bottle for good measure, then screwed the cap back on.

Milk's all right for babies. Apart from that, I can't see much point in it myself.

They raised their mugs – Tommy's had a slogan on it, I ♥ MY MUM – then drank a toast. Tommy smacked his lips and held out his mug as if he was going to break into a drinking song.

Ah! That's better!

Cal smiled weakly, not wishing to offend him.

Now then, Karl, what can I do for you? I can't imagine really, unless you want to buy some fish.

Cal stared at him. Buy some fish! Whatever did he mean? Off the back of a lorry? Or had he set up as a fishmonger? Cal looked at his greasy clothes and black-rimmed fingernails. He was a walking health hazard. Drinking tea with Tommy was risky enough, but buying fish from him would be positively dangerous.

No. It's about my dad.

I heard about that. He's had a stroke, hasn't he? How's he getting on?

He's recovering: slowly. But it's going to be a long job. It's doubtful if he'll recover all his faculties, though.

Brilliant man your dad, Karl. He was the leading light at our pit during the strike. He organized the strike committee, the picketing. He was brilliant.

Tommy walked across to the fireplace and picked up a packet of cigarettes from the mantelpiece. Fag?

No thanks.

Tommy lit a cigarette, then threw the spent match into the cold ashes which spilled from the grate across the hearth.

I'm making a few enquiries about my dad's arrest. What happened. My mother says it was totally unprovoked.

There's no doubt about that. It was disgraceful.

Tommy had a drink of tea, then placed his mug on the mantelpiece next to a framed school photograph of a boy and a girl.

Mind you. He wasn't the only one. There were

thousands of us arrested on trumped-up charges. It was par for the course during the strike. I was taken in a couple of times. They didn't half give me some bloody hammer as well when they got me in the cells. Two of them held my arms up, while a third copper thumped me under the arms. The bruises don't show under there, you see.

Tommy demonstrated the position with his arms stretched wide, his cigarette burning incongruously between his fingers. Cal winced. It was vicious stuff, but the brutality of the experience was comically impaired by the bizarre image of Tommy enjoying a smoke while he was being beaten up.

They photographed and fingerprinted me both times I was arrested. I said, You did this last time. They didn't take any notice, though. I said, You'll have more photos of me than my mother. Then the cheeky bastard says, Say cheese. I told him to fuck off, so I got another thump for that.

Tommy laughed and drew deeply on his cigarette. Bastards. But there was no rancour in his voice. He made the experience sound commonplace, as if it was all in a day's work.

Cal tried to imagine what it must be like to be beaten up in a police cell. Would he have said cheese, when the police photographer was taking his mug shot? Of course he would. He would have sung the National Anthem if they had asked him.

Cal watched Tommy hawking and spitting into the fire grate. The cigarette had brought on a coughing fit and Cal risked a sip of tea while he recovered.

I'll tell you what, though, Karl – hoarse and gasping, his eyes watering when he straightened up. I always thought your dad was a bit of a Commie.

He is a Communist. He's been a member of the Communist Party all his life.

Cal was surprised at his own interjection: his defiant tone in defence of his father's beliefs.

I mean he was a bit of a troublemaker at the pit. Always looking for a fight with the management and that.

Cal smiled. That sounded like his father all right.

I didn't agree with all his views. But I'll tell you one thing, Karl, everything he said about the strike was correct. I used to think he was exaggerating when he said that the government was out to destroy us, and that if we didn't win it'd be the end of the coal industry and the trade union movement. But he was right. That's what's happened. I mean look what happened to me. I worked at three pits since Foxmoor shut down and every one of them's closed now. I don't know if it's me that put a jinx on them or what.

He had another coughing fit, then wiped his eyes on his sleeve.

I did all sorts after that. Pea-picking down in Lincolnshire. God, what a job that was. A van picked you up about four in the morning. Then when you got there, there was no guarantee that there'd be any work. Then if they set you on you'd be working in the pissing rain all day. And the wages!

He finished off his tea and poured a splash of whisky into his mug. He held out the bottle to Cal.

Do you want a drop?

No thanks. I haven't finished this yet.

Finished it. He had barely started it.

They've got you over a barrel, of course. More men than jobs. Take it or leave it. And no union back-up. You can't believe it when you've been in an industry with a strong union. You just take it for granted. But when you're working on a job with no union protection at all, you've got nothing. You're on your own. They just treat you like shit and there's nothing you can do about it.

Tommy lit another cigarette off the glowing tab in his mouth. Cal couldn't remember the last time he had seen anybody chain-smoking. Perhaps Tommy had been watching a late night TV showing of Jean Paul Belmondo in *Breathless*, but he doubted it.

Anyway, in the end, I thought fuck this, working in the pissing rain for two quid an hour. So I finished up going down to London and working on the buildings. It was when the building boom was on down there and you could get work on the lump. I used to travel down on Monday mornings and come back at the weekend. It was all illegal, cash in hand, and they didn't care a fuck about safety. If you didn't like it, they just told you to fuck off then set somebody else on. They've got the whip hand, Karl.

Even if Tommy had never heard of Jean Luc Godard, he appeared to know his Dick Francis.

Anyway, you can guess what happened, can't you, being away all week? Weekends as well sometimes if I could get any overtime.

It wasn't a difficult question judging by the state of Tommy and the house.

The wife met somebody else and left me. Took the kids as well. That was the worst thing.

Tommy wiped his eyes on his sleeve again. Cal wondered if the tears were from his coughing fit, or fresh ones for the loss of his family.

Are you married, Karl?

No.

You've got some sense. More trouble than they're worth, families. Look at my son, Dean. He turned round and pointed at the school photograph on the mantelpiece. He's on about joining the Army when he leaves school. Well, I'm not too happy about that after what happened in the strike, am I?

What do you mean?

They were helping the police on the picket lines.

I never knew that.

Ask your dad. He'll tell you. I mean we couldn't prove it – they weren't wearing their uniforms and that.

Well, how did you know, then?

Because some of them were too little. You'd to be five foot eight to join the police force then and some of them were never that. And they were wearing big boots that didn't fit. They'd borrowed them, you could tell. And their hair was too short. And the way they marched about: the police never march like that.

Tommy gave an arm-swinging demonstration: three strides towards the sink, followed by a smart turn and a short march back to the table. It all sounded fanciful to Cal, but he knew that his father would have backed up Tommy's suspicions. He would have started with Churchill sending in troops against the Welsh miners at Tonypandy, then moved on to the Army being called in to preserve order at London docks during the 1926 strike . . . Grudgingly, Cal accepted these precedents, but he much preferred to listen to Tommy's unintentionally comic version of events than to his father's uncompromising analysis of history.

What are you doing now then, Tommy?

Tommy laughed. Oh, a bit of this and that. He hesitated. Come on, I'll show you something.

Cal followed him out of the kitchen into the hall, then into the front room. He stopped inside the doorway and looked round in astonishment. The walls of the room were lined with fish tanks. He had stepped into an aquarium.

Tommy laughed at his reaction. You didn't expect that, did you?

You could charge admission to come in here.

Tommy led Cal round the room looking into the tanks. It started off as a hobby. I've always liked fish. I used to spend a fortune when I was a kid trying to win a goldfish at the fair. Then I thought I might as well try and make a bit of money out of it, so I used some of my redundancy money from the pit and set this up.

You're a small businessman now, then? Enterprise culture and all that.

I'm small, all right. About five foot six in my stocking feet.

Tommy peered at the thermometer in one of the tanks and adjusted the thermostat.

Who do you sell them to?

Individual buyers. Hotels and pubs sometimes. I do a bit of business with the sauna in town. They have aquaria in the suites. Tommy laughed and shook his head. That's what Maurice Dee who owns the place calls them. They look more like fucking chalets at Butlins to me. He says the fish give the place a bit of class. He's right there, 'cos nothing else does. It's a right dump.

Cal listened with growing respect as they progressed slowly round the room, with Tommy naming the fish for him and supplying a brief history of fish-keeping . . . Records show that carp breeding was carried on in ancient China, and Aristotle – the father of all learning as he was known – left records of the types of fish that were brought to him to look at. Of course you'll know all about Aristotle, won't you, Karl, being an educated man? And do you know that when the Spanish invaders under Cortez were searching for the gold in Eldorado, they found goldfish in a collection of fish and fowl in the gardens of a Montezuman prince?

Tommy's words faded as Cal stared into one of the tanks and entered a silent, underwater world of vivid fish and undulating greenery. A stately angelfish explored a sunken galleon, then emerged through a porthole scattering a school of neon tetra in a fluorescent explosion.

Living pictures these, Karl. Works of art. You never get tired of looking at them.

Cal nodded, resurfacing. Do you sell enough to make a living?

I wouldn't say that. But to be honest with you, I get so much pleasure out of them, I'm reluctant to see them go.

As Cal watched Tommy feed the fish in one of the tanks, he considered what a hard life he had led compared with his own. Yet, in spite of everything that had happened to him, he remained unbowed, humorous and resilient. Cal felt proud to be in the same room as him, and he was glad that he had been the scorer of that winning goal in the rec. all those years ago, after Tommy's penalty save had saved their team from defeat. It established an affinity between them and rekindled a link with a past which Cal had tried his best to forget.

As Cal drove back to the hotel, he thought about what Tommy had said about his fish: living pictures, Karl. You never get tired of looking at them. Cal wished he could say the same about his work. He couldn't think of one film he had written that had been worth a second look.

EXT. LARGE HOUSE. WEALTHY SUBURB. NIGHT.

TOBY is searching for food. He looks through the gates of a large, expensive house with a swimming pool in the garden. He manages to slip underneath the gate, then crosses the garden and goes round the back of the house where the trash cans are kept. He stands up on his hind legs and manages to remove the lid of one of the trash cans with his nose, but he can't get inside so he pulls the trash can over. All kinds of leftovers spill out: half-eaten pizzas, scraps of meat etc, but the clatter of empty bottles plus the noise of the falling trash can wake up the inhabitants of the house. Lights go on and we hear voices inside . . . 'Who's there?' 'What the hell's going on?' etc. TOBY flees before he can get anything to eat.

EXT. BACK ALLEY. NIGHT.

TOBY continues his search for food. He is scavenging amongst the rubbish which has spilled out of the large overflowing bins in which the local shopkeepers and restaurateurs dump their rubbish. He finds a juicy bone and is just about to enjoy it when a big nasty-looking brute of a dog appears. TOBY snarls and growls at the intruder, but to no avail. He is no match for the vicious cur which rushes in, and, after a brief encounter . . .

Cal erased the last two words from the screen in case they evoked the film of the same name and raised unflattering comparisons with his own script.

He is no match for the vicious cur which rushes in, and, after a . . . short fight, drives TOBY away minus the bone.

Cal read through the scene, then switched on his tape recorder and went to the bathroom. As he unzipped his flies, there was a sudden burst of music and shouting from next door. Cal smiled when he heard Tommy's voice. It was as if they were still in the pub together.

TOMMY

Hey! Turn that bloody juke-box down, will you? We can't hear ourselves think here!

CUSTOMER I

Piss off, Tommy! What's the point in playing the fucking thing if you can't hear it?

TOMMY

(to Cal)

Do you want to go in another room where it's quieter?

CAL

No, This is fine.

(pause)

Would you like another drink before we start?

TOMMY

No. I'm all right for now, thanks.

(pause)

Well, there was a few of us stood about outside Phil Walton's house, exchanging a few words with the copper on guard . . .

(He starts to laugh)

CAL

What are you laughing at?

TOMMY

I was just thinking about an incident later on in the strike when another scab went back to work. He was a Czech called Jiri Skuhravy and two of the lads went round to his house one night to paint a slogan on his house. They intended to paint CZECHOSLOVAKIAN SCAB! but they couldn't spell it, so they painted POLISH SCAB! instead.

TOMMY and CAL laugh, but Tommy's laugh develops into a hacking cough.

CUSTOMER 2

It sound as if you could do with some Night Nurse, Tommy.

TOMMY

There's nowt I'd like better.
Any idea where I can find one?

There is laughter in the background from other customers.

TOMMY

Anyway, when Skuhravy sees it next morning – POLISH SCAB! all across the side of his house – he was bloody furious. But it wasn't being called a scab that made him mad. It was being called Polish.

The story amused Cal just as much the second time round in his hotel room as when Tommy had told it earlier in the pub. He sat on the bed laughing, and the general amusement on the tape was so prolonged that he had time to take off his shoes and stretch out before Tommy resumed his tale.

TOMMY

Anyway, to get back to your dad. He goes up to the bobby at the door and asks if he can go in and see the scab, Walton. They're chatting away and that, there's no trouble, then all of a sudden this police van draws up outside the house and a load of bobbies jump out and start moving us on, shoving us with their batons and that and insulting us. That Inspector Tolson was in charge. He was a right bastard, him. He's calling us lazy bastards and all the names under the sun. They were just looking for trouble, you could tell. Then one of the coppers starts shoving Helen Woofitt. She's got her little daughter with her as well. I mean, you're not looking for trouble, are you, when you have got your kids with you? Helen says to him, Hey, keep your filthy hands to yourself! I don't want you touching me! Something like that. The copper says, I wouldn't touch you with a barge pole. Of course her daughter, she must have been only about four or five, was terrified by this time and she starts to cry. So Helen says to the copper, I bet you feel right proud of yourself, don't you, pushing women around and making kids cry. And do you know what the bastard said? I can remember it to this day. He said, Call yourself a woman? You're just a miner's moll. I wouldn't piss on you. Well, you can imagine what happened next, can't you? It was bloody chaos. Helen went for him. Fights broke out. There was hell on. That's when your dad arrived on the scene. He came down the path and tried to calm things down. It made no difference, though. He just got truncheoned and thrown in the van with the others. They even arrested Helen Woofitt.

Cal listened to the rest of the tape, then opened the drawer in the bedside table and took out the envelope which contained his father's prison letters. He emptied them on to the bed and glanced through them.

I really miss the lads, you know. I think that's one thing people outside mining areas never understand, how close we all are and how working together develops a sense of comradeship and trust in each other . . .

When I'm really depressed I keep telling myself to put it down to experience and try to learn something from it. It's hard to learn anything in here, though, because being in prison turns you into a zombie if you're not careful. It's nothing to do with rehabilitation or anything like that. The idea seems to be to kill your brain . . .

One definite bonus, though, has been meeting people from different backgrounds. At one end of the scale there's young lads in for stealing televisions and stereos with no work and no prospects of getting any. And at the other end there's rich people convicted of fraud and theft whose only motive is greed. No doubt when they're in court, though, motives don't come into it . . .

I've just looked up and there's a mouse on the window-sill. I don't mind the mice, though, it's the cockroaches I can't stand. Can you remember that time when one of our Karl's mice ran up your sleeve?

Cal wondered if it was one of the unacceptable white mice which reminded him of the counter-revolutionary White armies which had almost overthrown the Bolshevik government in 1919, or one of the brown, politically correct substitutes. He glanced at his watch, replaced the letters in the envelope and, after a quick wash, hurried downstairs. Christine was waiting for him in the bar.

Sorry I'm late. I was working. I got carried away.

I was going to come up to your room.
Why didn't you?
I didn't want to appear too keen.
Would you like to go up now?
Before dinner?
Why not? We could work up an appetite.
Charlie (the barman) said: What's this, then – a family reunion?

Later, lying on the bed, Christine lit a cigarette and watched Cal kiss his way up her body. When he reached her face, she wrinkled her nose and sniffed at him.
You smell.
What of?
You know.
He kissed her mouth then lay on his back with his head on her stomach. You're incredibly sexy – do you know that? As soon as I see you I want to take your clothes off. When we were sitting in the bar, I wanted to kneel down and put my head up your skirt.
What, in front of everybody?
Yes. Would you like that?
He touched her thigh and Christine opened her legs for him.
Did you fancy me when I was going out with Joe and I used to come to your house?
I never really thought about it. You were Joe's girlfriend. Anyway, I only saw you a few times when I came home from university.
I met your girlfriend once. Do you remember?
Laura?
She was an art student, wasn't she? I'd never met anybody like her before. I was dead impressed.
Cal laughed and gently squeezed her fleshy lips. She was a student at Camberwell Art College.
Didn't you live together for a while?
Yes. When I graduated I got a job on the *Yorkshire Post*. We rented a cottage in a village near Leeds.

Christine finished her cigarette and took hold of his cock.

That was the last straw for my dad when I went to work for a Tory newspaper. He was convinced that I'd done it on purpose to spite him.

The sudden recollection of his father's fury and the ensuing row was so vivid that it left him impervious to Christine's fondling . . .

I'd never have believed it! A son of mine working for a Tory newsrag! Totally unprincipled, that's what you are. A traitor to your class. You should be ashamed of yourself! . . . And so on, ending in a hasty departure and his mother's tears.

Cal hadn't cared what his father thought about him then, and he was surprised how much he cared now, twenty years later. And his father was right. He was unprincipled. He had made a good living by it, too.

Funnily enough, though, he was wrong on that score. It was nothing to do with politics. It never crossed my mind. Laura had got a job at the City Art Gallery in Leeds. Then the job came up at the *Yorkshire Post*. It was convenience, that's all.

Christine was fondling his cock to little effect. I thought you fancied me.

Cal stared at her, puzzled. What do you mean?

This . . .

She held up his prick by the foreskin. It hung limply like a dead mouse. Cal laughed and enclosed her hand around it.

Did you fancy me when you used to come to our house?

I was too much in awe of you to even think about it. You were just Joe's clever big brother.

You're not in awe of me now, though?

I'm not in awe of anybody now. I've grown up.

If we'd been in the house on our own, would you have done this?

Cal tightened his grip on her hand and slid it up and down his stiffening cock.

Christine laughed. Not first time. Not straight away.

What about this then? He thrust himself towards her face.

Certainly not! I didn't even know people did things like that. I was a little innocent then.

She turned Cal on to his back and knelt astride him. I wouldn't have done this either. I always thought the man should be on top.

Afterwards, downstairs in the restaurant, Christine said: And this is something else I wouldn't have done.

What?

Let somebody seduce me *before* the meal.

Seduce *you*! You almost dragged me upstairs!

Cal cut into his steak.

The food's not bad here, you know. I'm pleasantly surprised.

Not as good as in France, though?

Well, no. Not quite.

When are you going back?

Cal paused, his fork half raised to his mouth. I'm not sure . . . I've got one or two things to clear up first. He avoided her eyes and looked at her plate. How's the fish?

Christine reached across the table and touched his hand. I'm not trying to put you under pressure, you know. I know you'll be going soon. Just be honest with me, that's all.

I am being . . . He picked up the wine bottle and topped up their glasses. Things haven't turned out as I expected, that's all. I thought I'd only be here for a few days. A flying visit.

So what's keeping you? And don't say me, because I won't believe you.

Cal smiled and squeezed her hand. I'm not sure. It's weird. Everything's changed.

Things have changed round here, that is for sure.

The people, the place. Everything's been ripped apart . . .

But Cal wasn't talking about the effects of the strike. He was talking about himself.

. . . It wasn't a total disaster, though, and a lot of people came out of it a lot stronger than when they went in. Especially the women. I mean, look at your mother. She was always a lovely woman, but totally dominated by your dad. She wasn't after the strike ended, though. They came out of it on equal terms.

I know. When I came back for their wedding anniversary I was surprised at the change in her.

She was fantastic. She started the Foxmoor Women's Action Group on her own. She said she was so fed up of hearing lies on television, especially that miners' wives were strike breakers and always trying to get their husbands back to work, that she decided to do something about it. So she wrote some notices out advertising a meeting in the community centre and stuck them in local shop windows. She said about six came to the first meeting, then the numbers grew as the strike went on . . .

Cal looked at the morsel of salmon poised on Christine's fork. She was so intent on her story that she had forgotten all about it.

Your dad was against it at first.

That's predictable.

He thought the women should stay out of it. A woman's place and all that. A lot of men felt the same way. But your mother was determined to go through with it. And there wasn't a lot your dad could do about it, really. What with picketing and meetings he was never at home. It was fantastic, Karl. In the end the women were the backbone of the strike. If it had been up to them, the men would never have gone back to work. They'd still be on strike now.

Cal laughed as the rising cadence of the last two words brought startled glances from a nearby table. It must have seemed like a bizarre injunction coming from someone eating *saumon en croûte*. Champagne socialists, they were probably muttering as they turned back to their dinners.

Cal transferred the scene into a script:

> CAL and CHRISTINE are arguing with the people at the next table.

TORY DINERS
(sneering)
Champagne socialists, eh?

CAL
(pouring the wine)
No. Chablis socialists actually.

He liked it. He would try to use it some time. But when would he ever write a script which included a political argument? He switched back to Christine.

I didn't get involved in the strike at first. In fact – and I'm ashamed to say it now – when they came out I *did* want Joe to go back to work. I didn't understand the issues then. I was more interested in the mortgage and the car and holidays and that. I thought they were stupid, coming out on strike. It just seemed like throwing money away.

Cal admired her candour. He would have made any number of excuses rather than admit to naked self-interest.

I don't know what I was moaning about, looking back on it. I mean it wasn't as if we were starving. At least I was working, so we had one wage coming in. A lot of families with kids and the wife at home suffered terrible hardship. I don't know how they stood it.

So how did you get involved, then?

It happened when Joe left me. I was devastated. Your mother suggested getting involved in the Women's Action Group to take my mind off things a bit. So I did. I threw myself into it: fund-raising, helping in the food kitchen, sorting clothes out that people had sent in. It was fantastic. I became independent. I started to think for myself.

Cal nodded towards her plate. Your dinner's getting cold.

She finished it swiftly and dutifully, eager to resume her story.

When we were collecting money in other parts of the country, we got some right abuse, you know. Lazy miners. Commies, enemy within, that kind of thing. You had to know your stuff to be able to answer back. I even began to speak at meetings. Can you believe it?

He could now. But not then. She hardly spoke in the house, never mind at public meetings.

But your mother, she was brilliant. It's amazing when you think about it. She went to Germany. All on her own. She'd never been out of the country before and there she was speaking at universities and public meetings to packed audiences. I've seen the photographs she brought back. This brave old woman standing there . . .

Her voice broke with emotion and she couldn't continue. Cal leaned across the table and kissed her. There were tears in his eyes too.

Harry was sitting in his armchair with the stray cat on his knee. He tried to stroke it but his hand fell heavily on its back and it jumped down. Maisie picked it up and stood in front of the fire nursing it like a baby.

Poor thing. He's not trying to hurt you.

The cat did not look too happy about being on its back either and it stared about wildly, ready to squirm free.

Did you say you'd got a cat, Karl?

No, a dog.

I didn't know you liked dogs.

He was Hélène's originally. I sort of adopted him when we started living together.

He watched the final furlong of a horse race on television.

Does my dad still have a bet?

Why don't you ask him?

Cal watched the horses slowing down, the jockeys relaxing in their saddles.

I was just saying, Dad, do you still have a bet on the horses?

It's no good talking to him from there. He can't see your face.

Cal got up from the settee and crossed the room.

And don't shout.

Cal knelt down in front of his father's chair.

Just speak slowly and clearly in your normal voice.

I was asking my mother if you still had a flutter on the horses, Dad.

Harry Rickards stared over Cal's head without replying. They resembled a tableau of a penitent son begging forgiveness from his pitiless father. Cal turned to his mother for help.

Ask him again. It sometimes takes a bit for it to sink in.

Dad? Cal touched his father's knee. Do you still have a bet on the horses?

Repeated a second time, with the racing having been replaced by the afternoon news, the question appeared increasingly irrelevant. Cal started to sweat. He wasn't sure if it was caused by the heat from the fire, or being on his knees while he waited for an answer. He couldn't prove it, but he was convinced that his father understood what he was saying, but was refusing to answer out of spite. He wondered what would happen if he left the room then peeped round the door and watched his mother ask the question.

He's probably too worked up or something to answer, Karl. Tell him that it doesn't matter and you'll speak to him again.

OK, Dad. It's not important. We'll leave it for now.

He stood up, relieved but disappointed that he had not been able to get through. His mother sensed it. She was still nursing the cat, which had fallen asleep in her arms.

Don't worry about it. He's better some days than others.

He certainly looks better.

Cal felt obliged to sound positive for his mother's sake, even though his father looked much the same to him. His face was still unbalanced with his eyes set diagonally like two spots on a domino.

Oh, he's a lot better. It'll be a long job, though. We'll just have to be patient, that's all.

They were drawn to an item on the television news about pit closures in the Nottinghamshire coalfield.

Cal glanced at his father for signs of agitation.

Hadn't we better turn it off in case it gets him worked up? We don't want him to have a heart attack as well.

Cal realized immediately that this remark could have been interpreted as levity, but his mother laughed.

It'll do him the world of good hearing that. Serves them right, doesn't it, Harry? Then to Cal: We'd have won the strike if it hadn't been for the Notts miners scabbing. Even with the government, the law, the police and the press against us, we'd still have won if we'd been united.

She spoke with such conviction that Cal understood why Christine had so much respect for her.

Have you seen Christine at all?

Cal was startled by the question. Not only was his mother an orator. She appeared to be psychic too.

We've been out once or twice. Why?

No reason. I was just asking.

She's the only person I know round here now.

His mother did not respond, but Cal felt there was something condemnatory in her silence.

Is it because of Joe?
What about him?
Me. Seeing Christine.
It's funny, isn't it, the way things turn out?
What do you mean?
Families. All those years ago when you were going out with Laura, and Joe was courting Christine. I suppose I thought you'd both get married and settle down. You know, like you do.
She rocked the cat in her arms and smiled down at it. Cal thought she was going to break out into a lullaby.
You're spoiling that cat. You'll never get rid of it now, you know.
Didn't you ever fancy having a family, Karl?
Cal stalled for a few moments by watching television and he was still looking at the screen when he answered her. Not really. I've moved round a lot. There's been one or two women along the way, but children never came into it.
What about Hélène?
What about her?
You've known her a long time.
Cal worked it out. Five, six years. Yes, I suppose that is a long time. For me.
Isn't she interested in children?
Hélène! His exclamation was loud enough to wake up the cat. No way. She's too interested in her career. Oh, by the way, I've got a little surprise for you tonight.
What is it?
Wait and see. If I tell you now it won't be a surprise, will it?
Why don't you stop for your tea then?
Cal tried to think of an excuse, but he couldn't come up with anything convincing. Yes. All right then. That'll be nice.
I'd better nip up to the shops. You stop here and look after your dad.

She placed the cat on the sofa next to Cal. There. Sit next to your Uncle Karl until I get back.

Cal stood up abruptly as if he was allergic to cats. I'll go to the shops for you.

What for?

Well . . . Save you a journey. Save your legs.

Maisie laughed. Save my legs! What for, a rainy day? Her mood changed. No. You stop here with your dad.

She had guessed his motive and was annoyed with him. Cal glanced at his father and felt ashamed of himself for making it so obvious. It was so easy to forget that he was in the room and probably listening to every word they said. Cal hoped not; otherwise it would confirm his father's low opinion of him.

Maisie went into the hall and returned wearing her coat. She stood in front of her husband and touched his arm.

Harry, I'm going to the shops. She pointed at her shopping bag. I won't be long. Our Karl'll look after you until I get back.

Cal wondered if this information might cause his father to have a relapse, but after a laboured reply which Maisie interpreted favourably, she left the room. The cat raised its head from the sofa as she opened the back door.

As Cal stood at the window and watched her walk up the path, he realized that it was the first time he had seen her leave the house since he had arrived back. So who looked after his father when she usually went shopping? A neighbour? The nurse? He had no idea. He had never thought to ask. His father had always accused him of being a selfish bastard who didn't care a shit about anybody else. Or a bourgeois opportunist. That was another favourite term of abuse. And when he was in full swing, he strung all the insults together and called him a selfish bourgeois opportunist bastard.

And he was right. Cal couldn't deny it. But his penitence lasted only the time it took his mother to reach the gate. As she closed it behind her, he hoped she wouldn't take too long.

The news bulletin had ended and the horse racing was back on television. Cal couldn't tell if his father was watching it or not. He had slipped down in his chair and it was difficult to make out where his eyes were focused.

Do you want to watch the racing, Dad, or would you like to watch something else?

Cal realized immediately that the question – two questions – were too complicated and he had asked them too fast. Speak slowly and clearly, his mother had told him, and keep any questions short.

Does our Joe still follow the horses, Dad?

No response.

Our Joe! (Don't shout.) He used to enjoy a flutter when he was younger. Can you remember?

Cal remembered the time Joe had phoned his digs (the only time) when he was at university and left a tip for the Derby with his room-mate. Tell our Karl it's a certainty, Simon had said when he got in, parodying Joe's accent. Tell him it's . . . what did he say? Tell him it's *barn* to win. Simon laughed unpleasantly. And what the fuck does that mean in plain English, *barn* to win? Cal felt a sudden rush of affection for his brother who cared enough about him to phone a tip through to London. He knew it wouldn't have come easily to Joe, and even though he was working hard to lose his own northern accent, he wasn't having this public-school poofter taking the piss out of his brother. Unlike Joe, and his father, he wasn't interested in horse racing, and normally he would have ignored the tip. But as an act of solidarity and gratitude, he placed a pound on the horse and it came in at 10–1. When he collected his winnings, he spread the notes like a fan and wafted them in Simon's face. There you are, look. The horse was *bound* to win, like Joe said. It fucking romped it.

That night, he spent some of his winnings at a Roxy Music gig. That was where he met Laura.

Cal remembered something else. He turned to his father. I'm going to the bathroom, Dad. I'll not be a minute.

Cal realized that he was nodding and grinning like a fool. He was glad to get out of the room. He couldn't stand the silence: that baleful stare. He was convinced that his father understood every word he said and was playing dumb to embarrass him. The old bastard. Cal preferred him in full spate. It was punishing. But at least it was out in the open and he could always fight back.

Cal went upstairs into the back bedroom which he used to share with Joe. It contained the same furniture he had grown up with: twin beds covered with candlewick bedspreads, two chairs and a matching wardrobe and chest of drawers. But it was more of a storeroom than a bedroom now and the place was cluttered up with carpet ends, spare bedding, his mother's pasting board and sewing machine, and the old aspidistra on its stand by the window.

The room felt damp. Cal touched the radiator. It was cold. A steely cold as if it had never been turned on. The central heating had been installed since he left home but they rarely seemed to use it. It was cold in the kitchen and in the living-room away from the fire. Perhaps they couldn't afford it. Perhaps he should sign them a cheque when he left. But it was more deep-seated than that. A lifetime of frugality had left them incapable of enjoying comfort. If they won a holiday in a luxury hotel, they would still turn off the radiators out of habit.

Cal turned the key in the wardrobe door and remembered to open it carefully. If he had swung it back, it would have banged against the chair. Inside hung a rail of his parents' old clothes: the overflow from their own wardrobe. Cal worked along the rail, separating garments with his hand. He recognized a dress, a blouse, a suit. It was a fashion museum, a sartorial calendar of his youth. These rejects had hung here for years, undisturbed and unworn. The next time they were removed from their hangers would be after his parents' deaths, when the house was being cleared.

Cal closed the wardrobe door and looked out of the window. He could see the rec. from here. He could see the goalposts and the swings. When he was at grammar school, he used to do his homework downstairs in case he was distracted by a football match. As he stared across the rooftops, Cal realized that he was rubbing one of the aspidistra leaves between his finger and thumb, the way he rubbed Bruno's ears when he was sitting in a deckchair by the pool, or working at his desk inside. He smiled at the thought of him. Anybody looking up from the back garden would have thought he was smiling at them and waved, but Cal wouldn't have noticed them straight away. He wasn't there. He was in the arrival lounge at Nice airport hugging Hélène, with Bruno jumping up at him for a share of his attention . . .

Cal had rubbed a shiny patch on the leaf. He took out his handkerchief and dusted all the leaves to restore their gloss. He pressed the soil. It was rock hard. Ants could have fallen to their death down the cracks. Poor thing. He felt sorry for it. Nobody had ever liked it, but it was a present from Auntie Maureen and she might have been offended if they had thrown it away. It became part of the furniture. Occasionally somebody would notice it and water it with dregs of coffee or tea, and sometimes Karl used to pour Joe's pop over it to tease him. But he did it once too often, and Joe finally cracked at the sight of his beloved Tizer fizzing on the soil. He snatched Karl's bottle of ink from the table and emptied it into the pot. Then he pissed on the ink to complete his revenge. Tizer, ink and piss. It was enough to kill an oak. Yet here it stood, neglected and half forgotten, but still alive. A link with the past, like the hat boxes on top of the wardrobe and the rail of clothes inside.

Cal turned away from the window and crossed the room to the chest of drawers, on top of which lay other familiar objects including the Evils of Capitalism bronze, and a picture lying face down. He turned it over. It was the photograph of Harry Pollitt. He would have enjoyed this discovery at one time and discomfited his father by asking ironically if the removal of his icons from the living-room meant that the class struggle had now been won. But not now. He was sad to see them relegated to the spare room. He knew that their displacement had nothing to do with the defeat of capitalism: it was a measure of his father's disappointment after a lifetime struggle against it.

Cal touched the bronze worker, who appeared to be grimacing even more painfully than he remembered as he pulled the chariot carrying the triumvirate of capitalist oppressors. He smiled as he noticed the repaired cigar which his mother had broken. As he was bending down to open the bottom drawer, he noticed something else: a tiny hole in the wall above the chest. He quickly traced the other three holes which completed the corners of a square. They had been made by drawing pins when he had put up a Rolling Stones poster. His mother was furious when she saw it and made him take it down. You're not ruining my wallpaper with that lot! she said.

Cal opened the drawer and took out the shoe-box containing the family photographs. He tipped them out on his bed then sat down and slid them apart until he uncovered the one he was looking for. It was a snapshot of Laura and himself taken in the back garden on a visit home from university. He had his arm around her, and in the background his father formed a third, unfocused, figure in the greenhouse behind them.

Cal laughed at his shoulder-length hair and platform shoes, but his smile faded as he concentrated on Laura. Christine was right: she did look arty. She was wearing a black T-shirt and jeans, but both garments looked faded compared with her long, glossy hair. Cal remembered her voice, the way she laughed, but above all, the texture of her skin, which felt as soft as the tissue paper which protected the illustrations in her art books.

Cal put the photograph in his pocket then replaced the others in the box. Seeing his father in it had made him realize that it was time he went back downstairs. As he picked up the envelopes containing the insurance policies and other family records, he noticed one with GERMANY printed on it in his mother's handwriting. He hesitated, but he couldn't resist it and he emptied the contents on to the bed. It contained letters and posters from Freiburg, rail and airline tickets and a writing pad with LECTURE NOTES on the cover. Cal opened it.

1. Stress that right from the beginning we'd decided that our group was going to be a campaigning group and not just a support group.
2. We wanted women to join who believed in what the miners were fighting for whether they were miners' wives or not. Because if the pits close the villages close with them and it becomes a depressed area for everybody who lives there not just for mining families.
3. Talk about support from all over Europe – food, clothes, money etc.
4. Stress that we're interested in campaigning. Holding rallies etc. In fact raising political awareness about the strike, not just money.
5. Talk about pressures from govt, police and media to break the strike. Bully boys, Marxists,

mindless hooligans, enemy within etc. Impossible for people not involved to understand what pressure we're under.

The notes went on for several pages but Cal didn't have time to read them. He closed the notebook and stared at the title, LECTURE NOTES. His own mother turned teacher. He would have been so proud to have listened to her.

He glanced at the airline tickets as he replaced the notebook and other mementos in the envelope: Manchester–Munich; Alitalia, Florence–Manchester. Florence? She hadn't said anything about fund-raising in Italy, and there were no photographs of her there in the box. Then he remembered the creased sepia photograph of the farmhouse on the hillside. That wasn't in the box either. It was a mystery, and judging by her embarrassment when she had snatched it from his hand and hidden it in her apron pocket, one which she was reluctant to disclose.

Cal watered the aspidistra then went downstairs. He could hear his father before he reached the bottom. He was making croacky, gurgling sounds as if his throat had been cut. Cal dashed into the living-room, nearly tripping over the cat which was dashing out terrified, making for the back door. Harry was sitting upright, gripping the arms of the chair as if he was trying to speak. He was in a state of extreme agitation. Cal thought he was having another stroke. He looked out of the window. Where was his mother? Why wasn't she back? Should he phone the doctor? The hospital? Why hadn't she left him the numbers? It was all her fault! He was furious with her for being so inconsiderate.

Then he smelled it. Oh, no! Please God, not that. Perhaps it was the cat. Perhaps that's why it was dashing from the room. But even as he scanned the carpet for the offending mess, he knew what had happened: his father had shit himself while he had been upstairs. He could feel his lips starting to quiver in disgust. He looked out of the window again. Should he get in the car and try to find his mother? If she had let him go to the shops this wouldn't have happened. It was all her fault! He blushed at his duplicity. How could he – his own mother? He had even blamed the cat. Anybody rather than face responsibility for his negligence. But he couldn't just let him sit there in his own mess or there would be hell to pay when his mother got back. He knew what she would say – You're irresponsible, Karl! That's what you are. Always have been and always will be. I leave you for two minutes and look what happens! He rehearsed a few excuses, but none of them were convincing and his mother blasted them away . . . There was nothing else for it:

Come on, Dad. Don't worry about it. (As if it was his own fault!) Let's get you cleaned up.

The stench intensified as Cal helped him to his feet and he felt his gorge rise. He thought he was going to be sick. He glanced down at the chair and was relieved to see that the cushion was unstained. He held his father upright wondering what to do next. He couldn't carry him upstairs to the bathroom because he was too heavy, and he couldn't risk giving him a piggy-back because he might fall off. But much more pertinently, he didn't relish the thought of supporting his father underneath the buttocks. Come on, Dad, lie down on the floor. That's it, steady . . .

Cal collapsed him gently on to the carpet and laid him on his back. He fetched several back copies of the *Morning Star* from the newspaper rack and spread them out underneath his father before removing his shoes and socks.

Right. Let's get you undressed, then.

Cal removed his father's shirt, then pulled down his trousers and underpants together. He decided there and then that nurses should be paid a thousand pounds a week. He could hardly bear to work. His face set in a grimace of disgust and he was relieved that he hadn't had his tea. The soiled garments smeared his hands. He rolled them up, took them outside and threw them into the back garden. They landed on the lawn. The little lawn where he had been photographed with Laura twenty years ago.

He hurried back inside, anxious not to leave his father for a moment now, placed a cushion under his head to make him more comfortable, then wiped off most of the excrement with sheets of newspaper.

There you are. I'll just go and fetch some water. I'll not be a minute.

He returned from the kitchen with a bowl of warm water, then knelt down beside his father and washed him all over. He had forgotten about the mosaic of blue mining scars and seared shrapnel wounds covering his body. What a brave life he had led: five years fighting in the war followed by a lifetime of danger down the pit: the Enemy Within. Cal was proud to wash his feet.

When Maisie returned from the shops, Harry was back in his chair by the fire, dressed in his pyjamas. Cal explained what had happened. He said they had been watching the racing on television when suddenly his father had become agitated. He said he thought it was the close finish to the race that had made him excited, but by the time he had realized what was wrong, it was too late.

Cal kept his back to his father and spoke quickly in a low voice, hoping that he couldn't hear, but nevertheless anticipating a tortured rebuttal at any second. But whether he was too exhausted by his ordeal, or had not understood what Cal had said, he did not respond and Cal escaped gratefully into the kitchen to help his mother prepare the tea.

Later that evening when Harry was asleep, Cal sat his

mother down on the sofa in front of the television and poured her a glass of sherry.

What's this in aid of? She smiled, enjoying being fussed over.

It's the surprise I was telling you about.

He switched on the television.

Why, what's on?

You'll see.

It was a foreign film on Channel 4.

Is this it?

Cal nodded. Maisie stood up.

Where are you going? He thought she was leaving already.

To fetch my glasses or I won't be able to read it.

The film was set in Lyon during the Nazi occupation of France.

That's where some of the women went fund-raising during the strike.

To Lyon?

To France. Do you live anywhere near there?

No. I live further south, in Provence.

Mrs Thorpe's daughter lives abroad.

In France?

No, in Spain.

The film opens in a back street with people queuing outside a bakery. The shop window is empty. Two German soldiers walk down the street. They notice an attractive woman standing in the queue and make suggestive remarks to each other in German. The woman looks away in disgust.

Cut to inside the shop, where the woman is buying bread. She is only allowed half a baguette in spite of strong protests that this is not enough. She pays the baker and leaves.

Can you understand what they're saying, Karl?

Yes.

I wish I could. I'm that busy reading the titles, I'm missing what's going on.

The woman arrives home, unlocks the door and goes inside. She takes off her hat and coat, then breaks the baguette and takes out a scrap of paper.

I used to have my hair done like that, waved with a parting.

That's Hélène.

Who?

Hélène. Who I live with.

Her?

That was the surprise.

Well, fancy . . .

Hélène unfolds the paper, reads it, then throws it in the fire. She looks worried. It is obviously bad news.

She's lovely, Karl.

Cal nodded. His mother was right. She was a good actress, too. When she read that note you knew she was in deep trouble.

Is her hair natural?

Cal glanced at his mother, startled. What do you mean?

The colour. Blonde.

Cal laughed. I thought you meant does she wear a wig.

Mrs Allsop's started to wear a wig. It's red. You've never seen anything like it. She looks like that mother chimp on the PG Tips advert.

Cal laughed again. Yes, it's natural.

It must be funny watching her from here. I can remember watching Orgreave on the news when our Joe was arrested. It seemed unreal.

Did you see him?

No, but I saw Charlie Thomas being helped away with blood pouring down his face.

There was blood pouring down the face of the baker in the film, as two Gestapo officers dragged him from his shop and threw him into the back of a car.

Is she nice?

Yes. Very nice.

Why are you seeing Christine then?

Cal watched Hélène making a telephone call. She was wearing a brown felt hat with a wide brim. She still wore it sometimes. She had kept it as a souvenir from the film.

I wouldn't say I was *seeing* her.

What would you say then?

He didn't say anything while Hélène was still on the screen.

I've told you before. We've been out for a drink once or twice. What's wrong with that?

It's a small town, Karl. People talk.

Yes. That was one of the reasons why he couldn't wait to get away. Everybody minding everybody else's business. You took a girl to the pictures and your parents knew about it before the lights went down.

Let them. They can talk as much as they like, for all I care.

Well, you should care.

What, about people gossiping?

No, about Christine.

I do care about her. I've known her since she was a girl. She's like family.

You're using her.

Using her?

Yes! Don't be so damned selfish, Karl!

Their raised voices disturbed Harry in his bed by the wall, but after a burst of gibberish he quickly settled down.

You've got time on your hands and it's convenient for you. It's as simple as that.

Look, I'm not forcing her to see me. She can always say no.

Yes, I know. But you'll be going back to France soon. She nodded towards the television. Back to Helen. I know you're both grown up and it's no business of mine, but sometimes you don't realize what you're getting into and you get hurt. You can't always rule your feelings, Karl . . .

Her voice faltered and she took out her handkerchief and blew her nose.

Cal couldn't understand why she was so upset. He wondered if she felt guilty, or responsible in some vague way because Joe had left Christine and she didn't want to see it happen again. Or perhaps she was concerned about Joe's feelings in case he found out. But why worry about him? He was the guilty party in the first place. Anyway, it had happened such a long time ago that he wouldn't care a damn who she was going out with. But it didn't seem to work like that. He remembered leaving Laura. It was all over. Finished. But when he heard she was seeing someone else, he was furious and wanted her back. His mother was right: you can't always rule your feelings.

Would you like another sherry?

No thanks. But I'd love a cup of tea.

As the film cut from a gloomy church interior to a sunny landscape and lightened the room, Cal could see that his mother was crying.

When he returned with the tea tray, Maisie had composed herself and was engrossed in the film. Hélène and her husband – who was the leader of the resistance movement – were making love before he departed on a dangerous mission. It was a passionate scene played with sexy intensity. This could be the last time they saw each other and they were making the most of it.

Cal was uneasy watching it with his mother. He thought she might be embarrassed by the nudity. But when he held out her cup, she was so involved in the action that he had to nudge her before she took it. There had been rumours in the French gossip magazines about an affair between Hélène and Roland Lafond during the shooting of the film. She had denied them, of course, but they were playing the scene with such conviction that it was possible to imagine how the rumours began.

Don't you get jealous, Karl, watching her like that with somebody else?

Of course not. She's playing a part. It's work.

But she was playing it so well that he began to wonder if there was anything in the story after all. It was a long time since she had made love to him like that, urgently, as if she meant it. She kissed Roland about the face. Kissed him! She was eating him! But then Hélène always saved her best performances for the screen, Cal told himself, as she stroked Roland's cheek, the way she used to stroke his.

Has she been in anything you've written, Karl?

No, not yet.

As if it was just a matter of time. But time had nothing to do with it. It was talent. She was too good to appear in the kind of films that he wrote. He couldn't imagine Hélène in *It's a Dog's Life* or *Jack in the Box*, or any of his other masterpieces which lay undisturbed on the shelves of the video shops. So what? He worked regularly. He was adaptable, reliable. He delivered on time. He wouldn't own a converted farmhouse in France if he sat around agonizing over every project like Hélène did. Was it worth doing? How would it affect her career? Fuck the career! It was worth doing if the money was right. It was as simple as that. He couldn't afford the luxury of a social conscience, and anyway who wants to pay good money to see films about unmarried mothers throwing themselves off the balconies of high-rise flats? Or some cunt freezing to death in a cardboard box?

Are you all right, Karl?

What?

You're muttering to yourself.

Have you got any beer in the house?

No, but I'll pop up to the off-licence if you like.

Cal wasn't sure if she was being sarcastic after what had happened when she had gone out earlier. He glanced across at his father in bed.

No thanks. I'm not that desperate.

It's a good picture, Karl. I'm enjoying it.

She was right. It was a good picture. It was intelligent and exciting and full of moral ambiguities. Not all the Germans were monsters, and all the French weren't heroes either. Should Hélène's friend have been beaten up and ostracized when she slept with the Nazi officer in exchange for medicine for her sick child? Cal wondered if he would have intervened when the Gestapo arrested the Jewish tailor. He wondered if he would have intervened when his father and Joe were arrested during the strike. Hélène was being arrested now. The Germans had discovered that her husband was the leader of the local resistance movement. Where was he? She refused to answer. Would she break under torture?

Yes, it was a good picture all right. Cal had to admit it. And in spite of his cynical bluster, he wished that he had written it.

It was strange watching the film in his parents' house. The last time he had seen it was at the Cannes Film Festival, where Hélène had won Best Actress Award.

Later, back at the hotel, Cal sat up in bed with a glass of Scotch and watched a late night American cops and robbers movie: the sort of thing that he might have written. Black cop and white cop are teamed up together. At first they hate each other. Gradually they develop a grudging respect for each other. And finally, they are prepared to die for each other.

Hélène could have played the classy foreign dame who is murdered by the psychopath in her elegant Fifth Avenue apartment. Except that she wouldn't have touched the role. It wouldn't have done anything for her career. It wouldn't have done anything for Cal's either, but it would have done a lot for his bank balance.

But could she have played the waitress putting down the two wise guys in the diner? Cal couldn't really see her in the apron and hat. She would have looked gorgeous, but gorgeous like a model on a catwalk, and that wasn't the same as a waitress being run off her feet. She would be too aloof for the part, too disengaged. She would have difficulty hiding her contempt for the two arseholes in the booth.

But the part wasn't written that way. It demanded a more conventional, Hollywood-type performance with the waitress giving as good as she got . . . Christine! Christine could have played the part. She would have looked just right, attractive yet accessible. The sort that the two jerks would have fancied their chances with after a couple of beers. She would have laughed off their suggestive remarks, then delivered a crushing one-liner as she walked away.

His mother was wrong about Christine. He wasn't using her, he was becoming involved with her, which was much more serious. Perhaps he should stop seeing her before things got out of control? Yes. Definitely. It made sense. He would ring her in the morning and explain that in the long run, etc . . . But at the moment he didn't care about the long run, or the medium run, he wanted Christine in the room with him: now.

Instead of watching the car chase on TV, he wanted to watch Christine undress. She enjoyed watching him watch her. It turned her on. She would slip her fingers underneath her suspenders and stroke her thighs, then put one high-heeled foot up on the bed and pull her knickers to one side . . . swampy, sticky, dirty stuff. Cal wondered where she had learned it. Perhaps there was more to Joe than met the eye.

It was never like that with Hélène. She was more restrained and self-absorbed when they made love. It was good, and she was so beautiful, but she always seemed to be aiming for some kind of higher, significant experience, instead of lowering her sights and enjoying a good fuck. There was never that raw, vulgar excitement that he felt with Christine, like sometimes wanting to crawl under the table and put his head up her skirt. Or watch her eating her dinner with her tits hanging out. He remembered the time she had pierced her knickers with the heel of her shoe as she was getting undressed. She laughed, then provocatively ripped them apart and threw them on to the bed.

Hélène always removed her knickers with one graceful stoop before getting into bed. Cal was always intimidated by her underwear, knickers and bra at a thousand francs a set. It was too expensive for rough handling and he was afraid of tearing the material when the hooks and eyes got stuck on her bra. Sometimes, depending on the position they were in, Cal could read the labels on Christine's knickers: size, brand name and washing instructions. The designer labels inside Hélène's knickers were more tasteful, but Cal wasn't interested in tasteful knickers. He liked tart's knickers, cut high up the sides and swooping down under the crotch. And dirty talk. He liked that too, but with Hélène it was all whispered endearments . . . *Oh, Cal . . . Je t'aime . . . Mon coeur* . . . Just like in a film. If he told her that he wanted to shove a candle up her arse, she would probably have a fit and call the police.

But sadly it all had to end. It wasn't fair on either Christine or Hélène. He would phone Christine in the morning and arrange a final meeting. Dutifully, he sat on the bed nursing his erection. He looked at his watch. It was too late to phone her now, or he would have asked her to come to the hotel and broken the bad news immediately.

Cal got up late. He felt ill. He had channel-hopped through the detective movie, and then because he couldn't sleep for thinking about Christine (the sexy women in the commercials made it worse) he had started to watch an even more risible film about two archaeologists called Charles and Catherine seeking a lost city in the jungle . . . He woke up to a buzzing screen and a litter of miniature whisky bottles on the bedside table. As he turned out the lights, he remembered that just before he had dozed off Charles had shot a tiger as it was about to attack Catherine. It was even worse than the films he wrote.

Cal had a shower and got dressed. He felt tetchy and out of sorts. He made a cup of coffee, then sat on the bed to consider his next move. His father was out of danger now, so there was no reason to stay any longer on his account. He was behind with the script. He blamed it on the room. There was no atmosphere. It depressed him. He couldn't recall anything particularly joyful about the hotel room in which he had written *Trouble in Store*, his most lucrative movie. But perhaps hotel rooms in Los Angeles were more conducive to creativity than hotel rooms in a clapped-out mining town. And Christine? Ripped knickers or not, there were other things to consider. Sex wasn't everything. He would be crazy to jeopardize his relationship with Hélène . . . He came to a decision. It was time to go home.

He stood up and put on his jacket. He felt better already, energized by his new resolve. But first he wanted to complete his investigation into his father's arrest. He suspected already that he was innocent, but his enquiries had kindled his interest in the strike itself and how it had affected the miners and their families. He had inadvertently been drawn back into the community which he had so readily deserted.

As Cal put the tape recorder into his jacket pocket, he found the photograph of Laura and himself which he had taken from the old shoe-box in his parents' house. He stared at the distant strangers and considered once more the problem which had been troubling him increasingly since his arrival. No. It would be too painful: destructive even. And was it worth the upset after all this time? No. Let sleeping dogs lie . . . But if he didn't find out now, he probably never would. Future visits would be fleeting, and when his parents died, he might never return . . .

Staring at the photograph confused him even further. He placed it in the drawer, next to the Bible in the bedside table, then phoned Hélène. He wanted to hear her voice. He wanted to hear her say how much she loved him and missed him. He wanted her to make the decision for him and tell him to come home. But all he heard was his own recorded voice and he banged down the receiver.

Cal drove slowly down Morrison Drive, where his father had been arrested during the strike. He had been to visit his parents first, to find out the scab's address. His mother wasn't sure which house it was; somewhere opposite the shops, she thought. When she asked his father, he became so agitated and incoherent that she had to fetch him a drink to calm him down. She thought it best to drop the subject after that and Cal left the house none the wiser.

Cal parked outside the row of shops and looked at the houses across the road. Perhaps the scab's house had a *black* plaque attached to signify the residence of an *infamous* person. He wondered if any of the shopkeepers had witnessed his father's arrest. It would be interesting to hear an account of the incident from someone less inclined to be as sympathetic towards his father as the family and friends he had interviewed so far. He knew that shopkeepers were notoriously Conservative and would probably have disapproved of the strike anyway because of the effect on their trade. They would have thought it only right and proper that the police should protect a working miner who was brave enough to defy the union bullies.

Cal got out of the car and walked past the shops: hairdressers (CLOSED), bookies, newsagent and supermarket (both fitted with grilles), and at the end of the row, an empty shop, its boarded frontage emblazoned with graffiti. It certainly wasn't Bond Street – there was no doubt about that.

Cal went into the supermarket. It was basic inside with limited meat and vegetable sections and sparsely stacked shelves. He approached the girl on the till. The other tills were unattended, their aisles debarred by sagging chains which, in addition to two elderly customers, emphasized the funereal atmosphere of the place.

Cal realized that the girl was too young to help him. She probably didn't even remember the strike.

Excuse me?

She was miles away. She hadn't even noticed him come in. He could have walked away with a Gro-bag on his shoulder and she wouldn't have raised the alarm. What was she dreaming about? Her wedding? (Cal had noticed her engagement ring.) Or the new house they were saving up to buy away from the council estate? A private house on a private estate . . . Like Christine and Joe.

Excuse me?

The girl turned towards him. Cal noticed the name badge pinned to her overall. They called her Lorraine.

I wonder if I could see the manager, please?

Lorraine turned back to the front and yelled down the middle aisle: *Mister Collins!*

The old woman standing directly in line with this blast was so intent on finding the cheapest brand of cat food that she didn't even look up.

A door marked STAFF PRIVATE opened at the back of the shop, and a man emerged, nipping out a cigarette. He blew on the blackened end, then tucked it into the breast pocket of his blazer which bore the corporate logo of the supermarket chain. As he walked down the aisle past the old woman choosing cat food, Cal recognized him. It was Jack Collins whom he had seen in the bushes with Mary Hanson all those years ago. Cal started to sweat with embarrassment. What if Jack recognized him and began to taunt him? . . . *Well, bugger me if it isn't Peeping Tom! What can I do for you? We've got a nice line in keyholes that you might be interested in . . .*

But he didn't, and Cal knew that his too-bright manufactured smile was the result of a customer-care course and not a natural smile of recognition. It was a Hollywood smile. Film producers used it a lot. Lorraine nodded at Cal.

He wants to see you.

Jack buttoned his blazer before he spoke. Yes, sir. What can I do for you?

Cal hesitated. It's a friend . . . I'm here on behalf of a friend of mine. He lives abroad. In France . . . Oh God! Why had he gone down this road? What did it matter if Jack did remember him? Why did he still feel embarrassed after all this time? His father was arrested during the miners' strike somewhere near here and he was put in prison.

What's his name?

Who, my friend?

No. The bloke who was put in prison.

Harry Rickards.

Harry Rickards? Oh, I know him. Everybody knows Harry round here. He used to be the branch secretary at our pit before he retired. He was a right firebrand, old Harry. Get your soapbox out, Harry, we used to say when he got going.

He shook his head and laughed. Cal had memories, too, of his father's oratory powers, but for him they were less amusing.

. . . You couldn't find a better man anywhere to fight your corner than Harry. He missed his way. He should have been a lawyer or something.

Jack dipped into his top pocket and fished out the half-smoked cigarette. He paused, glanced at Lorraine then put it away again.

His wife Maisie got involved in the strike an' all. She was one of the leading lights of the women's support group.

Cal remembered his mother's words: We weren't a support group, we were an action group.

They went fund-raising all over the country. I think Maisie even went abroad.

She did. She went to Germany.

Jack looked at him in surprise. Do you know her, then?

No. Not really. This friend of mine . . . He paused, diverted by the SPECIAL OFFER sign on the shelf above Jack's head. Standing below it, the special offer appeared to be Jack.

What are you laughing at?

What? Nothing. As I was saying, this friend of mine . . . He decided to risk it. He's Harry Rickards' son, actually. We were at university together.

He watched closely for Jack's response.

Who, Joe? I didn't know he'd been to university.

No, Cal. His other son, Karl.

Karl?!

He sounded as if Cal was making it up. He rubbed his chin while he tried to remember the lost brother. Cal noticed the blue mining scars on his hand.

That's right! I'd forgotten all about him. He went off to London, didn't he? Did well for himself.

It hurt Cal to be treated as an afterthought: a forgotten man. He was a non-person, airbrushed from his family's history like Trotsky from the photograph of the Bolshevik Party Central Committee.

He's a writer. He writes film scripts.

Cal said it forcefully, trying to compensate, trying to impress.

Writer! He should have been here when the fu — He caught himself just in time . . . when the strike was on and wrote about that.

He sounded so reproachful that Cal was relieved he was still in France. Jack turned to Lorraine.

Go and get yourself a cup of tea, love, while I have a talk to this gentleman.

Cal read the nutritional value on a packet of cornflakes to stop himself laughing at Jack's formal tone.

It isn't time yet, Mr Collins.

Never mind that. I'll look after your till.

Lorraine stepped down off her high chair and walked down the aisle to the staffroom. When she was inside, Jack took the half-smoked cigarette out of his pocket and lit up.

You're not supposed to, but she's not going to complain, is she?

He nodded towards a harassed young woman at the door, who was trying to convince her three small children that they didn't need a trolley and that a basket was big enough.

I let them have stuff when it's passed its sell-by date, if I know they're hard up.

Jack unbuttoned his blazer and sat on the conveyor belt at the side of the till.

Who'd have thought I'd have finished up with a job like this?

He shook his head and blew cigarette ash off his sleeve.

When my mates come in, they're always taking the piss out of my blazer. Hey up! they say. I didn't know you'd got a job at Butlins. I wish I had, I tell 'em. At least I'd be getting plenty of cunt. He laughed and shook his head, ruefully. They're nearly all out of work now. It was a bastard of a place, the pit, but you couldn't beat it for solidarity. That's what the strike was about, you know. The miners were the only people Mrs Thatcher was scared of. She knew that if she could beat the miners, the rest of the unions would cave in and they'd be able to privatize everything. They had it all prepared. Did you ever read the Ridley Report?

Read it? Cal hadn't even heard of it.

It was all in there, the preparation for battle. Power stations should be well stocked up with coal in case there was a long strike. Plans for importing coal and recruitment of non-union drivers for haulage firms. Welfare benefits cut off and specially trained police. They were well prepared for it and they didn't half make us pay. I mean, look at Harry Rickards. Look what happened to him! He dropped his tab end, rubbed it out, then nudged it under the till.

Did you know he'd had a stroke?

Who, Harry?

Cal nodded.

No, I didn't know that. Was it serious?

Yes. He's recovering now, though, slowly.

You never hear anything now. It's not the same round here any more. When the pit closed it knocked the spirit out of the place.

Two customers came in and uncoupled a trolley.

Jack stood up and brushed down his blazer. Bloody hell, we've got a rush on. I'd better fetch Lorraine back.

Before you go, I wonder if I could ask you something? This friend of mine, Karl, Harry's son, he's making enquiries about his father's arrest. Apparently he was badly beaten by the police and he's trying to find out what happened.

Jack didn't look shocked at the suggestion of police brutality. He knew it was true. He had experienced it himself.

It happened all the time. The police just made things up. When I went to court after being arrested in Nottinghamshire, the cop said I'd thrown a brick and it bounced up and hit him on the hand. We were in a field at the time. My solicitor said, What was it made of – rubber? It was a farce.

I understand that Karl's father was arrested along this road somewhere. He'd gone to talk to the scab, Phil Walton.

That cunt! It came out louder than Jack intended and he glanced around to see if anybody was staring at him. I'd better watch my fucking language or I'll be getting the sack. He pointed towards the shop window. He lived over there, look, across the road. That house with the tree.

Cal had to stand on his tiptoes to see over the cut-price offers plastered across the glass.

They should have hung him from its branches, the scabbing bastard.

It was a cherry tree. One grew in Cal's garden in France. A hammock hung from the branches of his.

He doesn't live there now, though. He flitted. Nobody'd talk to him. I felt sorry for his wife and kids, though. It wasn't their fault but they copped it just the same. Selfish bastard. Scabs are all the same. They only think about themselves.

Were you there when my dad was arrested?

Your dad?

Sorry. Karl's dad. I've become so involved since I started this research that I almost feel like one of the family.

Why doesn't he come and find out himself?

He's away. In America. Working on a film.

What's it called?

Cal hesitated. *It's a Dog's Life*.

It's a fucking dog's life here, without going to America.

Jack picked up some discarded till receipts. They looked like a collection of bus tickets.

I wasn't there when Harry was arrested, but I heard about it. It was that bastard Tolson that caused it. If he'd have let Harry talk to Phil Walton there wouldn't have been any trouble. He was the same on the picket line. He provoked you to get you arrested.

Jack started to laugh. Cal stared at him, perplexed. His amusement seemed at odds with his subject-matter.

We didn't half get our own back on him, though, one day on the picket line. It had been snowing – bloody freezing it was. We were stood round the brazier trying to keep warm when two of the lads decided to build a snowman. When they'd finished, one of them goes into the cabin and brings out a toy policeman's helmet that somebody had brought down. You know, one of them that you buy at the seaside that says KISS ME QUICK, or summat like that on the front. We used to put it on sometimes to take the piss out of the coppers on duty at the pit gates.

Anyway, one of the lads brings it out of the cabin and pops it on the snowman. Even the two coppers on duty had to laugh. I shouts across to 'em, What about your mate here? He's changed sides. One of them shouts back, I hope he's not from the Met. or you'll be in trouble. They were right bastards them, the Metropolitan Police. Fucking brutal they were. They used to wave handfuls of fivers at us and jeer through their van windows when they knew we hadn't two halfpennies to rub together. His face flushed and he clenched his fists. He was back in the strike again.

Cal restrained a smile as he imagined a customer approaching Jack with a complaint and seeing his staring eyes and raised knuckles.

Anyway . . . Jack relaxed and began to smile. Just then, a police Land-Rover drives up and Tolson gets out to have a word with the coppers on duty at the gate. As soon as our lads see him, they start shouting across at him: Hey up! You've got a new recruit here – pointing at the snowman. Aren't you coming to have a word with him?

When Tolson sees the snowman with the helmet on, he's furious. Get that helmet off it! he shouts. What for? It's not one of yours, young Craig Bailey says. Never mind whose it is, Tolson says. Take it off! We all start taking the piss out of him then. Asking him if the snowman would get done for obstruction, because it meant that we'd got seven men on the picket line now, instead of six. Or would he get nicked for stealing NCB property, because his buttons were made of coal? One of the lads said they'd have to put him in the fridge at the police station.

Cal was laughing so loudly that customers were staring at him from the aisles.

Anyway, Tolson's getting madder and madder and in the end he says, Are you going to take that helmet off that bastard snowman, or do you want me to take it off? I said to him, What are you getting so worked up about? It's only a joke. He says, Right then, don't say you haven't been warned.

So he strides back to the Land-Rover, climbs in, and we can see him talking to the driver and pointing at the snowman. Then right enough, the driver starts the engine and drives straight at it. Then whack! Jack thumped his fist into his palm to illustrate the impact. There was this almighty crash and snow everywhere. I've never seen anything like it. There's Tolson and the driver sat there dazed and we're rolling about pissing ourselves laughing – even the two coppers on duty at the gate were laughing. What Tolson didn't know was that Craig and Scott had built the snowman round a concrete bollard to give it a bit of strength.

Jack couldn't continue for laughing. He wiped his eyes on his sleeve. He hadn't enjoyed himself so much since his days at the pit.

When the Land-Rover backed out, all its front was dented in. It was a right mess. I thought Tolson was going to have a fit, he was that angry. His face was purple. He leans out of the cab shaking his fist at us. I'll get you, you bastards! he shouts. Don't you worry about that!

As Jack roared his threat across the supermarket, the customers looked round and saw a demented-looking figure leaning sideways and shaking his fist. But they soon lost interest and turned back to the shelves, as if such wild behaviour was an everyday occurrence in their lives.

The old woman, who had worked her way up and down the aisles as if she was browsing in a bookshop, placed her goods on the conveyor belt, then defined them with the NEXT CUSTOMER block even though there wasn't one behind her. Jack looked towards the staffroom as if he was going to call Lorraine, then changed his mind and squeezed on to the high chair. He pressed the foot pedal and four items moved towards him: baked beans, sliced bread, fish fingers and a small tin of cat food.

Jack tapped out the prices and slid them down the chute.

Not much on the belt today, love – it must be a bad seam.

She made no immediate response to this mining metaphor, but as she was loading her bag she said:

My husband was killed down the pit. We'd only just got married and we were living with his parents. When I opened the door and the union man said, Can I speak to Mrs Foster, please? I thought he meant George's mother. I hadn't even got used to my new name.

Cal left the supermarket and went into the newsagent's next door. The owner was unwrapping a bundle of newspapers on the counter. As he cut the tape, the pile expanded slightly as if it was breathing out.

Excuse me.

The newsagent glanced at the headlines of the top copy before looking up.

My name's Cal Jones. I'm researching a film about the miners' strike and Jack, the manager of the supermarket, said you might be able to help me.

In what way?

Well, apparently there was an incident across the road when some striking miners were arrested outside the house of a – outside the house of a working miner. Jack said you might have witnessed it.

What's it for, television?

Yes. That's right.

I thought you were from the telly. You don't look as if you're from round here.

Cal was tempted to tell him his real name to restore his local credibility, but decided against it in case the newsagent made the connection with his father and took against him.

Let me tell you something. What did you say your name was – Karl?

Cal.

The newsagent cleared away the tape and wrapping paper from the counter and threw them into a wastepaper basket. Cal detected something aggressive in his manner and suspected that he was clearing the decks for a lecture denouncing the miners, the breakdown in law and order, and the need for stiffer penalties for criminals, including chopping off the hands of children who stole sweets from his shop.

I've always been a big supporter of the police, Cal . . .

Cal wondered if he could stand it. Perhaps he could excuse himself by saying he was late for a meeting with Arthur Scargill back at the hotel.

. . . but I got a rude awakening during the strike, I can tell you.

Cal paused. Perhaps Arthur could wait.

Mind you, the miners weren't all angels, either, and I certainly didn't agree with the strike. If it had gone on much longer I'd have gone out of business. But having said that, there was no excuse for some of the things the police got up to.

Like what?

They took the law into their own hands. And when the miners wouldn't give in, they tried to intimidate them back to work.

In what way?

Well, when what-do-they-call-him across the road went back to work. He pointed towards the shop window. There was trouble every time the police drove him through the picket line. After one battle down at the pit they decided to teach the pickets a lesson and they chased them up into the village. I've never seen anything like it. They were totally out of control. They went berserk. There were mounted police chasing men down the streets, lashing out at them with their batons. One young lad ran in here to escape and one of them tried to follow him in! The horse's head and front legs were in the bloody shop, but luckily the doorway was too low for the rider to come in. This lad ran behind the counter and nipped out through the back door. Old Mrs Jackson was in the shop at the time. She nearly had a heart attack, I can tell you. I was bloody furious. I shouted to the bobby, What do you think you're doing? You can't invade people's property like that! Do you know what he said?

Cal had a rough idea. He knew that he wouldn't be shocked.

He told me to fuck off. And with a woman in the shop at that! And when he backed his horse out, he smashed a window with his truncheon just because that lad had got away.

He was so involved in his story that he did not notice Cal take his tape recorder out of his pocket and hold it concealed below the level of the counter.

They terrorized the village: surrounded it. They were marching through the streets with combat helmets on and big riot shields. I was so disgusted with the way they were carrying on that in the end I put a notice in the window: NO POLICE PLEASE.

A man came into the shop, nodded to the newsagent, then walked across to the magazine shelves against the wall. He looked up at the top shelf, where the sex magazines were displayed partly concealing each other like a hand of dirty playing cards. As he reached towards them, his T-shirt came out of his jeans, revealing a pale, hairy back. He worked quickly along the row, exposing the front copy of each title, then sliding it back into place.

The newsagent lost interest in Cal and watched him.

What you looking for, Gary?

That one that specializes in big tits.

That's what they all specialize in, isn't it?

Do they fuck. She hasn't got big tits, has she?

He held up a magazine, but the newsagent and Cal were too far away to make out what size the woman's tits were. Gary gazed at the cover and shook his head in wonder.

These birds. You could fucking eat 'em, couldn't you?

He replaced the magazine and continued along the row.

Big Uns! That's what it's called.

The newsagent shook his head.

I've sold out.

Dirty bastards. It only came out yesterday. What did they do – queue up all night? They're a load of sex maniacs around here, that's the trouble.

He worked back along the shelf, glancing inside one or two magazines before choosing an alternative title and taking it to the counter. He placed it on the pile of newspapers then felt in his pocket.

Give me twenty Capstan and a box of matches as well.

Cal looked at the pin-up on the cover of the magazine while Gary paid the newsagent.

He could imagine Christine posing like that and fixing him with the same knowing leer. He could see her on his bed at the hotel, provocatively changing positions, mocking the convention yet being excited by it too. He thought of Hélène. She would never have posed like that. Cal had seen a portfolio of austere, black-and-white nude studies of Hélène taken by a famous French photographer. But they were more suitable for an art exhibition than for wanking off to.

Gary tucked his cigarettes and matches in the pocket of his T-shirt, picked up the magazine and left the shop. The newsagent watched him walk past the window and shook his head.

Poor sod. His wife's just left him. He's on the dole and they're about to repossess his house. I suppose he needs some consolation with that lot on his mind.

Cal wasn't listening. He was wondering whether to buy a magazine and telephone Christine.

When the strike was on, there were police from all over the country billeted around here. They used to buy girlie magazines all the time until I stopped them coming in. I suppose they'd nothing else to do, being away from home.

After the newsagent had told him about the disturbance outside the scab's house, Cal bought a road map of the region and left the shop. He was still thinking about the incident when he almost collided with Charlie Thomas coming out of the bookie's next door.

Hey up, Karl, what you doing here? Going to put a bet on?

I've been making a few enquiries about my dad's arrest. This is where it happened.

I can tell you what happened.

I thought you weren't there.

I didn't have to be. It happened all the time.

Charlie pointed to a taxi parked in front of Cal's car.

Do you want a lift into town?

Cal looked surprised: bookies? taxi? Charlie's luck must have changed.

Have you come into some money, then?

Charlie glanced at him, puzzled. Then he realized

what Cal meant and thumped him playfully on the arm.

I'm the driver, you silly cunt, not the passenger. The window-cleaning fell through, so I managed to get a bit of part-time driving while one of the regular drivers is off sick.

Cal sat on the bed and spread out the road map across the cover. He studied it for a while, then walked slowly about the room, pausing occasionally and gazing down at the map, his eyes drawn compulsively to the red line which wound its way across a patch of dun-coloured contours.

He decided to do some work on the script and make the decision later. But first he made two phone calls. Christine wasn't in. He still hadn't told her that he was going to stop seeing her. Perhaps at the end of their next meeting? Hélène was cool and sarcastic. Had he gone back to live in England now? Should she pack his things and send them on? He tried to reassure her that he would soon be home. Yes, he realized that he said that every time, but he felt guilty about neglecting his parents in the past and he was trying to make amends. He was helping to nurse his father, too. He had even washed and changed him the other day while his mother had gone shopping. He owed it to them after all they had done for him. They were old now and this might be the last time they spent some time together . . . Pure corn, but it worked, and when Hélène replied, her tone was softer and more conciliatory. She told him how excited she was about her new film and how much she was looking forward to Berlin. Then she asked him about his own work, but his thoughts were elsewhere as he stared at the map on the bed.

. . . What? Yes. Yes, of course I'm listening to you. It's a bad line. I couldn't hear what you said, that's all . . . Yes, it's going well. Apart from looking after my parents, there isn't much to do here, so I'm really making it crack. Cal laughed at her alarmed response. No, I didn't say I was taking crack. I said *making* it crack. It's a local expression. It means things are going well . . . Yes, of course, you can read it. He laughed. No, I don't think there's anything in it for you.

There never was. But Hélène always read his scripts anyway. She said it brought them closer together, sharing each other's work. But he wasn't sure about that. When he read the scripts which arrived from Hélène's agent, he usually fell into a jealous sulk and had to take the dog up the mountain to work it off.

. . . Yes. Put him on.

Cal grinned when he heard Hélène call Bruno to the phone. He could see the dog getting up from the cool tiles and padding across the room.

Hélène was laughing when she spoke. He's here. The phone is to his ear.

Bruno?

Cal paused instinctively as if expecting a reply.

Bruno. It's me.

He couldn't say any more for laughing. Hélène came on the phone. She was laughing too.

You should see his face, Cal. His tail is wagging but he looks confused.

I'm not surprised.

Cal wondered if he could use the idea in *It's a Dog's Life*. TOBY is on the telephone. But how could he be? Perhaps he could break into somebody's house, knock the phone off the hook, then dial home by pressing the buttons with his nose or something. And what was he supposed to say when somebody answered – woof fucking woof? It was a stupid idea but it amused him and he smiled as he developed it further, with TOBY up on his hind legs holding the telephone in one paw and tapping out the number with the other like a cartoon character.

Yes. Yes, I'm still here . . .

But his smile quickly faded when Hélène told him that she was meeting Roland and Alain for a script conference in Nice. They had flown in that morning and she was meeting them at their hotel. She had to go now or she would be late.

Cal replaced the receiver and stared at the map on the bed. But he was no longer thinking about the high road across the moors; he was thinking about Hélène driving to Nice.

Why were they meeting there? Surely the director would have enough time for script conferences during rehearsals in Berlin. What if she was lying and Roland had come on his own? Perhaps there was something in the rumour about an affair between them after all.

Cal snatched up the receiver and stabbed the digits furiously. He imagined her preening and pampering herself in the bathroom, selecting her slinkiest, most expensive underwear; then changing her mind and sliding oiled and naked into a skintight dress (the blue one – his favourite). Well, if she thought she was going to meet that bastard frog actor wearing no knickers and a frock that came up to her arse, she had another think coming!

In his fury he pressed a wrong button and had to start again. But as he concentrated on the numbers, selecting them deliberately this time, he calmed down and realized that he was in danger of making a fool of himself. If she was seeing Roland surreptitiously, why bother inventing a script conference? She didn't need to mention him at all. He wouldn't know. Just like Hélène didn't know about Christine . . . He heard the familiar French dialling tone, quickly pressed the rest before Hélène picked up the phone, then called Christine with the receiver still pressed to his ear.

She was still out. Where was she? Who was she with? She was a bit of a dark horse, Christine. Never said much about her private life. Never invited him back to her house. What if she'd got another feller? He felt himself going into free-fall again, but fought back and told himself not to be so stupid. What if she *has* got another feller? So what? What if she's got two fellers? What if they were queuing round the block?! It's none of your business. You're not going to marry her, are you? In another few days you'll be back in France and you'll never see her again. How dare you criticize her, you selfish, hypocritical, unfaithful bastard? But it didn't work and his madness raged on. She's using me. She's stringing me along. She's trying to make me jealous so that I'll stay . . . He searched desperately for a reason why she would want to do this. She didn't love him, he knew that. (He wasn't even sure if she liked him.) Sure, the sex was good, but not that important. And if she was so crazy about him, why didn't she ever phone him up? It was illogical. It made no sense. In a film script, the producer would have asked him what her motivation was, then sent him away to do some rewrites.

He thought of Hélène and Roland (and Alain?) discussing their script over dinner in Nice . . . *I think we need to expand the train scene a little. Perhaps one of the other passengers could chat Eva up* . . . He'd chat her up if she was wearing that blue dress with no fucking knickers on. They all would. They could have a gang rape in the carriage. That'd pack the punters in . . . Steady on. Calm down. Cal wished that he was with them, discussing one of his scripts. Which one – *It's a Dog's Life*? He slammed down the telephone. There wasn't a dog's chance. Fucking dogs. He'd been savaged earlier on, when he visited one of Phil Walton's neighbours after meeting Charlie outside the bookie's. It started barking as soon as he knocked on the door, then went straight for his legs when the woman opened it. Luckily, she was holding a cup of tea which she threw on its back just as it was going for his ankles. That took its mind off him, although the woman wasn't too pleased. She said it was a waste of a good cup of tea.

Cal folded up the map on the bed. Fucking TOBY. Perhaps somebody could throw a cup of tea over him. Or shoot him. Or tie a brick round his neck and throw him in the river. He had lied to Hélène. He was nowhere near the end of the first draft. He hadn't looked at it for days. He was losing interest in the project. Fast. He poured himself a Scotch from the mini-bar then sat down at his word processor and looked back at the last scene.

TOBY had been ambushed by a stray cat just as he was about to tuck into the remains of a hamburger . . . Cal shook his head. It was shit. Complete and utter. There was no other way to describe it. But well-paid shit nevertheless. He had a drink and cleared the screen.

EXT. DERELICT LAND. NIGHT.

A pack of stray dogs are sniffing around a bitch on heat. They are growling and fighting over her and one or two mount her.

TOBY arrives on the scene and mingles with the other dogs. They snarl and bark at him, but he has got the scent now and won't be driven away. He manages to get a good sniff at the bitch's arse, then, when a general mêlée breaks out amongst the pack, he seizes his chance and tries to mount the bitch.

Unfortunately, the bitch is too tall for him, and when he gets up on his hind legs, he can't get his cock in. The bitch loses interest and starts to walk away, but TOBY is determined if nothing else and clings to her hindquarters with his front legs and they walk around like some hideous circus act.

Cal couldn't type any more for laughing. He read it through. It was the best scene in the script so far. But it wasn't that kind of film. It was a family show. He wiped the scene and started again.

EXT. DERELICT LAND. NIGHT.

A BAG LADY is sitting by a fire chewing a chicken leg. She is muffled up in many layers of old clothes and her possessions are by her side in two bin liners. In the background a pack of stray dogs are snarling and fighting. Suddenly we see TOBY break from the pack, pursued by a brute of a dog. He manages to escape, then, whining pathetically, he approaches The BAG LADY.

The BAG LADY watches him approach. There is no indication from her expression whether she is hostile or friendly towards him. TOBY is wary. He has had enough ill treatment from humans by now to expect the worst. The BAG LADY throws him the drumstick with a bit of meat attached. TOBY devours it ravenously. When he has finished, The BAG LADY holds out a chunk of bread towards him.

BAG LADY

Come on, boy.

Cautiously, his hunger overriding his fear, TOBY approaches The BAG LADY and takes the bread from her hand.

BAG LADY

Poor mutt. You're starving, aren't you?

She pats TOBY on the back and strokes him.

BAG LADY
So what happened to you then?
You get lost? Or did your owner
sling you out? Looks like we're a
couple of rejects together, old pal.

TOBY whines pitifully and settles down with
his head on his paws staring into the fire.

The moor, scoured by a continuing wind, stretched into the distance and met the dark clouds which slid across the horizon. It was a winter landscape except for the shorn sheep, which looked pitifully exposed as they nibbled the short grass by the roadside.

Cal drove slowly in case they ran out in front of the car; especially the lambs, which panicked and dashed to their mothers as he approached. But he was driving slowly for another, more important, reason: he was afraid of reaching his destination, and the closer he got, the more convinced he became that he should turn back.

He approached a pub standing by the side of the road. It was the first building he had seen for miles and he tried to remember the name before he reached it. But he was too late and he had to read the sign as he drove by. They used to walk up from the village and visit it sometimes. It was a cosy place, with a fire in the snug and a few local farmworkers in the bar. It looked different now, though. An extension had been added, the car park enlarged and there was a board outside advertising bar snacks and evening meals.

The road reached the edge of the moor and Cal's stomach turned over as the valley came into view below him. It looked much the same as he remembered: a familiar patchwork of woods and fields – so lush compared with the moorland behind him – and the village at the bottom of the steep, winding hill.

He pulled in at the side of the road and considered

whether to go on. What was the point after all this time? Why reopen old wounds? It was unfair. Cruel. Disruptive. He couldn't think of one good reason to justify his visit. He started the engine and continued down the hill.

He parked on the main street outside the butcher's shop and looked through the window to see if Mr Gage was inside. No, it was a younger man behind the counter and when he got out of the car he noticed that the name above the shop door had been changed.

Cal walked along the street past the shops. Some of them he recognized, but others had been converted into tea shops and gift shops, and the cobbler's on the corner of Beech Hill was now an estate agent's. Cal stopped and looked in the window, whistling softly in amazement as he compared house prices to what they had been twenty years ago. Even allowing for inflation, there was nothing they would have been able to afford straight from university. Not even the stable, RIPE FOR CONVERSION.

Cal turned up Beech Hill. Had it always been as steep as this? Or was he walking slowly on purpose to delay his arrival? When he reached the cottage, he walked straight past and continued up the hill. He had a sudden urge to visit the church, and to see if the little tadpole pond behind the old barn was still there. And the horse chestnut tree which had been split by lightning and you could squeeze inside . . . Anywhere would do to postpone raising that worn brass fist and rapping on the door.

Cal reached the church and looked over the wall into the graveyard. He smiled when he saw the mounting block just inside the gate. She used to clamber up the steps, then jump on to his back and hang on with her chubby little arms around his neck, squealing and laughing, while he galloped about between the gravestones, neighing and trotting his tongue like a galloping horse . . . The sudden striking of the church clock made him jump and brought him back to the present. He waited for the chimes to fade, then walked back down the hill to the cottage and opened the gate.

As he walked up the path, Cal wondered if the rose bushes in the garden were the ones which he had planted when they had first moved in. And if those primroses had spread from the first clump which they had guiltily dug up from the meadow behind the farm. He paused at the door, looked at the number, looked at his watch. If he had had a mirror in his pocket he would have looked at that. Finally, he raised the brass fist and knocked twice.

A girl opened the door. She was eating a doughnut and icing sugar was spilling down the front of her jumper. Cal stared at her, totally nonplussed, then began a calculation which was too absurd to finish. Of course it wasn't her! The girl before him was only about twelve.

Is your mum in, please?

But what if he had mistaken the voice on the phone and this girl's mum wasn't the mum he had come to see? Had he committed a hideous blunder? He became aware of music playing somewhere in the house as the girl continued to eat her doughnut and scrutinize him. He was about to apologize and tell her that he must have got the wrong address, when she turned round and called over her shoulder.

Mum! There's somebody to see you.

Cal identified the music. It was Bach. One of the Six Little Preludes.

Who is it?

But he hadn't made a mistake. It was *her* voice.

I don't know. A man.

The music grew louder as an inner door opened and a woman entered the room. Cal looked past the girl and watched her approach. She was wiping her hands on a paint-stained cloth and humming along to the music. She looked composed, at ease with herself, and in that brief time before she saw him, Cal hated himself for shattering her peace.

Hello, Laura.

She stared at him. The colour left her face, then rushed back like blood through a bandage. Cal tried to smile but it wouldn't set. He started to sweat. He could feel the drops trickling down his arms. Laura placed her hand on the girl's shoulder. Standing side by side, they blocked the doorway.

I was driving by . . .

That didn't work either. The girl looked shrewdly from one to the other and thoughtfully popped a penny chew into her mouth. Laura tucked a strand of loose hair behind the girl's ear then brushed the icing sugar from her jumper. The girl shook her off, annoyed at being treated like a child in front of a stranger.

Mum! Stop it!

Is this your daughter?

What do you want, Cal?

I was driving by.

You've already said that.

I was on my way to see Joe. He lives in Manchester.

He could tell that she didn't believe him. No wonder, Manchester was in the opposite direction; but he couldn't think of anything else to say. If only the girl would go inside he might be able to explain himself. But she had no intention of disappearing. She could sense the drama and Laura appeared to have no intention of sending her away. She was using her daughter as a shield.

I wanted to see you. It was his turn to blush now. He looked at the girl. What's your name?

Jessie.

Do you mind if I have a word with your mum, Jessie? In private.

Jessie looked up at Laura, willing her not to agree.

I don't think there's anything to see me about, do you?

Jessie linked arms with her mother and gave Cal a sweet smile. We're going to the Garden Centre when Daddy comes in.

Make sure you buy some hemlock, Cal felt like replying.

What is it, Cal? What do you want?

Cal shrugged and shook his head. He could have cried. Sorry. It was stupid. Bye, Jessie.

He turned and walked down the path. Laura and Jessie stood in the doorway and watched him go.

Who is it, Mum?

Cal!

He paused at the gate and turned round. Laura was walking towards him, followed by Jessie.

You stay here.

Oh, Mum.

Do as you're told. I won't be a minute.

Laura continued down the path. When she reached Cal, Jessie went inside and slammed the door.

Laura shook her head. Little madam.

It's understandable, I suppose.

What do you want, Cal?

He stared past her towards the cottage. Laura waited. Cal continued to avoid her eyes. Then he turned abruptly and opened the gate. I'm sorry. It was a mistake.

You bastard!

He looked at her then.

You turn up after twenty years with a cock-and-bull story about going to see Joe. Give me the fright of my life. Then walk away without a word of explanation. It's unbelievable!

It's not that simple.

That's typical of you, starting something and then not having the guts to finish it.

She glared at him over the gate. He didn't deny it.

Was it you that rang the other night, then put the phone down?

Cal watched a bee disappear up a foxglove. He wished he was going with it. Yes.

I thought so. It's the sort of devious thing that you'd do.

I'd no choice. You'd have hung up if I'd identified myself.

What did you expect – tears of gratitude?

I wasn't even sure you'd be here.

So why have you come? I think you owe me an explanation.

Cal looked at her. Her hair was cut short now, with a fringe.

OK, I'll try. I came back from France to see my dad. He's had a stroke. They thought he might die.

He spoke quickly, in case Laura changed her mind and sent him away before he could finish.

I'm sorry.

Well, as you know, my dad and I were never very close.

Laura looked round at the cottage. Jessie was watching them through the kitchen window.

Look, you may as well come in. The damage has been done now.

Thank you. I won't stay long.

Cal followed Laura back along the path. When they reached the cottage, Jessie withdrew from the window. Cal had been in such turmoil since his arrival that he hadn't even thought about the girl's father. He looked at Laura's hand as she opened the door and felt a peevish pang when he saw her wedding ring.

Come in.

The door led into a large kitchen which stretched the width of the house. It had a low ceiling and a flagged floor with a window at each end. Except for the stone fireplace, Cal did not recognize anything else in the room.

Sit down.

Thank you.

He sat in the Windsor chair by the fire, then hurriedly stood up and moved to the sofa.

I thought it might be your husband's chair. He might not like it if he came in and saw me parked in it. Some people are funny about their favourite chairs. They get possessive. If we sat in my dad's chair, he made us get out and sit somewhere else when he came into the room.

Tim's not like that.

I'm glad to hear it. Old habits die hard, I suppose.

Would you like a drink: a cup of tea or something?

No thanks. I've got to go soon.

To Manchester?

She laughed. Cal looked down in embarrassment and studied the pattern in the rug.

You were always a rotten liar.

Perhaps that's why I keep practising.

You were saying about your father?

Yes. He had a stroke, so I had to come back from France.

You mean he spoiled your holiday?

He sensed the sarcasm. No. I live there.

You live in France?

Cal nodded. He wished he had said Bosnia in case she was envious and turned nasty on him.

Whereabouts?

He considered saying Lille. In a high-rise flat, next to a steelworks.

The south . . . Provence.

Provence! Gosh, I am impressed.

It's just an old barn, that's all. I bought it dirt cheap before the property boom and did it up.

We went camping last year in Provence before Becky – Too late! She had said it. Cal looked away, hoping that the mention of their daughter's name wouldn't bring on a fit of resentment . . . Before Becky went to university. There are some lovely campsites in that area.

Cal nodded. Not that he knew of any. The last time he had been inside a tent was when he was in the cubs.

We stayed near Mougins.

Cal knew the village well. He often visited the restaurants there. It was twelve kilometres from his house. Perhaps they had driven past the gates on their way to the campsite.

I was really shocked when I saw my dad. You know what a strong man he was? My mother has to do everything for him. He can't walk on his own, or feed himself. My mother maintains that it was caused by a blow from a truncheon when he was arrested and imprisoned during the strike. I don't know if there's any truth in it, but she says he never fully recovered from the experience.

Cal glanced up at the sudden burst of rock music from overhead. Laura didn't seem to notice it.

Well, it would have seemed a bit heartless to have gone straight back, so I decided to stay on for a few days and find out what really happened when my dad was arrested. I had a vague notion of taking out a complaint against the police, or trying to claim compensation or something. But my mother wasn't keen on the idea. She said it was too long ago and that my dad had had enough of the law during the strike.

He made it sound like a crusade: one of those movies in which the successful son (usually a lawyer) returns home to clear the family name. He didn't say anything about suspecting that his father probably deserved everything he got.

But it didn't work out like that. I stayed longer than I intended. I got involved.

With a woman?

Don't be cynical.

Why not? I'd say it was about par for the course.

Cal resented the accusation, especially as it was true. But why should she be sympathetic after the way he had treated her?

It's nothing to do with a woman. It's the family. The place. It's hard to explain . . .

The music upstairs grew louder and overwhelmed the Bach in the other room. Cal suspected a teenage manoeuvre to drive him out of the house.

You know how much I hated it at home and couldn't wait to get away?

If she did know, she didn't show it.

Cal struggled on. But since I came back . . .

You mean you're trying to redeem yourself?

Something like that.

Is that why you're here?

In a way.

You came to see Becky, didn't you?

Not only Becky.

You came to tidy up the past.

No. To discover the past.

She's not here.

I gathered that.

If she had been, I wouldn't have let you in.

Cal glanced around at the paintings on the walls to deflect the pain. Are they yours?

Some of them.

Cal stood up for a closer look. I recognize this one.

It was a watercolour of a turbulent sky dominating a strip of moorland.

Yes, I did it just after we arrived here. There are no family portraits, I'm afraid.

Cal took the knife in the back and looked at the other pictures without comment. He paused in the doorway of the other downstairs room and looked through at a large unframed canvas standing on an easel by the window.

You've still got your studio, then?

He remained in the doorway looking through at the picture. It was an oil painting of a horse race, but the canvas was so dark that it looked as if the meeting was taking place at night.

Do you mind if I take a look?
If you like.
Cal walked into the room and stood by the tall stool in front of the easel. Laura watched him from the doorway like a gallery attendant.
I'm restoring it.
Is it yours?
Do you mean do I own it? Or did I paint it?
Well, you obviously didn't paint it, unless you've gone in for faking old masters.
He regretted using the word before he had finished the sentence.
No. Faking's not my business.
It was an obvious retort which she contrived to turn into an insult. Cal kept his eyes on the canvas, pretending he hadn't heard. Laura crossed the room and stood next to him in front of the picture.
I'm cleaning it. I've started taking the varnish off. That's what I do now, clean and restore pictures. She indicated the jars of solvents and swabs on the window-sill. It needs a bit of retouching here and there where the paint has cracked and flaked, but it'll look beautiful when it's finished.
What is it – a Stubbs?
Laura laughed. Cal enjoyed the sound of it.
Not quite. It's a good picture though, full of life.
Who owns it?
A Derbyshire family. Private collection.
I didn't realize you could restore pictures.
I couldn't. But I decided I needed another string to my bow – especially with Becky to bring up. So I took the diploma in picture conservation at Gateshead.
What about your own work?
This is my work. I haven't done any painting for years now.
Why not? You were good.
No I wasn't. I was competent. Working with good paintings made me realize my own limitations. There

are enough mediocre painters around without me adding to the numbers.

Cal was shamed by her integrity. If he had applied the same stringent standards to his own work, he wouldn't have written enough to fill a postcard.

Seems a shame.

Not at all. There's no point in doing it unless you've got something to say.

She crossed the studio and turned around an ornately framed picture leaning against the wall.

Look at this.

She revealed a winter landscape of a woman in bonnet and shawl walking towards a farm. The cool colours of the sky were mirrored in the wet road, and streaky clouds balanced the snow-lined furrows of the ploughed fields. A plume of smoke from the farmhouse angled across the sky towards the bare branches of a solitary tree, cleverly framing and focusing the lone figure at the centre of the painting.

Do you like it?

Cal crossed the studio for a closer look. Yes. It's good.

It's wonderful! Look at the brushwork. So confident. So bold. And the furrows in the fields. You could plant seed in that lovely thick paint. Perhaps that's why the owner wants it cleaned, in case corn sprouts from the dirt.

She laughed, enjoying the opportunity to share her enthusiasm for the picture, even if it had to be with Cal.

But it's not just the technique, it's the story.

It's like a scene from a Thomas Hardy novel.

Yes. Who is she? A servant girl? The farmer's young wife? Where has she been? Why is she wearing only a bonnet and shawl when it's obviously so cold? Perhaps she's the disgraced daughter of the household, returning home after a disastrous affair . . . I can't wait to start work on it.

Cal started work on it too.

EXT. COUNTRYSIDE. DAY.

Winter, late afternoon. There is snow on the ground and the light is fading. SARAH is walking along a muddy road towards a farm. Even though it is bitterly cold, she is wearing only a shawl over her shabby dress and she is shivering. We hear the distant cawing of rooks, the only sounds in a desolate landscape.

SARAH reaches the farm and looks over the gate at the house, where a light is glowing in the kitchen window. She licks her lips, swallows nervously, then opens the gate and crosses the yard. The creak of the gate being opened brings a sheepdog out of the barn. It rushes at SARAH, barking fiercely, but she is unafraid of the dog. She smiles.

SARAH

Hello, Ben. It's me. What's the matter – have you forgotten who I am?

The dog eventually stops barking, then whines and begins to wag its tail.

SARAH

That's better. That's a good boy.

The farmhouse door opens and a man steps outside. He is middle-aged, burly, wearing a collarless shirt, gaiters and boots.

TOM

Who is it? What do you want?

He starts when he realizes who it is. SARAH approaches him.

SARAH

Hello, Tom. It's me. I've come back . . .

I read your novel.

Cal didn't hear her. He was still at the door of the farmhouse with Sarah and Tom. Laura was right. It was a good story. It certainly knocked *It's a Dog's Life* into a cocked hat.

Cal?

He turned away from the canvas.

I said I read your novel.

Oh that? God, it's such a long time ago, I'd forgotten all about it.

I enjoyed it.

It was crap. Derivative. Didn't I send you a copy?

I threw it on the fire.

I don't blame you.

I read it later. I borrowed it from the library when things had settled down.

Cal turned back to the canvas to hide his shame. How could he have been so insensitive as to have sent her a copy of the book which he had written in this house, in this very room, just before he had walked out?

I needed to get away. To be on my own.

But you weren't on your own. You went to live with that journalist in Belsize Park.

No. That was later. After the novel was published.

She didn't dispute it. Her silence was more effective.

Cal stared at the picture. Perhaps he could use the scene in the farmyard. TOBY has been captured by a brutal farmer and turned into a vicious guard dog . . .

Do you know what I liked about the book? . . . Cal?

Yes?

It was honest. Astonishing really, coming from you.

Are you going to keep on insulting me?

What did you expect – a fly-past?

Perhaps I should go.

That's the trouble with you – you can't face up to things. As soon as things get tough you walk away.

I am trying to face up to things. That's why I'm here.

Cal looked at the picture again and felt a pang of empathy with the young woman walking towards the farm. She was returning after many years away. She had done things she was ashamed of, but was determined to face the consequences . . . Cal turned and faced Laura.

Look. I know it doesn't make sense, but I wanted to know what had happened to you. His eyes slid back to the canvas. The woman was still heading towards the farm. She hadn't turned back . . .

There was the sound of footsteps coming down the stairs, then Jessie appeared in the doorway.

When's Dad coming home, Mum?

I'm not sure. I think he said he'd got a meeting.

When are we having tea?

Soon. Go and make yourself a sandwich or something if you're hungry.

Jessie didn't move and Laura had to give her a hard look before she obeyed. Seconds later, there was a blast from the television in the kitchen.

Jessie! Turn that down!

She did. But not much.

Perhaps I'd better go. I don't want to cause any trouble.

You should have thought of that before you came.

I did.

And what if Tim had opened the door?

I'm not sure.

He looked at the horse-racing picture on the easel. The nose of the leading horse was tantalizingly short of the winning post.

I know this doesn't make much sense, but even though I realized you'd probably be married and have children, I somehow refused to accept it. I always saw you as you were, in this house as it was then and with Becky still a baby. And for one absurd moment when Jessie opened the door, I thought she was Becky.

The silence between them was punctuated by the pointed slamming of doors and rattle of crockery from the kitchen.

What does your husband do?

He teaches History at Leeds University.

Will you tell him I've been?

Of course. If I don't, Jessie will.

I don't suppose Jessie knows who I am?

She hasn't a clue.

Cal looked again at the winning horse on the painting. Its eye was wild and bloodshot. It was about to receive a final crack from the jockey's whip.

And Becky?

As far as she's concerned, you don't exist.

Cal sympathized with the hard-ridden horse.

You mean she thinks that your husband's her father?

No. When she was about twelve or thirteen and I thought she was old enough to handle it, I told her everything: about you and what had happened.

What did she say?

She took it really well. She'd always regarded Tim as her father anyway. He'd been around since she was a baby – he was lovely with her – and she couldn't remember you. Then when we got married, she took my married name. It seemed the obvious thing to do, especially as we intended to have children of our own.

Cal hated Tim for being so agreeable. He hated Becky for not giving him hell. He hated Laura for being so sensible and he hated Jessie for hating him. He hated the whole fucking family!

So what do they call you now, then? What's your married name?

Jordan.

Cal tried out the names to himself. Becky Howard. Becky Jordan. Becky Rickards . . . Pity.

Which university is Becky at?

Sheffield. She's reading Modern Languages.

What's she like, you know, as a person?

Lovely. She's a lovely girl. But I'm bound to say that, aren't I – I'm biased.

Cal read the unfamiliar titles of the books on the shelves in the alcove. He had written his novel in this room. He wondered what had happened to his desk.

And she never asked about me? Not once?

Cal, you're not thinking of seeing her, are you?

Of course not. Why?

Because that's why you're here, to find out where she is. After all these years you're suddenly full of concern. Or is it guilt?

It's natural enough. Blood ties and all that.

Listen, Cal: don't. I don't want you to – do you understand? She's settled. She's happy. She's come to terms with the past. Don't you realize what it could do to her if you suddenly appeared on the scene? It could destroy her. It could upset her whole life! Cal, are you listening to me?

He nodded, but he didn't look as if he was.

He was staring out of the window into the garden, thinking about when he used to stand here with Becky in his arms and point out the flowers and the birds, and how he planned to hang a swing from the apple tree on the lawn.

Cal was so affected by his meeting with Laura that as he drove back across the moor he had to stop the car and sit quietly for a while to unburden himself. How could he have been such a shit? Laura hadn't even wanted the baby. She valued her independence. She was more interested in being a painter than a parent. He had persuaded her to have it. It would be a meaningful experience. It would seal their relationship and all that bollocks. He even wanted to get married, but they postponed it when the newspaper he was working on offered him a job in the London office. He couldn't refuse, could he? It was a good move. It would mean more money. He would rent a cheap room and travel home at weekends . . . Eighteen months later, he left her to live with a woman he hardly knew, except in bed.

He knew that it wouldn't last, even after he had confessed to a distraught Laura and tried to justify the affair in spiritual terms. But it didn't wash, and calmer, after a sleepless night, she told him that unless he broke off the relationship and came back home, she never wanted to see him again. He knew that she meant it. Unless he agreed, there would be no turning back. But he still left. He threw everything away for a good fuck. How could he have done such a thing to Laura and their baby daughter when he loved them so much? It was unbelievable, irresponsible, indefensible! He must have been crazy!

Cal felt a pain in his chest as he recalled packing his suitcase in the bedroom. Laura kept out of his way. He could hear her murmuring to Becky downstairs and Becky squealing and yelling as if it was any other day. He paused in the hallway. Should he go into the kitchen and say goodbye? No, it might upset Laura again, and if she started crying Becky might start crying too. (What consideration. He should have been awarded a medal for gallantry.) Then walking down the path, glancing at the roses and primroses he had planted. Starting up the car engine. One last look at the house, hoping to see Laura and Becky at the window. Hoping that Laura would come to the door and call him back . . .

Cal was sweating. He wound down the car window for air. Why had he admitted his affair with . . .? He couldn't even remember her name. With Andrea. He knew it was no big deal. They just fancied each other, that was all, and when the novelty wore off that would be the end of it. In that case, why hadn't he ended the affair when Laura had asked him? Because he knew that Laura and Becky and life at the cottage wasn't enough for him. He wasn't sure what he wanted, but in spite of all its attractions, it wasn't that. He wanted to be free, to do as he wished with no responsibilities. But he didn't have the courage to admit it. He needed the affair as an excuse. He wanted Laura to throw him out so that he could blame her for being rigid and unreasonable.

Cal got out of the car and slammed the door in a fury. What a bastard! What a selfish, cowardly bastard he was! Startled by his sudden appearance, a hefty, thickly coated lamb rushed to its mother in alarm. It ducked underneath her and appeared to be tupping her as it attacked her teats. The sight of the sheep, shorn naked and exhausted by suckling, patiently enduring the rough attention of its burly offspring, upset Cal even more. He glanced about at the other lambs and sheep grazing near by and noticed that there wasn't a ram in sight. It was too much for him. He couldn't take any more. He got back into the car and drove away, along the same road which he had taken on that dreadful day all those years ago, towards the motorway and London.

Cal lay on the bed with his hands behind his head, a glass of Scotch balanced on his chest and his gaze fixed on the ceiling. He was thinking about what Laura had said about his novel. It had been published such a long time ago that it was hard to believe he had written it. But even though he had derided it in front of Laura, at least he had cared about it at the time, which was more than he could say about most of the work he had done since.

When he returned to the hotel after the distressing journey back across the moors, there was a message asking him to ring his agent. Was he interested in writing a pilot for a new American cop series? How much? Thirty thousand dollars for a three-page treatment. The producer's keen to talk. Let me sleep on it. I'll give you a ring in the morning . . . But it hadn't been like that at the beginning. He had started out with high hopes and serious intentions. His novel, like many first novels, was thinly disguised autobiography. It was about a sensitive, working-class grammar-school boy who is bullied by the other boys on a council estate, somewhere in the provinces. He then goes off to university, never to return. The usual stuff. He had exaggerated the brutality dished out to the budding Aubrey Beardsley for dramatic effect. But Laura was right. It was truthful in essence if not in detail, and the passages dealing with family conflicts and the corrosive effects of a divisive education system were painfully accurate.

He had called the main character Leon, after Trotsky, the arch-enemy of Stalinists, in order to get his own back on his father. This rebuff, combined with the prominence on the dust jacket of his own name, which he had changed from Karl to Cal, was also fitting retribution for all the playground insults he had suffered as a child.

He thought it rather waggish at the time, but now, looking back, it seemed petty and vindictive. Cal had sent a copy home, but his mother told him later that his father had looked at the cover then put it down. He hadn't even opened it. That hurt; for despite the animosity Cal felt towards him, he would still have welcomed his criticism.

His mother read it. She liked it, she said, and she didn't seem to be offended at the kind but compliant portrayal of Leon's mother. Perhaps she didn't recognize herself. Perhaps she thought it was just a story. But Cal hadn't cared what she thought. Not then, before her emancipation. But he would have valued her opinion now.

Except for his mother, and Laura, and a few old friends, nobody else seemed to have read the book, and the only reason *they* had read it was because he had given them complimentary copies. It received a few passable reviews, but the paperback rights remained unsold and it was obvious that nobody would get killed in the rush when his next novel appeared. It was all such a let-down, and the final humiliation occurred when he walked into a remainder bookshop on Oxford Street and saw piles of his book only a few months after publication. There were hundreds of them, white-edged, unopened, virgin books. If he had been approached by a colleague from the office as he stared gloomily at his name, repeated mockingly on each spine, he would have denied authorship as emphatically as Peter had denied Jesus. He left the shop convinced of his failure and determined never to write a novel again.

Christine could tell that something was worrying him when he didn't put his hand up her skirt in the lift. They had met in the hotel bar, then gone up to his room. He usually enjoyed watching her undress, but tonight he sat on the edge of the bed and looked at her in a curiously detached way. When she was down to her red underwear and he still hadn't taken his cock out, she knew it was serious.

What's wrong?

Nothing.

She wondered if he was building up to the big goodbye speech. You're leaving, aren't you?

Cal shook his head and told about his visit to Laura's.

But why? It doesn't make sense.

It might have done if he had told her about Becky.

She must have been mortified, seeing you on the doorstep after all that time.

She was.

He had intended to tell Christine the full story, but in the end he couldn't go through with it. He had never told anybody about Becky and it seemed inappropriate that Christine should be the first to know.

I was going to Leeds to meet an old friend: a guy I used to work with on the *Yorkshire Post* years ago. It was on the way.

To Leeds? Not on my map it isn't.

I took the scenic route.

You should get a job driving mystery tours.

I had a sudden urge. I wanted to see how she was getting on; what had happened to her.

But it wasn't fair, dropping in on her like that.

I know.

So why did you do it?

It was a bizarre scene with an indignant Christine in her underwear, attacking the repentant Cal sitting on the bed fully clothed.

Didn't you consider her feelings? What she must have felt like when she saw you? She's built a new life for herself. Got married, started a family. Then you turn up out of the blue and all the old memories come flooding back.

I know it doesn't make much sense, but I went to apologize, to make amends somehow.

But Christine was having none of his sanctimonious posturing. Make amends! After twenty years? Make trouble, more like. She removed her dress from the armchair and sat down. Have you ever loved anybody, Karl?

He looked at the high curved instep of her shoes and the sheer promise of her stockings and did not reply.

I have. I loved Joe. I never wanted anybody else. When he left me, I thought it was the end of the world. If it hadn't been for your mother getting me involved in the women's group, I think I'd have gone mad.

She crossed her legs and Cal gazed at the smooth

plane of her outer thigh and the taut suspender tugging at her stocking.

He loved me too. He was nice to me. I don't mean this – she touched her lacy knickers scornfully. This is just the icing on the cake. I mean he cared about me.

Some icing. Some cake, Cal thought as he followed the line up between her overlapping thighs.

Haven't you ever wanted to get married, Karl?

She could see where he was looking. He wasn't even listening to her.

Haven't you ever wanted a family?

He looked up from her legs but still did not reply.

I never really wanted any children when I was married to Joe. We were happy on our own. But I've regretted it since. If we'd had children, they might have kept us together. It would have been nice for your mother too; she would have loved grandchildren.

It's not too late.

What isn't?

For you to have children.

He was admiring her breasts, the way they swelled out of her bra above the lace trim.

It's too late for your mother.

Well, Joe then. Perhaps they'll have children.

They can't. His wife's infertile. Your mother told me.

She stood up and put on her dress. Cal thought she was trying to titillate him by undressing again from scratch. It was only when she picked up her coat that he realized her real intention.

Where are you going?

Home.

Why?

I'm depressed.

What about?

I'm not sure.

Would you have married me, instead of Joe?

No.

Why not?

Because I didn't trust you.

Would you marry me now?

No.

Why not?

Because I still don't.

You like me, though?

I fancy you. That's not the same thing.

Isn't that enough?

As I said before, it's the icing on the cake. The trouble is with you, Karl, you're all icing.

As Cal drove along, he switched on the tape recorder lying on the seat beside him and listened to Helen Woofitt's version of his father's arrest.

... I mean I wasn't even involved, not at first anyway. I'd just gone to the supermarket with our Rachel when I saw this crowd outside his house. There was no trouble, people were just standing around. One or two were shouting scab and that, but it wasn't nasty. I mean they weren't going to burn his house down or anything.

Then your dad arrived and walked up to the house to see if he could have a word with Phil Walton, but the bobby wouldn't let him. There was no argument or raised voices or anything between them – in fact you could see the bobby was embarrassed. He was from round here. I've forgotten his name now, but he didn't like what was going on either. Not all the police were bastards. It was mainly them from other parts of the country that were the worst. There was no come-back for them. The local police had to live with it when it was all over.

Anyway, we were stood around talking when suddenly this police van draws up and all these coppers jumped out and started ordering everybody about and that. That ... What do they call him? Hang on a minute, it'll come back ... Taylor ... Tolson! That's it. Inspector Tolson. He was a right clever bastard, him. He was just looking for trouble. Come on! Move on! he starts shouting, or you'll be arrested. And then the coppers started pushing us around. I mean, it gets your back up that, doesn't it? Especially when you're not doing owt. It wasn't that there was a riot going on or anything.

Anyway, as you can imagine, the whole thing turned nasty. Scuffles broke out and they started making arrests. Our Rachel started crying. But I'd got my rag out by then. I know I shouldn't have, but I wasn't having anybody pushing me around, especially when I hadn't done owt. And the things they called us! I'll not repeat them, but you can imagine. I just told them to eff off. Fight fire with fire, that's my motto. Our Rachel was terrified by this time. She was screaming and hanging on to my legs. She was only three at the time. She was in a right state.

Anyway, your dad comes down the path from the house and tries to calm things down, telling us not to retaliate and to keep calm and that. A fat lot of good it did him. He just got truncheoned and thrown in the van with the rest of us. The worst thing though was – and I'll never forgive them for this – our Rachel was hanging on to me for dear life. She could see they were going to take me away. But instead of letting her go with me, they dragged her off and left her in the street. When the van drove off, I could see her through the window running after the van, her little face terrified. I mean . . . Sorry about this. It's all coming back . . . Take your time, Helen . . . (his own voice on the tape) . . . What sort of people are they who can do a thing like that? But they did. And they would have done anything. Anything to break the strike, because they were under orders from the government to.

Your dad was brilliant during the strike, Karl, the way he went round people's houses giving advice when they were in trouble. I mean people were getting into terrible debt. They didn't know how to cope with it. They'd never been in that position before. We had our electricity cut off. I'll never forget Graham's face – that's my husband. I'll never forget his face when he came home and I was sat in the dark with a candle lit. He'd been kicked to pieces on the picket line all day, then when he comes home the electricity's been cut off. I thought he was going to burst into tears, poor sod. The trouble was, we'd only got an electric cooker so we finished up having to cook on the fire. Not that there was much cooking to do, mind. I don't know how we'd have managed without the food kitchen.

Anyway, your dad came round and advised us to go round to the Electricity Board and claim special circumstances because of the baby and that. He said he'd bring our case up on the committee and see if he could get us anything out of the strike fund. It was horrible. It was like living on charity. The only consolation was that everybody was in the same boat. People got behind with their mortgages. Televisions had to go back. Furniture. Cars. Everything. I can remember Alec Todd next door. He got a snotty letter from the bank about missing a repayment on his car. So he picks up the phone and says, Is this the listening bank? Right. Well, listen to this. If I get any more letters like this one, you're getting eff all. And he slams the phone down. Joyce Grayson used to put all her bills into a hat and draw one out. She said it was the only way she could decide which one to pay. It was heartbreaking. You'd worked hard to build a decent life, then suddenly it was all taken away from you. But we stuck it out because it was a just cause, Karl. And I said to your dad when he called round, They'll not force him back to work, Harry. I'll burn the furniture first to keep warm.

Cal turned left at the road sign pointing towards the university, then switched off the tape recorder. And now Helen. They all told the same story. It looked as if his mother was right after all and his father hadn't been the aggressor.

He parked in a side street then sat staring through the windscreen. Anyway, who was he to doubt his mother's word? Where had he been when his father was being truncheoned and thrown into the back of a police van? Ten thousand miles away in Hollywood writing yet another adaptation of *Jack the Ripper*.

He got out of the car and looked around, wondering which way to go. A cold wind blew down the narrow street and the tall buildings cut out the sun. Cal shivered. What was he doing here? He remembered Laura's warning: *Don't you realize what it could do to her if you suddenly appeared on the scene? It could destroy her. It could upset her whole life* . . . He had been going to turn back throughout the journey. It still wasn't too late.

Two girls walked down the street towards him. One of them was carrying an armful of books, the other a shoulder bag. They were obviously students: like Becky. Would her hair be long, like the girl with the books? Or short, like the other one? And what colour would it be? Dark like Laura's? Or fair like his? And her eyes? He hoped she had Laura's dark blue eyes . . . Laura was right. It could destroy her. It could destroy them all. He took his car keys out of his pocket ready to drive away. The girls drew level.

Excuse me?

They stopped and looked at him.

Are you at the university?

The girl with the long hair nodded. The girl with the short hair said: Yes.

Cal paused. There was still time to change his mind and ask them where the town hall was, or the museum.

Could you tell me where the Modern Languages Department is, please?

The girls looked at each other. The one with the long hair said:

It's in the Russell Building, isn't it?

The one with the short hair nodded and pointed up the street. Go to the end of the road and turn right. You can't miss it. It's a tall building. A skyscraper sort of thing.

I'd hardly call it a skyscraper.

It's the nearest you'll get to a skyscraper round here.

They both laughed.

Cal laughed too. Thank you. I'm sure I'll find it.

As Cal walked away, he realized that he would have been about the same age as the two girls when he met Laura. So young. So long ago. He could have cried as he listened to their fading laughter across the lengthening distance between them.

At the end of the street he turned right as instructed. The Russell Building was directly before him. As he walked towards it, his head gradually went back as he looked up the towering glass façade. It certainly wasn't the Empire State Building, but, as the girl said, it was the nearest you'll get to a skyscraper round here. He walked up the steps and pushed through the glass doors.

The foyer was crowded with students. Cal stepped back against the wall trying to look casual, as if he was a lecturer, or a mature student waiting to meet someone. He scanned the faces of the girls walking past. What would she look like? Perhaps that was her, with the brown legs and tight shorts standing by the noticeboard. He strayed from the gravity of his mission for a moment or two before forcing himself to look away. Or the girl in the army boots with the shaven head, reading a copy of *The Socialist Worker*. Guiltily, he hoped not. As he glanced around, he was surprised how many of the girls – especially the attractive ones – appeared to take after him. There was something about the eyes of that one . . . And what about that one over there? Yes, she definitely had his lips. Tall blondes were included whether they looked like him or not with the excuse that they had inherited their height from his father. On the other hand, he wondered how he would feel if he saw a girl who was the spitting image of Laura and there was no doubting whose daughter she was. It would be a weird sensation, seeing his daughter and ex-lover simultaneously.

He crossed the foyer to the lift and looked for Modern Languages on the board. There was still time to turn round and go back, but when the bell rang and the doors slid open, he allowed himself to be carried into the lift among the crush of bodies, then carried out again when the lift reached the fifth floor. The students around him dispersed quickly down the corridors before he could compose himself and he was left standing on his own, wondering what to do next. It shouldn't be too difficult to find her now, though. He had narrowed down his search to her department; somebody here would be able to help him.

He walked slowly along the corridor looking at the lecturers' names on the doors. Some of them would know Becky. Some of them would teach her. All he had to do was knock on a door and ask. He continued down the corridor, then paused outside the open door of the departmental office and listened to the tapping of computer keys inside. When they stopped, he was determined to go in and ask the secretary how he could contact Becky Jordan. But she would want to know who he was, which would lead to embarrassing explanations, or, more probably, straight lies. It was too complicated, and he walked away before somebody came out of the office and discovered him lurking there.

At the end of the corridor, he stopped and looked at the German Department noticeboard which contained the class lists, tutorial groups and timetables for all three years. He worked out which year Becky was in then started to work through the tutorial groups . . .

John Aston, Damien Barnwell, Rosemary Hill . . . He could feel his heart bumping . . . Clare McKinnon, William Morton, Rowena Shaw . . . He was short of breath . . . Andrew Birch, Nazia Ali, Rebecca Jordan. Rebecca Jordan! There she was, his Becky. Tears blurred his sight. She might not bear his surname but she was still his daughter, whatever she was called now.

A door opened behind him and a group of students emerged noisily into the corridor. Cal ignored them and tried to work out where Becky would be by co-ordinating the class lists with the various timetables on the noticeboard. But it was too confusing and in frustration he turned away and approached a boy and girl standing with their arms around each other outside the recently vacated lecture room.

Excuse me?

They turned towards him. The smell of petunia oil took him back to his own student days. He wondered if they still burned joss sticks in their rooms.

Do you know Rebecca Jordan?

There was a pause, then the girl laughed.

You mean Becky? Yeah, she just left.

She freed an arm from the boy's embrace and pointed along the corridor. Cal realized that Becky had just walked past him at the noticeboard; had been within inches. It might even have been her bag that had brushed his sleeve as he had been trying to decipher her whereabouts from the timetable.

Have you any idea where she's gone?

The boy nodded. Every time he moved, his leather jacket creaked. Yeah, they've gone for a drink.

Any idea where?

Yeah, the Cross Keys.

Thank you.

Cal turned away without asking directions. He didn't have to: he had noticed the pub on his way to the Russell Building. The name had registered because it was the same as his father's local in the village. As he turned the corner to the lift, he glanced back along the corridor. The boy was manoeuvring the girl into the empty lecture room. Cal hoped that he would take his jacket off first, or they would be heard all over the campus.

When Cal reached the Cross Keys he paused at the door. The juke-box inside was playing 'Layla'. Cal knew it off by heart. He stood there anticipating the piano break, desperately trying to convince himself that he shouldn't go in. His car was just around the corner. It would be better for everyone concerned if he carried on walking and drove away. He stared into the alcove which contained facing doors. Which room would she be in? He selected the door on the left, but it made no difference because the interior had been renovated and both doors now opened into one large room.

Cal walked straight to the bar without looking round. He would look more natural with a drink in his hand. Anyway, he needed it, and not just as a prop. He ordered a Scotch and soda and had a drink before turning round. The room was occupied mainly by students, except for a couple of tough-looking local youths, with cropped hair and tattoos, playing pool. 'Riders of the Storm' replaced 'Layla'. Cal knew this record off by heart too, but he wasn't listening as he scanned the faces of the girls in the room . . . He soon found her. She was sitting amongst the group by the window. He recognized her immediately. She looked just like the old sepia photograph of his mother when she was Becky's age.

Cal placed the shoe-box on the table and removed the lid. His mother, moving around watering the pot plants, watched him take out a handful of photographs.

What are you looking at them again for? Are you getting nostalgic in your old age?

Cal glanced through the snapshots: his cousin Julie's wedding, one of himself in his school blazer holding Fidel the dog, Christine and Joe on a beach somewhere, his father in his Army uniform, smiling with his arms folded . . . Cal looked across the room at him, then back at the photograph; from the slack-jawed wreck of a man asleep by the fire, to the confident young soldier in front of the Nissen hut.

What are you looking for, anyway?

Cal kept his head down to hide his tears and picked out another batch of photographs. The top one showed a stern-looking woman wearing a black frock and black lace-up boots, sitting stiffly on a studio chair. Cal didn't even know who she was; must have been a great-aunt or somebody. He slipped it underneath the pile, then paused and stared at the next one. This was the one he was looking for. It was a photograph of his parents taken before they were married. They were sitting on a gate in a field with their arms around each other. His mother's fair hair was cut short with a fringe – like Becky's. Cal gazed at her, transfixed. If anyone had questioned him later about the colour of his father's hair, or what he was wearing, he would have had no idea. He could have removed his arm from around Cal's mother's shoulders, jumped down from the gate and walked out of the photograph and Cal wouldn't have noticed just then.

Glancing across as she moved the plants around on the window-sill, Maisie noticed Cal's preoccupation with the photograph.

What are you looking at?

He didn't hear her.

She tidied up a geranium, then walked across to the table and looked over Cal's shoulder.

That was taken just after your dad and me got engaged. You can see my ring – look. Ben Robinson took it for us. He'd been all through the war like your dad, then he got killed down the pit soon after.

They studied the photograph in silence with their heads together. Maisie smiled at her handsome young fiancé with his arm around her. Cal stared at the young woman with the fair hair.

It was taken in the mushroom fields. That's what everybody called them. I can't think why, though – I can't remember anybody picking any. It's hard to imagine it now. There was only the village then and it was all surrounded by fields. The mushroom fields disappeared when they built this estate after the war. When we moved here after that old house in Platts Lane opposite the rec., we thought we'd moved into Buckingham Palace.

She reached into the shoe-box and took out another photograph.

I loved that coat. I can remember. I saved up ages to buy it . . .

Cal continued to stare at the photograph in his hand. He could feel his heart pounding. He was sweating. If he didn't say something soon he would faint.

. . . And here's your Uncle Geoff looking like a spiv. She laughed.

Mother, I want to tell you something.

He didn't half fancy himself with the women, your Uncle Geoff – he thought he was Errol Flynn.

She reached towards the box for another photograph but Cal took her hand.

I want to talk to you. Come and sit down.

Still holding her hand, he led her across to the sofa and sat her down.

Talk to me? What about? She waited anxiously. It must be serious if she had to sit down to hear it. What's the matter? What's happened?

I've got something to tell you.

He couldn't look at her. He looked at his father instead to make sure that he was still asleep. It shouldn't have been like this, furtive and shamefaced.

He had transformed a joyous event into a guilty secret.

I should have told you years ago. Anyway . . .

She was waiting, waiting, and judging by her expression, still expecting the worst.

I went to see Laura the other day.

Laura? Laura who?

You know. We met when I was at university. We lived together for a while.

Oh yes. I'd forgotten about her. It seems such a long time ago. She visited a couple of times. I think our Joe was quite taken by her on the quiet. He'd never met anybody like that before. Christine had a bit of a sulk about it, if I remember right.

Well, I drove out to Bradley to see her. She still lives there.

What happened between you two? You never told me. Mind, you were always secretive, weren't you?

Cal nodded impatiently. He would have agreed with any criticism just then. Now that he had started his confession, he didn't want to be side-tracked.

Well, Laura, she had a baby.

That's nice. Still, I suppose she'll be married now.

I'm not talking about now, I'm talking about then. We had a baby . . . Laura and me.

She stared at him. Then, when she realized the full implication of what he had said, her face turned the colour of wax and Cal could see what she would look like when they finally laid her out. She was so pale that Cal wondered if she was going to expire there and then.

Would you like a drink? A cup of tea, or a brandy or something?

You've got a child?

Cal nodded. A girl.

And you never told us?

Her colour returned with a rush. Cal recognized the

signs. He leaned away towards the arm of the settee in case she took a swipe at him.

I couldn't . . .

You rotten devil!

I couldn't!

His anguished denial startled both of them and they instinctively glanced across the room at Harry who was still asleep by the fire.

What are you trying to do – wake your dad up as well? It's a good job he's not a fit man, or he'd give you a damned good hiding as big as you are.

Things were difficult. He was pleading now, in a whisper. Laura and me split up.

What's that got to do with it? You could have still told us.

She was crying now, wiping her cheeks with her hand. To think that I've had a granddaughter all these years and never known about it. I'll never forgive you for this, Karl. You can get out. Now! Go on!

Wait a minute. I haven't finished yet.

You've finished with me, that is a certainty. I don't understand it. I mean, what did she think? What did you say to her when she asked about us, her grandmother and grandad? Were you ashamed of us or something because her grandad and uncle worked down the pit? Because we lived on a council estate? Is that what it was?

Don't be ridiculous . . .

I used to defend you against your dad. But he was right. You are a snob.

That's nothing to do with it.

What is it to do with then?

Cal licked his lips and tried to swallow. Have you got any beer? He sounded as if he had just staggered in off the desert.

Beer! I wouldn't give you a drink if we'd a brewery in the kitchen, after what you've just told me.

It wasn't like that. I never saw her.

What do you mean?

Cal looked around the room, desperately seeking a diversion – a telephone call, a knock on the door, an electricity cut. Anything. But nothing happened. His mother was still waiting.

A few months after Becky was born – that's her name, Becky – I left Laura and I never saw either of them again until the other day.

You mean you abandoned your own daughter? She made it sound like murder. How could you, your own flesh and blood?

It wasn't like that. I intended to keep in touch but it didn't work out. After a while I decided it would be better for Laura and Becky if I stayed away altogether. It was too painful.

Don't try to make it sound like a sacrifice. You probably disappeared so that you didn't have to pay maintenance, something devious like that.

Every blow found its mark. If it had been a boxing match, the referee would have stopped it to save Cal from further punishment.

You shouldn't have told me. What's the point in knowing now, when she's grown up?

I meant to tell you! I should have told you when she was born, I realize that. But we'd lost touch. I was living in London. I was having a bad time . . . He was having a bad time now. He wiped his brow, then looked at his damp fingers. Are you sure you haven't got any beer?

Maisie just stared at him, pitilessly, forcing him to go on.

As time went by it became more difficult. Then, when Laura and I finally split, I thought it would upset you knowing you'd got a granddaughter who you couldn't see.

How do you know I wouldn't have been able to see her?

Because it wouldn't have been fair to Laura. You would have been a link with me: a constant reminder. After I'd left, she had to break that link and try to forget all about me.

Cal did not dare look at his mother, but he could tell that she was shaking her head.

I don't blame her. She should have broken your neck while she was at it.

Maisie cranked herself up from the sofa and walked across to the fireplace. Cal watched her warily as she picked up the poker. She jabbed at the cokes in the grate then added a few lumps of coal from the scuttle. Cal relaxed only after she had replaced the poker in its stand: a spent shell case which his father had brought back as a souvenir from the war.

So why did you go and see Laura, then, after all this time?

I didn't go to see Laura. I went to see Becky.

Maisie sat down at the table with the shoe-box in front of her and photographs scattered about the tablecloth.

And did you see her?

Eventually.

What do you mean?

Laura mentioned that she was a student at Sheffield University, so I went to find her.

He glanced across at his father and wished he was awake. Suddenly, he was proud to be a father, and he wanted his own father to know about Becky despite the distressing circumstances.

It was crazy really. I started asking around, trying to find out where she was. In the end, I traced her to a pub. She was sitting there with some friends.

How did you know it was her? Did somebody point her out?

They didn't have to. I recognized her straight away. He stood up and walked across to the table. She looked just like you in this photo. He picked up the photograph of his mother and father sitting on the gate in the mushroom fields. Her hair. Her eyes. Everything. I couldn't believe it.

As Maisie stared at the photograph, tears spilled down her cheeks on to her dress. It was an outpouring of grief for the lost, lovely girl smiling out at her, and for the granddaughter she had never seen.

Cal placed his hand on her shoulder. I'm sorry, Mother.

Lend me your handkerchief.

She dabbed her cheeks and blew her nose, then handed it back to him. What did she say?

What do you mean?

When you made yourself known.

She didn't say anything. I couldn't go through with it in the end. It would have been unforgivable, turning up like that. It nearly killed me, though, I can tell you, when I left that pub and walked back to the car. I've never felt so unhappy in my life.

His mother continued to look at the smiling girl in the flowered dress.

It's something you'll have to live with, Karl, and I can't say I feel sorry for you. But at least you'd the decency to consider somebody else's feelings for a change.

She replaced the photograph in the box and picked up the one of the young soldier standing against the Nissen hut. She stared at it in silence then, unexpectedly, she began to cry again: silently, barely noticeably at first, then openly, loudly, with an outpouring of long, shuddering sobs which racked her whole body. Cal thought she was crying over the loss of Becky again, but however much he apologized and tried to comfort her, it made no difference and eventually he gave up and stood back, appalled and ashamed that he had caused her so much pain.

*

INT. LIVING ROOM. TOBY'S HOUSE. DAY.

Two detectives, GOODING and CARDARELLI, are discussing TOBY's disappearance with his parents. PATTI, their young daughter, is lying on the carpet watching TV.

MR and MRS DUNCAN are fraught with worry.
TOBY has been missing for days now, and there is still no clue to his disappearance.

DET. GOODING

OK, Mr Duncan. Let's go through it one more time.

MR DUNCAN

(angrily)

What's the point? We've told you everything we know. You should be out there looking for the goddamn boy instead of wasting your time sitting around here!

The DETECTIVES glance at each other. They are familiar with MR DUNCAN's frustrated response.

DET. CARDARELLI

We understand your frustration, Mr Duncan. But we're doing everything possible, I can assure you. We're following up every possible lead.

MR DUNCAN

But the boy's got to be somewhere. Can't you get some more men on the case or something?

MRS DUNCAN, who is sitting on the sofa, bursts into tears. MR DUNCAN sits down beside her and comforts her.

MR DUNCAN

Don't worry, honey. Everything'll be OK.

DET. GOODING

(checking his notebook)

You say he left home about five?

MR DUNCAN

That's right. He said he was going to call at the library, then visit his pal Ronnie.

Cal's eyes drifted away from the screen to his tape recorder at the edge of the table. He pulled it closer and switched it on.

... There were mounted police chasing men down the streets, lashing out at them with their batons. One young lad ran in here to escape and one of them tried to follow him in. The horse's head and front legs were in the bloody shop, but luckily the doorway was too low for the rider to come in ... This lad ran behind the counter and nipped out through the back door. Old Mrs Jackson was in the shop at the time. She nearly had a heart attack, I can tell you. I was bloody furious. I shouted to the bobby, What do you think you're doing? You can't invade people's property like that! Do you know what he said? He told me to fuck off. And with a woman in the shop at that ...

Cal laughed in spite of himself then fast-forwarded the tape and listened to a snatch of Helen Woofitt's account – vivid, chilling stuff which roused the emotions. He switched off the tape recorder and placed it in the drawer out of sight; otherwise he would have been tempted to play the tape all the way through.

He returned to the screen. Where was Toby? Who the fuck cared? He read Mr Duncan's last speech then began to type:

DET. CARDARELLI

Well, he visited the library all right.
We checked that out. The librarian
caught him defacing pictures in a
book, adding tits and cocks etc, and
when she scolded him he told her
to fuck off.

DET. GOODING

Nobody seems to have seen him
after that. We suspect that the
librarian may have enticed him
down to the storeroom on some
pretext and beaten his head in with
an encyclopaedia.

Cal deleted the last two speeches then stared glumly at the screen. He was making little progress and delivery date was approaching fast. There was only one thing for it: he would have to stay in his room until it was finished. He would have the television removed, use room service for his meals and tell switchboard to refuse all telephone calls. He had done it in the past. He had done his best work under pressure. He settled himself, flexed his fingers, then keyed in.

DET. GOODING

(checking his notebook)

Well, he went to the library all right.

We checked that out. The librarian remembers seeing him. She couldn't give the exact time, but she guessed it was somewhere around five thirty. He seems to have disappeared after that.

PATTI

(still watching TV)

Maybe he visited that weird guy.

MRS DUNCAN

What weird guy?

PATTI

He lives on the next block to Ronnie Cutts. He's some kind of professor. He's nice really, but all the boys tease him and tie cans to his dog's tail and stuff. They call him Professor Fruitcake.

The telephone rang. Cal snatched up the receiver, pathetically grateful for the diversion. He vowed that this would be the last call he would take until he had finished the script. Definitely. It was solitary from now on.

Hello?

He hoped it was Hélène or Christine. It was his mother. He feared the worst, but she reassured him that his father was fine but she would like to see him.

What, now? . . . Not particularly, I was just doing a bit of work . . . No, honestly, it's not urgent. It can wait . . . Positive. I'll come straight away.

He replaced the receiver and picked up his jacket. What else could he do? She was his mother, after all. He left the room and walked along the corridor towards the lift. And he hadn't been much of a son when it came down to it. He hadn't been home for years and even then it had taken an emergency to bring him back. The lift arrived. He stepped inside. He hardly wrote or even telephoned: neglectful, downright selfish, that's what he was. He walked past reception and out through the door. (He would tell the receptionist about the incoming calls when he got back.) He might never see her again after this visit. Anything could happen at her age. She might even die before his father. Invalids often hung on for years. He unlocked the car door and ducked inside. But why couldn't she tell him on the phone? He fastened his seat-belt and started the engine. Anyway, a spot of fresh air would clear his head. The room was stuffy. Hotel rooms were always like that, really difficult to work in. Perhaps it might be better to leave the script until he got home . . .

Where are you taking me?

You'll see.

What is it, then – a mystery tour?

Cal knew that it must be somewhere special, because his mother had dressed up for the occasion. She was wearing powder and lipstick and he could smell her perfume when they got into the car. He smiled as she fussed over the seat-belt, grumbling that it was creasing her dress. When she had finally settled, he started the car and drove off.

They left the estate and drove along the main road through the village: past the shops and the primary school which Karl and Joe had attended, past the rec. and the old Plaza cinema which was now boarded up; then out into the open countryside and past the derelict colliery, where Harry Rickards and most of the men from the village had worked. Maisie stared out of the window in self-absorbed silence like an emigrant returning to her homeland after a lifetime away.

Suddenly, she roused herself and pointed through the windscreen.

Turn off, there.

Cal slowed down and turned into a narrow, twisting lane with high hedgerows which obscured the views round the bends.

Don't drive so fast, Karl. It's not the Monte Carlo Rally.

The Monte Carlo Rally's a lot more dangerous than this.

Have you been?

Only once. I was researching a film, but it never came off. He slowed down and drove on to the grass verge to allow an approaching tractor to pass by. Weren't you brought up round here?

Yes, Highfields village. She pointed across the fields. It was more of a hamlet than a village, though. Just a few houses and a pub.

I wish I knew where you were taking me.

You'll soon see.

The road cut through a wood where the overhanging branches came together and formed a dense canopy. It was like travelling through a tunnel and when they reached the other end it was as if somebody had switched the light back on.

Maisie laughed. That takes me back. I used to hate going through there when I was a girl. I was always scared of somebody jumping out on me.

I used to come round here occasionally on my bike.

Stop here, Karl.

Here?

He pulled up in front of a gate. The road was flanked by meadows with a scattering of trees; but it was hardly a beauty spot, and Cal presumed that his mother had been taken short and needed to go behind a hedge. She got out of the car and stood staring into the field.

When she didn't move, Cal looked past her through

the bars of the gate. Perhaps she was scared of the cows? He leaned across the passenger seat and wound down the window.

Do you want to go somewhere else?

Get out. I want to show you something.

Cal turned off the engine and got out of the car. He stood next to his mother and looked into the field. A few grazing cows raised their heads and stared back at them. Cal wondered what he was supposed to be looking at. Not at the cows, surely? It wasn't as if they were a vanishing species, the last six Friesians on earth.

There used to be a prisoner-of-war camp here.

Cal glanced at her in surprise. What, in this field?

This field and the next one. It was all one big field then. There were two rows of Nissen huts surrounded by a wire fence. She dotted out their positions in the air, then drew a square around them. The gate was up there – she pointed along the hedgerow – next to that tree.

What nationality were they?

Italians. She laughed. Eyeties, as they called them round here. They made a garden over there in that corner. And they used to play football across there at the back of the huts.

How long were they here for?

A couple of years till the end of the war. Then they went home.

She continued to gaze into the field. Cal gave her a sideways glance. Was that it, then? Had she dragged him all the way out here, just to tell him that? It was an interesting little story, but it hardly justified the urgency of her telephone call with its hint of important revelations. Or, perhaps in his eagerness to escape from the script, he had misinterpreted her tone, and all she wanted was a trip into her past, and the opportunity to share a few memories with him before he returned home.

But when he turned to ask her if she was ready to leave, and saw the tears in her eyes and her lips twitching, he knew that she hadn't told him anything yet.

Are there any pubs near here, Mother?

There's one in Highfields. Or there used to be.

Do you fancy a drink? Or a sandwich or something?

She looked at her watch and nodded. That'd be nice.

Cal took her arm. We've plenty of time. You said he's not due back from the hospital until four.

My dad never came in here. He was a strict Methodist, you know. He didn't approve of drink. It wasn't like this in his day, though. Maisie shook her head and looked round at the gleaming horse brasses decorating the walls and low beams. It was a right scruffy hole then. Most of the miners came in straight from work in their pit muck and stopped until closing time. She paused and took a bite from her sandwich. Jim Gregory the landlord used to wrap kippers in greaseproof paper and throw them on the fireback to cook. It was a big Yorkshire range then. She laughed and pointed to the new stone fireplace with its basket of gas-fired logs. You couldn't cook many kippers on that. She finished her drink. Some of the miners would have slept here if Jim had let them. I used to come in with his daughter, Bessie. We went to school together. My dad would have killed me if he'd known . . .

Cal sat back and let her talk. He bought her another drink, hoping that she would relax enough to reveal the purpose of their excursion.

The Italian prisoners of war weren't allowed in here. I don't know if it was against the law, but I know they were banned from coming in, in case there was any trouble with the locals.

Do you mean they were allowed out of the camp?

Oh yes. They worked on farms during the day:

harvesting, potato picking, that sort of thing. Then they were free during the evening.

And they just wandered around on their own?

Yes. They didn't go very far, though. They kept to the woods and fields round the camp. It wasn't a real prisoner-of-war camp like in Germany, with armed guards and barbed-wire fences.

But didn't they try to escape?

Did they heck! Maisie laughed. Just imagine trying to get back to Italy from here in them days. Anyway, they didn't want to. They were better off here than fighting.

Cal shook his head and finished his beer. Curious.

What is?

The whole story. It's crazy.

Would you like another drink, Karl?

He looked at his watch. Have we time?

Yes, I think so.

Cal stood up but Maisie caught hold of his sleeve before he could leave the table.

You sit down. I'll go.

He didn't argue. As he watched her ordering the drinks at the bar, he remembered when his parents used to visit the Working Men's Club on Saturday nights when he was a boy. He couldn't imagine his mother ordering a round in there. His father wouldn't have allowed it. His socialism didn't extend to that kind of liberty. He could imagine it now, though. Even before his father's stroke, the balance of power between them had shifted.

Maisie returned with the drinks. It was her third glass of beer.

Cal smiled at her. You'll be getting drunk.

What if I do? It's a special occasion.

You were telling me about the prisoners of war.

She looked past him through the window, back into the past. They used to march to work in the morning, singing. It was lovely, Karl, you could hear them for miles . . .

She paused, listening . . . Then, when she heard the stirring marching song drifting across the quiet countryside, she dabbed her eyes and blamed it on the smoke-filled room.

But who ran it? Who ran the camp?

She replaced her handkerchief in her handbag, and had a drink to compose herself. They ran it themselves, mainly. There were two English sergeants in charge, and there was an English cook. Bernardo was always complaining . . .

She stopped, but it was too late.

Who's Bernardo?

He was one of the prisoners. I'd forgotten all about him.

She blushed and tried to laugh it off. Cal placed his hand over hers on the table.

Why don't you tell me about it, Mother? That's what you've brought me here for, isn't it?

Cal sat staring at the screen of his word processor. But how could he work now after listening to what his mother had told him? TOBY would have to stay on the run a bit longer. He couldn't rescue him just yet. He decided he needed another drink. He had already had a couple in the hotel bar after dropping off his mother at home. But there had been a redundancy party going on and it was too noisy. He wanted to be on his own where he could think. It was time to start raiding the mini-bar.

. . . Bernardo? The first time she had seen him was at the football match in the rec.

Which football match?

Somebody organized a football match – don't ask me who – between a team of local lads and the prisoners of war. There were posters up in all the shops in the village: ENGLAND VERSUS ITALY, as if it was an international match or summat. I think the word had gone round that the Italians fancied themselves a bit at football. As I've already told you, they used to play a lot in the camp. So some of the locals decided to show them who was boss, that sort of thing.

Anyway, it turned into a big do. What with the war being on, there wasn't much in the way of entertainment, so a lot of people turned up, as much out of curiosity as anything else, just to have a good gawp at the Italians. It was the first time some of them had seen a foreigner except on the pictures. Italy was a long way off in them days. And there was no real antagonism towards them, as there would have been if they'd been Germans. People didn't regard them in the same way. They were still the enemy, but they weren't as bad somehow.

Everybody thought our lads were going to give them a pasting, England being the birthplace of football and all that. They were properly kitted out in shorts and shirts and some of them were good players. Not that I knew anything about football – I'd just gone along for the fun of it with my friend Bessie I was telling you about. But I could hear some of the spectators saying that one or two of them had had trials with professional clubs before the war.

The Italians marched from the camp, singing as usual. You could hear them coming along the road. It was a good two miles to the village from there. It's a wonder they weren't worn out before they started. They were a bit shocked when they saw the size of the crowd. You could tell by the looks on their faces. I don't think they realized it was going to be such a big do. They thought it was going to be a kick-about and not a serious match. They'd no proper kit, either. They were wearing the same stuff as they always wore, a kind of grey uniform and army boots. They looked like Fred Karno's army when they lined up.

Cal had no idea who Fred Karno's army were, but

he didn't ask. He didn't want to interrupt his mother while she was seeing it all so clearly.

It was funny, really. She shook her head and laughed. They all looked like you'd expect Italians to look: you know, swarthy with black hair. Except for one who was fair with ginger hair. Well, when the crowd saw him, you can imagine.

Cal could, and he started to laugh too.

EXT. RECREATION GROUND. DAY.

A group of spectators are standing behind the goal watching the Italian team warm up before the match.

GEORGE

Hey up, look at that one!

FRANK

Who?

GEORGE

Him there with the ginger hair.

FRANK

He's not a bloody Italian. He looks like one of ours.

CLIFF

He looks like old Billy Spencer from down Victoria Street.

GEORGE

Perhaps Billy fought in Italy in the First World War and got friendly with one of the mademoiselles.

CLIFF

Mademoiselles? They're French, aren't they?

GEORGE

What do they call Italian women, then?

CLIFF

Fuck knows. But it looks as if Billy managed to get across one of them.

They weren't laughing when they started playing, though, Karl. The Italians soon wiped the smiles off their faces. When they lined up for the kick-off, you could see our lads looking at each other and grinning. They looked bigger and stronger. You could see they thought they were going to murder them. I didn't know the first thing about football, but it was obvious even to me that they played a different kind of game. Our team kicked it up the field and chased after it, but the Italians dribbled it about more and they enjoyed doing tricks with the ball. The crowd soon went quiet, I can tell you, when they saw it wasn't going to be a walk-over.

Maisie went quiet, too, and stared into her glass.

Cal got up from the table and walked across to the mini-bar.

I was standing on the touch-line with Bessie Gregory, and Bernardo – I didn't know they called him Bernardo then – was playing right next to us on the wing. He was lovely. You could see that all the girls had taken a fancy to him. He'd got lovely eyes and once, when the ball went over the line, I picked it up and handed it back to him. He said, Thank you, and smiled at me. I can't remember the score; I think me and Bessie had to go before the end. But I remembered Bernardo, and when I went to bed that night, I could see his face when I gave him the ball back.

After that, I started making detours past the camp on my way home from work hoping to see him again. It was silly, really. I mean what would I have done if

I had met him – fallen off my bike so that he could pick me up?

But you did meet him again?

Yes, but not there. I was working for Dr Allison at the time as a maid. He lived in a big old house near Highfields. It was lovely. It had wisteria growing up the front and a big lawn and a gravel drive. It's the nicest house I've ever been in, even to this day.

Cal wondered what she would think of his house in France.

Then, one day, the doorbell rang. I can remember exactly what I was doing at the time. I was polishing the dining-room table and I didn't answer it straight away, because I wanted to finish the table off first. Then Mrs Allison shouted from the drawing-room.

Maisie!

Yes, ma'am! Just going!

She stepped back from the table, then bobbed about, inspecting the surface from different heights and angles to see if she had left any smears. One last quick rub, then she hurried from the dining-room into the hall. She usually checked her appearance in the hall mirror before answering the door, but because of the delay, and the reminder from Mrs Allison, she opened it straight away.

Bernardo was standing on the broad bottom step looking up at her. He was wearing the regulation grey uniform, but one of his sleeves was rolled up and his hand was bandaged with a bloodstained kerchief.

Posso vedere il dottore, per favore?

Maisie just stood there, transfixed.

Bernardo held up his injured hand to attract her attention. Doctor?

Maisie could feel herself blushing as she tucked loose strands of hair behind her ears.

(Later, Bernardo used to tease her about their first meeting. *Faccia* . . . Face, squeezing her cheeks. *Rossa*. Red like fire.

Was it heck! Laughing and blushing again.
Heck? What is heck?
I'd been working, polishing the dining-room table. That's why my face was red).
I'm sorry. The doctor's not in. He's out on his rounds.
Aspetti . . .
With his left hand, Bernardo felt awkwardly into his tunic pocket and produced a folded sheet of notepaper. From sergeant . . .
Maisie unfolded the note and read it. Wait here.
Mi scusi?
Wait here!
She held out her hand as if she was restraining a mob. As she turned to go back into the house, Mrs Allison appeared in the doorway.
What is it, Maisie?
She looked surprised to see a lone figure standing before her, and a sorry-looking one at that.
I was just coming to fetch you, Mrs Allison. It's one of the Italians from the prisoner-of-war camp. He's cut his hand.
She gave the note to Mrs Allison. When she had read it, she looked down the steps at Bernardo.
I suppose he'd better come in. Come along.
She beckoned Bernardo into the house and Maisie closed the door behind him.
Where shall I take him?
Into the waiting-room – where else? The enemy or not, he'll be treated like any other patient in this surgery. Medicine doesn't take sides, Maisie.
Chastened by this rebuke, and relieved that Bernardo didn't understand English, Maisie pointed to a door across the hall. This way, please.
Wait a minute, Maisie, I think we'd better take a look at his hand. I'm sure that filthy rag can't be doing it much good.
Mrs Allison opened an adjacent door and led Maisie

and Bernardo into the surgery. She pointed to a chair in front of the doctor's desk. Sit down.

Grazie.

Behind the desk, french windows opened on to a long lawn with wide herbaceous borders, and a summer-house at the bottom of the garden.

Bernardo raised his hand appreciatively and smiled at Mrs Allison.

Bellissimo. Bellissimo.

Yes, it is rather pretty, isn't it? I don't suppose you go in for lawns very much in Italy. Far too dry, I would imagine. Now then. Let's have a look at that hand . . .

She untied the knot on the stained kerchief, but when she tried to unwrap it, Bernardo pulled away his hand and winced in pain.

Run the tap, Maisie. The blood's dried and stuck it to his hand.

Maisie turned on the cold-water tap and Mrs Allison guided Bernardo to the sink.

Now then, put your hand under there. That should fetch it off.

The running water gradually softened the congealed blood and after a minute or two, Mrs Allison carefully peeled away the kerchief from his hand.

Right, let's see what we've got.

Painfully, Bernardo straightened his fingers, revealing a deep gash across his rough palm. All three of them winced when they saw it.

Mmm. You've certainly been in the wars, haven't you? She laughed at the unconscious irony of her remark. In more ways than one, I should add. What did it say in the note, Maisie?

He cut it on the threshing machine.

He's lucky he didn't cut his hand off, by the looks of it. It's going to need stitches, I'm afraid. Boil a kettle of water up, Maisie, and let him soak it in a bowl of hot water with a drop of Dettol in it. I think that's as much as we can do until the doctor gets back.

Yes, ma'am.

They watched Bernardo gingerly touching his injured palm.

Perhaps you could wash his other hand for him, Maisie? We don't want to risk infection.

Yes, ma'am.

And make him a cup of tea, poor chap. He looks all in. I'll be in the drawing-room if you need me.

As she crossed the room, Bernardo looked up from his hand and called after her, *Grazie, signora.*

Mrs Allison turned and looked back at him in surprise.

You're very welcome, young man. I only wish some of our people had such good manners.

She left the room, closing the door behind her.

Bernardo pointed after her. *E' una signora molto gentile.*

Maisie nodded, uncomprehending, as he continued to speak in Italian. But even though she could not understand him, she could tell by his tone and gestures who he was talking about, and when she picked out '*mamma*' a couple of times, she wondered if he was comparing Mrs Allison with his own mother.

I'll just pop the kettle on, then I'll wash your hand for you.

It was Bernardo's turn now to nod and smile dumbly as she filled the kettle and lit the gas.

Give me your hand, then. She took his hand and placed it under the tap. Hold it there and I'll wash it for you.

Maisie raised a lather between her palms and enclosed his hand between hers. She concentrated hard to avoid his eyes and she felt herself blushing when her fingers slipped between his. They were so close together that Maisie could smell the hay on his clothes and feel his breath on her face. Hurriedly, she rinsed his hand, then turned off the tap.

That should do it.

She dried his hand briskly on the roller towel, then sat him down on the chair in front of the desk.

Wait there, while I go and fetch some tea.

Bernardo looked up at her and smiled. *Grazie*.

Maisie hurried from the surgery, hoping that Mrs Allison wouldn't see her and remark on her flushed cheeks.

And that's how it started, Karl.

You mean you had an affair with him?

Well, yes. But we didn't call them affairs in them days. I started going out with him.

Cal stared at her. This old woman. His own mother having an affair with an Italian prisoner of war! He glanced at the drinkers at the next table and wondered if they had overheard.

I think we'd better go. My dad'll be back soon.

Maisie placed her hand over his on the table. What's the matter – are you embarrassed?

Well, it is a bit of shock.

It's a long time ago, Karl. Before you were born. Before I met your dad.

But shocked or not, Cal was already working on the pitch . . . The movie opens in the bedroom of . . .? Amy, a servant girl. The room is sparsely furnished, with whitewashed walls. It is early morning; Amy is asleep. We hear singing in the distance, barely audible at first – something stirring, perhaps an aria from an opera? The singing grows louder and we hear the sound of marching boots. The noise wakes Amy up. She gets out of bed, runs across the room and pulls back the curtain. Below her, a group of Italian prisoners of war are singing lustily as they march to work at a local farm. One of the prisoners – a handsome young man – glances up and sees Amy at the window. Their eyes meet. The Italian smiles. Amy blushes and lets the curtain fall. She stands there, all of a flutter, listening to the singing fade away . . .

Let me show you something, Karl . . .

He didn't hear her. He was busy working out the next scene.

Maisie opened her handbag and took out what appeared to be a folded handkerchief. She moved her sandwich plate to one side, brushed away some crumbs, then deliberately unfolded it on the table. She looked like a conjuror performing a trick, but when the handkerchief was spread out, there was nothing inside. Cal stared at the pale blue square. Creased neatly in four, it reminded him of the window that Amy had looked out of. What could he call the Italian prisoner of war? Luigi? Marco? Then, suddenly, he realized what his mother had spread out on the table before him. It was the kerchief which Bernardo had wrapped around his hand when he had visited Dr Allison's house.

Cal smiled at his mother. Did he give it to you?

Well, sort of. I found it when I was emptying the wastebin in the surgery and I took it home and washed it. When Bernardo came to have his hand dressed again, I offered it back to him, but he wouldn't take it. He said . . . She laughed. I couldn't understand what he said, but it was obvious that he didn't want it back and that he'd like me to keep it. It was his way of saying thank you, I suppose. I was really touched. He didn't have much to give away. He'd only got the clothes he stood up in . . . Her lips started to quiver.

Cal thought it best to keep her talking to prevent her from crying. So how did it start – this affair? What happened after that?

Maisie picked up the kerchief from the table. The creases were so deep that it folded itself.

He'd been to have his stitches out. I'd just finished work and I passed him walking back to the camp as I was cycling home. When he saw who it was he waved, and I got off my bike and walked with him part of the way. I could tell he liked me. And I liked him. We took to each other straight away. He was different to the lads round here. He was funny and good-natured and he paid attention to me. He made me feel nice . . . Well, one way or another, we arranged to meet. God knows how, looking back on it, because he could speak hardly any English and I couldn't speak a work of Italian . . .

They walked up the lane towards the church with Maisie wheeling her bicycle between them. Bernardo was trying to explain how he had cut his hand on the threshing machine. Maisie couldn't understand the first part of the mime: he appeared to be dragging something heavy, probably a bale, or a sheaf of corn. But there was no doubting when the accident happened. Bernardo leapt back and stared at his open palm in horror. *Mamma mia!* His performance was so melodramatic that Maisie almost laughed, and in order to hide her amusement she grimaced and contrived a matching expression of exaggerated concern.

When they reached the church, Maisie stopped and mounted her bicycle. Bernardo fiddled with the bell, ringing it quietly without resonance.

Go? You?

Yes. Maisie pointed along the road. I'm going home.

She turned and pointed to a path which led across the fields facing the church.

The camp's across there. That way.

Camp. *Si*.

Across the fields.

Si.

Past the pond.

Si.

It's a nice walk.

Si.

I've got to go now.

Si.

I'll be late for my tea.

Si.

My mother'll be worried about me.

Si.

Goodbye.

But she still kept her foot on the upraised peddle and did not push off. They stood there, tense and uncertain, avoiding each other's eyes. The clamour of rooks in the grounds of the vicarage emphasized the silence between them, and a magpie, head cocked on the roof of the lychgate, appeared to be enjoying their discomfort with mischievous glee.

Suddenly the church clock struck the hour and made them jump. Bernardo patted his heart in mock concern and Maisie laughed, the tension broken between them. Bernardo gestured towards the clock tower and picked up the count . . . *tre*, *quattro*, *cinque*.

Five o'clock! I'd better go. My mother'll wonder where I am.

Maisie turned the handlebars and straightened up the front wheel.

Bernardo placed a hand on the saddle as she prepared to push off. *La posso vedere di nuovo?*

Maisie glanced back at his hand on the saddle. I don't know what you mean.

Bernardo pointed at Maisie, then at himself. *Tu. Io.*

I still don't understand.

Bernardo shuttered his hand rapidly between them in frustration, then pointed to his eyes.

Eyes?

No . . . See! See! Then back to gesticulating between them. You! Me!

He became so agitated that Maisie grew alarmed in case anybody walked past and thought he was threatening her. Then, suddenly, she understood what he meant. She smiled and nodded vigorously.

Si! Yes! Yes!

She grasped his hand which was still fluttering between them and touched them both with it.

You. Me. Yes!

Laboriously, using their hands, the church clock and pidgin English, they worked out a date, a time and finally, pointing emphatically at the ground beneath them, the place where they would meet. Bernardo gave Maisie a push to start her off, then ran beside her as she rode away. Maisie pedalled faster, Bernardo responded and they raced along the lane laughing together until Bernardo pulled up exhausted and Maisie left him behind. She turned and waved. Bernardo waved back, and in the quiet country air, she could still hear him calling after she had ridden out of sight. *Arrivederci! Ci vediamo a presto!*

Did your parents know about it?

Did they heck! Mrs Rickards laughed. My dad'd have killed me if he'd have known.

They stared at the folded kerchief on the table.

But didn't it . . . Wasn't it . . .? Cal paused, trying to phrase it as tactfully as possibly. He didn't want to make her sound like a POW groupie, or a good-time girl, as they were called in those days. Wasn't it a bit scandalous going out with a prisoner of war?

Cal wasn't sure whether he was scandalized by his mother's behaviour or not. It wasn't as if she had faced the same dilemma as Hélène in *La Terre Dangereuse*. She had fraternized with the enemy in an attempt to save her husband from being executed by the Gestapo, but his mother had done it of her own free will. It was like finding out that she had been a whore.

I suppose it was, but there weren't many people to scandalize up here. There were only a few houses and farms. In fact I doubt if anybody saw us together. It'd have been different if I'd lived in the village: everybody would have known about it. But it was two miles away, and two miles was a long way in them days when there was no public transport and nobody had a car.

Did you find out where he came from? Or ask him anything about the war? For example, where he was captured?

It was difficult not being able to understand each other very much. But from what I could gather, he was captured somewhere in North Africa; but I don't know where. I didn't know anything about North Africa.

Cal did. He had spent three months there, researching a film about the battle of El Alamein; but the producer hadn't been able to raise the money and the film was never made. The following year, he had written a script called *Dangerous Dudes* for the same producer, which won an Oscar for best musical score.

Why are you telling me all this, Mother?

Why, is it embarrassing you?

I'm not sure what it's doing. It just seems a bit late in the day, that's all.

Better late than never, as they say. She picked up the kerchief from the table and replaced it carefully in her handbag. I suppose I wanted to get it off my chest, but the opportunity never arose. Then, when you told me about Becky, I thought it only right that you should know.

Does my dad know?

No. I never had the courage to tell him. How could I, when he'd fought in the Italian campaign himself?

They finished their drinks and stood up.

I'd like to call at Ashwell church on the way back.

What for?

Oh, for old times' sake, that's all.

Cal was relieved to get outside. His mother's revelation had brought on a headache. He felt offended and depressed. But why? It was a charming story of innocent, young love between a pretty country girl and a handsome young soldier. It sounded like the synopsis for a film. Perhaps he should ring his agent . . . No! Forget it! He knew why he was offended. He was offended for his father. His mother had betrayed him. But that was ridiculous. She hadn't even met him then. It didn't make sense. But even so, he still felt resentful as they drove back along the narrow country lanes.

Maisie grabbed his arm instinctively as a rabbit dashed across the road in front of the car. Cal almost wished he had hit it to spite her. He couldn't remember the last time he had taken sides against his mother, and he realized that if she had revealed all this when he had just arrived from France, he probably wouldn't have taken against her then. But a lot had happened in the meantime and he felt differently towards his father now.

As they drove towards the church, Maisie continued the story of her friendship with Bernardo, pointing out places they had been together.

You see that farm? I used to help him carry the milk up to the camp from there . . . And that tree! That one! That oak tree in the field. We once sheltered from a storm under that. What a shame, looking back over her shoulder as they left it behind – it's all rotten now. It's nearly dead . . . And that wood over there across the field. She paused, her memory overpowering the words. It used to be full of bluebells. You weren't supposed to go in. It was private. They used to breed pheasants. We used to sneak in and lie down in the bluebells. It was lovely and peaceful with the birds singing in the trees. She laughed. But we weren't interested in them. And the smell. That lovely sweet smell. It used to get all over your clothes. It was like being drenched in scent. When I got undressed to go to bed, the smell of bluebells used to fill the bedroom.

Cal glanced across at her. An innocent story of young love? It was turning into *Deep Throat 2*.

You'd have liked him, Karl.

(No, I wouldn't.)

He was good at sports.

(Yes, it sounds like it.)

He used to do tricks for me: handstands and somersaults and things. He used to make me laugh.

(Macho clown.)

I used to take him little treats . . .

(I bet you did!)

A homemade cake. Or a fresh egg or two. They only had powdered egg at the camp. But guess what he liked best?

Cal shook his head. He didn't even want to think about it.

Onions.

Onions!

He couldn't get enough of them.

What for, juggling with? Cal almost added.

They used to hate the food they got at the camp: mashed potatoes, bully beef, that sort of thing. So they did their own cooking when they could. They used to collect herbs from the fields and do a bit of poaching, and beg a few vegetables from one or two of the farmers. It was a real treat to get hold of a few onions or carrots.

Cal nodded reluctantly. He could sympathize with them there, having enjoyed French and Italian cooking for the past ten years; they weren't the only ones who found English cooking bland. He could imagine the doleful expression on the prisoners' faces as the dollop of mash thudded down on their enamel plates.

They drove up the lane towards the church then stopped outside the lychgate.

Do you want to get out? He hoped she would say no.

Just for a minute or two.

Cal got out of the car, walked round the bonnet and helped his mother out of the other side. She stood with her back to the church and looked across the open countryside.

It's changed since me and Bernardo used to meet

here. There was no golf course then. It was all fields. There was a stile over the wall and a path which led to the prisoner-of-war camp.

She walked along the lane, then stood on her tiptoes and looked over the wall into the grounds of the rectory.

Goodness . . .

What's the matter?

Come and look, Karl.

Cal joined his mother at the wall and looked across the garden of the Victorian rectory. It looks as if it's been converted into a restaurant.

Reverend Francis used to live there when I was a girl. There used to be an orchard where they've made that car park. Bernardo once sneaked in through the hedge and stole me an apple . . .

While Maisie remembered her youth, Cal watched a waiter setting the tables in the dining-room and decided to bring Christine here before he returned to France . . .

You see where that big lawn is, Karl?

. . . A final night out together. A passionate farewell.

There were some trees there and rooks used to nest in the branches. She looked high into the sky with her head tilted back. They used to circle around and you could hear them cawing miles away.

Cal followed her gaze and thought about the eagles planing the sky above the mountains behind his house and the long climb through the pine forest with Bruno.

It's sad, really. I wonder where they went when the trees were chopped down.

Poor Bruno . . . Would he still be pining? Or would he have forgotten him by now?

I want to show you something, Karl.

What?

You'll see.

They walked back to the church and Cal followed his mother into the graveyard.

If I can find it, that is.

Find what?

My parents' grave.

They walked up the worn flagged path towards the church. Cal looked up at the clock on the tower then glanced at his watch.

The clock's stopped.

I'm not surprised. It looks as if time's stood still in here.

The church door was padlocked and the graveyard had reverted to a meadow. Poppies, buttercups and dog daisies formed random tributes on the graves, and when Maisie stepped off the path into the long grass, she disturbed a skylark which sprang up singing at her feet.

She placed her hand on her breast and laughed. It made me jump.

Be careful, it might have a nest.

Cal stayed by the church door and made no effort to help his mother find the grave. It wasn't as if she was looking for a cricket ball – it wasn't that kind of search. It was personal. She needed to find the grave on her own.

While Maisie was reading the inscriptions on the headstones, Cal looked for the skylark's nest in the grass. He quickly found it, and when he saw the blotched, brown eggs lying in the grass-lined hollow, he felt a childlike thrill of triumph. It was like discovering treasure. He thought of Tommy Johnson, who was the best bird-nester in the village. He could climb the highest trees, and during the nesting season the backs of his hands were always criss-crossed with scratches from searching bramble patches and hawthorn bushes.

I've found it, Karl!

Cal rearranged the flattened grass around the nest, then followed his mother's trail across the graveyard. She scraped away the lichen from the headstone then stepped back and they read the inscription together in silence.

I didn't realize they'd died so close together.

Yes, they died within three years of each other. My mother was only forty-five.

What did she die of?

Maisie bent down and pulled up a few weeds from the grave. I should do something about it. It's a disgrace.

When she stood up, Cal noticed that her hands were trembling and she was sweating.

Are you all right?

She nodded and supported herself on Cal's arm. It must be the sun.

Cal glanced up at the cloudy sky, then smiled and tried to make a joke out of it. The beer more like.

Could be. I'm not used to it. Let's go and sit down a minute.

Cal led her back through the long grass and they sat down on a weather-beaten bench at the side of the church.

That's better.

But she didn't look it. Cal noticed the beads of sweat along her top lip. Maisie opened her handbag and rummaged about inside.

Have you got a handkerchief, Karl? I seem to have forgotten to put one in.

I should have one somewhere . . . He patted his pockets then produced a ragged tissue. That's no good. I've got a box in the car – I'll fetch them.

But Maisie wasn't listening. She sat motionless, staring towards her parents' grave.

Mother?

She ignored him and Cal watched her with increasing anxiety as she continued to stare straight ahead.

Mother, are you all right?

Again no response, then, mechanically, as if under hypnosis, she took Bernardo's kerchief from her handbag, unfolded it and held it to her cheek. The touch of the material on her skin unlocked her emotions and she began to cry. Her tears soaked the cloth and stained it deep blue, like the time Bernardo had held his injured hand under the cold-water tap in Dr Allison's surgery.

Mother, what's the matter?

She couldn't speak. Her sobs convulsed her body.

Mother, what is it? What's wrong?

Cal was in a panic. He thought she was having a fit, or a nervous breakdown.

I killed her!

What? Killed who?

My mother! You asked me what she died of. She died of a broken heart!

The words came out in spurts, loud and uncontrolled.

What do you mean? What happened?

Maisie pressed the soaking kerchief to her eyes.

I had a baby. I had a baby and she never got over it . . .

Even now, sitting at his word processor in his hotel room, the recollection of his mother's disclosure was still explosive enough to bring Cal to his feet, as it had done in the churchyard earlier in the day. He opened the door of the mini-bar and took out a miniature Scotch . . .

. . . Cal stood by the bench and stared down at his mother sobbing into the damp kerchief. Her hair was thinning on top and he could see her scalp through the silver strands. A baby! When? How old was he? (He never considered that it might be a girl.) His mind was befuddled. He couldn't work it out. If he'd had a piece of chalk in his pocket, he would have done a rough subtraction on a gravestone. He closed his eyes and concentrated. If the baby had been born at the end of the war, say in 1945 or '46, today he would be . . . He worked it out . . . No! It wasn't him! He was too young. Bernardo wasn't his father after all. He relaxed, relieved. But what if he had been? What a film that would make! INT. PRISONER-OF-WAR CAMP. DAY . . . Forget it! (Well, until later anyway.)

Cal sat down on the bench beside his mother and put his arm around her.

Calm down now. It's all right . . . He held her for a while, then stood up. I'm just going round the back. I think the beer's gone straight through me.

But he didn't really want a piss. It was just an excuse to give his mother the opportunity to compose herself in private, and to give him time to accommodate her astonishing disclosure. What was his name? What happened to him? Cal half read some of the inscriptions on the graves, then focused on Timothy Hanson, 1819–83, and wondered if he was a distant relative of Mary's. He imagined her sucking him off in the long grass behind a gravestone. Not as a girl, when he had seen her with Jack in the bushes at the bottom of the rec., but now, with his mother in tears at the other side of the church.

He picked a bunch of wild flowers to take his mind off it and to get rid of his erection, then returned to his mother and presented her with the bouquet.

A present for you.

Thank you. They're lovely.

She smiled up at him. She had stopped crying and was sitting upright and composed with her handbag on her knee, as if she was waiting for a bus.

Are you ready to go?

Sit down, Karl. I might as well tell you the full story now.

Feigning indifference, and working hard on his role as the tactful son, Cal sat down on the bench. He couldn't wait for her to start.

You don't have to, you know.

I want to. I've kept it bottled up too long. And after you'd told me about Becky . . .

Is that why you were heartbroken the other night?

That's right. It brought it all back. A lost son followed by a lost granddaughter: it was too much.

Haven't you told anybody?

No. Except for my parents. They knew, of course.

What about Bernardo – did he know?

She looked at him, sharply. Of course he knew. He was the father.

Yes, I gathered that. What I meant was, if you got pregnant at the end of the war, he could have been released and gone back to Italy without ever knowing about it.

How do you know he went back to Italy?

Well, where did he go?

I know what you're thinking, you know. You think I was a silly young girl taken in by an Italian Romeo who deserted me when I got into trouble.

Cal remained silent. She wasn't far off the mark.

I wasn't a bit like that. When I told Bernardo, he was glad. He wanted to get married. He wanted me to have the baby.

But Cal remained cynical about Bernardo's motives. Didn't she realize that he wanted to get married so that he could take out British citizenship and remain in England?

He came to see my parents. They didn't even know I'd been going out with him until I told them I was pregnant. Well, you can imagine their reaction, can't you?

Cal nodded. It wasn't difficult. He could imagine the scene in detail from location to dialogue.

My mother had hysterics. She was always bad with her nerves but that tipped her over the edge. And my dad . . . She stared at the flowers. Cal thought she was going to start crying again. He smacked me across the face. It was the only time he ever hit me in his life.

Cal hadn't imagined that in his scenario: the smack. That was far more shocking than the reaction which he had imagined.

I told Bernardo what they'd be like, but he still insisted on going to see them. He didn't want them to think that he was just a fly-by-night.

She plucked the dead leaves off the stems of the dog daisies. The poppies were wilting already.

We met here at the church. Bernardo was sitting over there on the wall, waiting for me. I tried to tell him that it'd be hopeless but he wouldn't listen. It was terrible. She shook her head as it flooded back. My dad wouldn't let him in the house. As soon as he saw us coming he rushed out, dragged me inside and locked the door. My mother was having hysterics, my dad was shouting at me and poor Bernardo was in a right state outside. In the end, my dad completely lost his temper and went out to him. He was calling him every name under the sun: pit-talk, as women called it. It was shocking really. I'd never heard my dad swear before. He was such a religious man. Then he attacked him and tried to beat him up. It was really upsetting.

Cal was upset too. He wasn't sure whose side he was on, but it was heart-rending stuff.

It was pitiful, really. My dad was only little. He was as quiet as an old sheep usually and he'd got silicosis from working down the pit. He kept swinging out at Bernardo and you could see him gasping and his chest heaving. I though he was going to kill himself. And Bernardo, he never tried to hit him back, not once. He kept taking the blows on his arms and trying to explain himself. He was embarrassed and upset by it all and I could see the tears in his eyes. He was sorry. He was trying to apologize. It was as if his own father was giving him a good hiding and he couldn't fight back.

Cal sat back and closed his eyes. The emotional pummelling was too much for him. He was exhausted.

I left home then. I couldn't stop there after that. I went to live at Dr Allison's for a while. I explained what had happened. I thought they might give me the sack, but they were lovely to me. They used to let Bernardo come and visit me, and Dr Allison even offered to go and talk to my parents. But I wouldn't let him. I knew it'd be hopeless. I thought it was best to let things calm down a bit and then see what happened.

Cal imagined Bernardo sitting on the wall looking down the lane waiting for Amy . . . No, Maisie. It's Maisie! Stick to reality! Waiting for Maisie to arrive. Here she comes! Standing up on the pedals, dying to see him again in spite of the trouble they're in. They wave. Bernardo jumps down off the wall and runs to meet her. They laugh as Bernardo grabs the handle-bars, then they embrace with Maisie still standing astride the bike. They are so pleased to see each other. To be together again. To be in each other's arms. They love each other so much. No one else matters in the whole world. And they are going to have a baby. And Bernardo wants to marry her. He's not just saying it. He really does. And he's going to see Maisie's parents to prove it. A prisoner of war. The enemy. He is going to see Maisie's outraged parents to try to explain himself in pidgin English.

Cal opened his eyes and looked towards the wall where Bernardo had sat. He was a brave man. Grudgingly, he had to admit it. He was an honourable man too. Cal had to admit that. What would *he* have done in the circumstances? He concocted all kinds of principled actions, but in the end he had to face up to it: he would have run away. He would have made tearful vows and declarations of undying love and then, after a faceful of kisses and an emotional farewell, he would have sailed away into the distance thanking his lucky stars for his narrow escape.

Cal continued to stare bitterly towards the wall. He was neither brave nor honourable, but at least he was learning to face the truth. It was a start.

What happened?

I had the baby in February, just before the war ended and Bernardo went back to Italy. We called him Gerald after Dr Allison who delivered him. It seemed the right thing to do after they'd been so good to me. Bernardo called him Geraldo, of course.

Cal could hear him saying it: Ger-al-do, his voice dipping on the last syllable. So he had a half-brother: – how strange.

Maisie laughed, then started to cry again. Every time I heard Geraldo and his orchestra on the wireless it reminded me of him.

So he did go back to Italy, then?

There was a note of triumph in Cal's voice. His cynicism was justified after all.

Yes, he wanted me to go with him.

(A likely story!)

He'd written to his parents explaining and they agreed. He used to read me their letters and we tried to translate them together. They had a farm in Tuscany and they wanted us to go and live there. It sounded lovely.

Why didn't you go, then?

Maisie shook her head.

Why not?

I was going to, especially after what had happened with my parents . . .

Did you ever go and see them, after the baby was born?

No . . . I sent them a letter to let them know, but I never heard anything back. It was as if they were dead . . .

Her voice faded and broke. She was still shocked by the rebuff, even now, fifty years later.

Cal placed his hand on her shoulder to comfort her. Why don't you leave it if it's too painful?

No. She squeezed his hand. I want to finish it now.

She gazed across the churchyard in the direction of

her parents' grave. After a while, Cal began to wonder if she had forgotten about him.

It was all arranged. Bernardo went back to Italy when the prisoners were released to get things sorted out, then me and Geraldo were going to follow him.

And then you got a Dear John letter, Cal felt like adding.

But it didn't work out like that.

Here it comes!

She paused. It seemed callous to be gloating over her betrayal, but Cal had to admit to a certain sneaking satisfaction at being proved right after all.

My dad came to Dr Allison's house one day to see me. I knew then that something was wrong. I can see him now standing at the bottom of the steps. It was strange. When I opened the door, he took his cap off as if I owned the house instead of just being the maid. It was as if he didn't know me. The funny thing is, I didn't recognize him for a split second either. He was like a stranger standing there.

He'd come to tell me that my mother had had a nervous breakdown. He'd a cheek really, looking back on it. He just stood there and said it as if he expected me to go home with him there and then. As if nothing had happened between us. As if I'd never met Bernardo and had a baby. As if he hadn't forced me out of the house. I wasn't sure if he'd come to make me feel guilty, or if he was genuinely concerned and thought I should know.

Anyway, I'd no choice really: I had to go and see her. The doctor had been. He'd given her some sedatives. Not Dr Allison, Dr Warren – he was our doctor. I was glad I didn't work for him. The way he used to look at you. He gave you the creeps. And his breath always smelled of drink. She gave a little shudder at the thought of him.

When I got home, my mother was sitting by the fire with a shawl round her. I was really shocked when I saw her. She'd aged ten years in six months and her hair had gone white. She looked like a little old woman. She didn't even look up when I walked in. She just carried on staring into the fire. Whether it was the tablets she was on, or because she didn't want to look at me, I wasn't sure, but she was a pitiful sight. I felt terrible. I could have drowned myself for what I'd done to her.

But it wasn't your fault. If they'd have been more sympathetic she wouldn't have got herself into that state.

That's easy to say now, Karl, but things were different then. It was a scandal to have a child out of wedlock in them days. And my mother and dad were religious people. I'd been brought up a chapel-goer. In their eyes, I'd brought the family into disgrace.

So much for Christian forgiveness – that's all I can say.

Anyway, it was obvious she was in a bad way. She was vague. You'd say something to her and she wouldn't answer you. She could potter about the house, but she was in no condition to do any housework or cooking or that . . .

She was distracted by a magpie landing on the roof of the lychgate. It cocked its head and cackled at them, then flew away.

She needed somebody to look after her, I could see that straight away.

Meaning you?

What else could I do? My dad did his best, but he couldn't afford any time off work. So when I'd finished work at Dr Allison's, I'd cycle home and do what I could to help: get my dad's dinner ready for him and do some washing and that. It was too much for me, though. It wore me out.

And what about the baby . . . Gerald? (He felt curiously bashful saying his name for the first time.) Did you take him with you?

No. I couldn't.

Why not?

Well, after all the trouble we'd had, I thought it best to keep him out of the way for the time being. I explained everything to Mrs Allison and she was marvellous about it. Her children were grown up and had left home and she really missed them, so she was glad to look after Gerald while I was away. She loved him. In fact I used to get jealous when I came back sometimes and I saw her feeding him. It was as if she was his mother, not me.

But you told them? You told your parents about him?

I told my dad. It was no use telling my mother anything. She was like somebody in a trance most of the time. Anyway, even if she had been able to take it in, I'm sure it'd only have made her worse.

But what did your dad say?

Nothing.

What do you mean? He must have said something.

He didn't want to know about him.

But he was his grandson, for Chrissake!

He reached over the arm of the bench and swiped at a head of hedge parsley, exploding a shower of white flowers on to the grass.

Maisie took his arm to calm him down. I know he sounds terrible. But he wasn't, not really. He was a good husband to my mother and he'd been a good father to me. He was unbending, that's all: strict. That was his way, and a lot of people would have acted like that at that time.

Cal was able to predict the outcome now . . . Bernardo was back in Italy: *arrivederci* Maisie. Maternal Mrs Allison, missing her own children and recognizing Maisie's plight, offers to adopt Gerald. Tears all round, but Maisie finally agrees that it's in everybody's best interests etc. It was a stock narrative, but potent all the same; especially as it featured his own family.

I wrote to Bernardo and explained what had happened to my mother, and that I was going to have to move back home and look after her for a while. It was a big disappointment. He'd made all the arrangements for me to go over, but he was ever so understanding and he suggested that he should come over and take Gerald back to Italy and I should follow as soon as my mother improved. You know what Italians are like about family?

Cal nodded. He wasn't sure if he admired Bernardo for his integrity, or resented him for making him feel guilty. He thought of that terrible journey across the moors after he had deserted Laura and Becky. And then seeing Becky sitting in the pub with her friends . . .

I didn't like the idea of it at first, being separated from Gerald altogether and all that distance away. But I came round to it in the end. I knew he'd be well looked after, and it'd be a weight off my mind and it wouldn't be long before I could join them . . .

. . . How could he approach her? He couldn't just walk across the room and say, Excuse me, I'm your father. He tried to work out alternative advances, but as he watched her chatting and laughing and fooling around, he knew that none of them would work. Whatever he did could blight her future. Becky picked up her glass; Cal mirrored her action at the bar. Then, as they raised their glasses, Cal proposed a silent toast to his daughter, drained his glass and walked out.

. . . I was looking forward to it. It was an adventure. Italy was a long way off in them days, Karl. A lot of people emigrated to America after the war, but that was different, they spoke the same language and they'd an idea of what it was like from going to the pictures. But Italy, it was foreign parts, a different language. Nobody knew anything about it except that it looked like a boot on the map . . .

Would he ever see Becky again? Would she enquire about him when she grew older? Would she try to find him?

. . . I went to meet Bernardo and his mother off the boat at Liverpool. She'd insisted on coming with him to look after Gerald, and Bernardo had told her so much about me that she said she couldn't wait to meet me. Mrs Allison was heartbroken when I went to fetch him. She'd bought him a new little romper suit and a knitted bonnet and shawl. He looked a picture when he was dressed . . . What's the matter, Karl?

He shook his head.

Are you all right?

He nodded and turned away, but not before she noticed the tears in his eyes.

You said you wanted me to tell you.

He nodded again. He was too upset to speak.

Liverpool was a right trek from here. You'd to go to Leeds on the bus, then catch a train to Manchester, then change for Liverpool. It took all day. But it was exciting, though, looking forward to seeing Bernardo again, and I kept telling Gerald that he was going to see his daddy. He was as good as gold. I suppose he'd have been just over a year old then.

Just over a year. About the same age as Becky when he had walked out on her.

I can't tell you what I felt like when I saw the ship coming in. There were a lot of other people waiting on the docks and all the passengers were on deck, and when they saw who they were waiting for, they started waving. I couldn't see Bernardo at first, and then it struck me: what if he's not on board? What if he's changed his mind? You know, like you do – a thousand things crossed my mind. But then I saw him. He was leaning right over the rail. I think he'd seen me first and he was waving like mad. Oh, Karl, I'll never forget that moment as long as I live. Then I held Gerald up for him to see, and I kept saying, Look, it's your daddy! It's your daddy, look, up there!

And she held out her arms with her fingers spread, as if she was holding her baby.

I couldn't wait for them to tie the ship up and get the gangplank down. And when he came off the ship and ran towards me . . .

It was too much for her and she began to sob violently. She opened her handbag and took out the damp kerchief to stem her tears. Cal gazed across the churchyard towards an ancient beech, which appeared to be sighing in sympathy as the wind soughed through its branches. He fumbled in his pockets and Maisie handed him the sodden rag.

Bernardo threw his arms round us both and hugged us so tight that it frightened Gerald and made him cry. Poor bairn, he must have thought he was trying to smother him. We were both laughing and crying and trying to say things to each other. I can't tell you how glad I was to see him. Then his mother stepped forward. I think Bernardo had forgotten all about her in the excitement. He'd left her behind when he ran to meet us, and she was hanging back to give us a few moments on our own. She was a lovely woman. I took to her straight away. She put her arms round me and kissed me on the cheeks. I was amazed! I wasn't used to that sort of thing from a complete stranger. I wasn't even used to it from my own mother, come to that. We didn't go in for that kind of thing very much in our house. And when they saw Gerald, well . . ..!

She shook her head, her eyes tearful with laughter now. Cal could imagine it. He could have written the scene. But not as well as his mother was telling it.

I've never seen anything like it. Talk about excited! Bernado's mother took him off me and kissed him and hugged him, and then she passed him to Bernado and it was all *Bello di nonna!* and *Bello di papà!* and the way Bernardo looked at him and held him to his chest – I'd never seen a man hold a baby like that before. You could tell he was really proud of him and it made me feel proud too.

Then they started discussing who he looked like. I didn't realize what they were talking about at first, but I soon guessed by the way they kept pointing to Gerald's face and touching their own noses and pointing at their eyes. They kept saying *si* and *no*, and mentioning *Papà* and *Tino* and *Mario*, who I knew were Bernardo's brothers. Mrs Allison said Gerald was the spitting image of me, but you wouldn't have thought it the way they were carrying on. It was funny watching them – they'd forgotten all about me. I was like a stranger all of a sudden. Then Bernardo laughed and held him up in the air and shouted: *Piccolo Geraldo! Mio figlio! Mio figlio!*

It would have been a surprising announcement even on a busy quayside, but in a quiet country churchyard the effect was startling and a pair of wood pigeons crashed out of the beech tree in alarm.

Cal stared at his mother. His safe old mum: or so he'd thought. He'd been wrong about his father too. This trip hadn't turned out at all as he had expected. There was the business with Christine. And what about Hélène? He hadn't spoken to her for days now, except through messages on the answerphone. Then there was the problem of *It's a Dog's Life*. Delivery date was due and he was way behind schedule. He hadn't even reached the scene where Toby rescues the blind girl, yet. He blew his nose on the kerchief. Things were falling apart.

We had a night in Liverpool before the ship sailed next day. We stayed in a hotel. I'd never stayed in a hotel before. I've never stayed in one since, if it comes to that. I thought I was really going up in the world. I shared a double room with Mrs Rossi and Gerald, and Bernardo was in a single room down the corridor. I was embarrassed at first. I'd never shared a room with anybody before, never mind a bed. But Mrs Rossi soon put me at ease. She was a grand woman. She sang Gerald to sleep. It was lovely listening to her.

Cal wondered if she had visited Bernardo's room when Mrs Rossi and Gerald were asleep. She would have done in a film; it would have been an obligatory scene – the old woman snoring, the creaking floorboard as Maisie crossed the room. Then down the corridor and a passionate love scene on the narrow bed . . . But this wasn't a film, it was real life, and in the circumstances she would have stayed in her own bed.

But next morning, Karl, when they left, it was terrible. I'd tried to build myself up to it, but it didn't work. When we were on the quay I nursed Gerald for as long as I could; I couldn't bear to let him go. Bernardo and his mother were ever so patient; they knew what I was feeling and they were starting to move the gangplank when they finally took him on board. I gave him a last kiss before I handed him to Mrs Rossi, then me and Bernardo hugged each other and his mother kissed me. We were all in tears, as you can imagine.

When I saw them walking up the gangplank I panicked. I wanted to run after them and fetch Gerald back. But it was too late. I felt terrible. I felt as if I'd deserted my own baby, even though he was with his father and grandmother. They waved from the rail. Mrs Rossi was holding Gerald. Bernardo was shouting to me and blowing kisses. Do you know, Karl, I've never felt as empty in my whole life as when that ship sailed away. And the journey back home on the train: I was in a daze, I couldn't remember anything about it.

When I got home, I washed a couple of dirty nappies that I'd brought back and hung them on the clothes horse in front of the fire to dry. I can see my mother now. She didn't say anything. She just pretended they weren't there. I could have strangled her.

A bank of cloud passed across the sun, turning the

deep shade under the beech tree to darkness. Cal glanced up at the sky.

It looks like rain.

Maisie wasn't listening. She was an age away, back in her parents' house, grieving for her baby.

Things got worse after that. I was resentful and guilty at the same time. I'd a job on to speak to my mother. I thought she was putting it on to spite me and keep me at home. She made no effort to shake herself at all. She just moped about. She was like a wet lettuce around the house.

But didn't they ever ask about Gerald? I can understand them being angry at you and Bernardo. But that wasn't the baby's fault. And he was their grandson, after all.

My dad asked after him once. He presumed he was still at Dr Allison's. I told him I'd had him adopted. It seemed simpler. That shook him a bit. But he didn't want to know any details and it wasn't raised again after that.

Cal shook his head and brushed a few hedge parsley flowers off the bench.

Weird.

It was. And what made it worse was that my mother wasn't getting better. Bernardo kept sending letters asking when I was going over and I could never give him a definite answer. I'm sure he thought I was reneging on him.

And were you?

She turned on him indignantly. No! I was not! What makes you think that?

Cal blushed. He wasn't sure. Instinct probably, being a natural reneger himself.

Sorry.

I was determined to go. There was nothing in the world I wanted more than to join Gerald and Bernardo. I used to cry myself to sleep thinking about Gerald growing up without me.

I didn't mean it like that. I meant, well . . . memories fade. You can't help it.

That's true enough. As the months went by I began to wonder if it had all been a dream.

It must have been fantastic when you saw them again. He was eager to know what had happened when she arrived in Italy, and why she had returned.

I didn't go.

What?

I didn't go in the end.

I thought you said . . .

My mother died.

Cal hadn't been expecting that either.

That settled it. I couldn't go then.

Cal shook his head sympathetically, but the more he thought about it he couldn't see why not. There was the question of her father to consider, but surely she couldn't be expected to sacrifice herself indefinitely?

She took an overdose of sleeping pills.

That complicated matters, there was no doubt about it.

You mean she committed suicide?

It was impossible to tell. The doctor said that she might have forgotten that she'd taken her dose and taken some more. She'd become terribly vague and absent-minded. My dad realized there was something wrong when he got up for work. He said her arms and legs were cold. But it was too late by then: she'd died in her sleep.

Cal read the inscription on a nearby gravestone in oblique respect.

What do you think happened?

She committed suicide.

You can't be sure, though.

I'm certain. She lost the will to live and put an end to it all.

And you blamed yourself for her death?

Who else could I blame?

Don't you think you were a bit harsh on yourself?

Looking back, perhaps I was. But at the time I was devastated. It was like a punishment for my sins. I couldn't have left my dad on his own then.

Her degree of self-sacrifice made Cal uncomfortable. It wasn't a virtue he was familiar with.

I wrote a letter to Bernardo explaining what had happened and that I couldn't go.

But your dad died three years later. Couldn't you have gone then?

It was too late by that time. After that last letter, I never heard from Bernardo again. I suppose I'd hurt him too much. He might even have been married: who knows?

She stood up and brushed the back of her skirt. Anyway I'd met your dad by then.

EXT. PROF. KNUTT'S HOUSE. DAY

A police car pulls up in front of the house and DETECTIVES GOODING and CARDARELLI get out. The house is shabby and needs painting and the yard is full of wrecked cars and machine parts etc. DET. GOODING rings the doorbell. Then, instead of the usual chimes, we hear a blast of 'The Ride of the Valkyries'. GOODING and CARDARELLI shake their heads and raise their eyes in world-weary fashion. The guy was obviously some kind of screwball.

Cal sat staring at the screen of his word processor. He had been staring at the same six sentences for the past half hour. He couldn't concentrate. He couldn't think. He couldn't get the professor to answer the door. He couldn't get the detectives inside. And when he did, whatever they found out about TOBY would be of no consequence compared with what he had learned from his mother earlier in the day.

There was a knock on the door.

Come in!

The barmaid entered the room carrying a bottle of Scotch.

Where would you like it, sir?

He glanced round, hopefully. But no, there was no provocative leer on her face. Pity, he felt like it. It would relax him and then he might be able to get on with some work. He had phoned Christine several times since arriving back at the hotel, but she wasn't in.

Over here please.

He could hear the swish of her tights as she crossed the room.

Put it on the table.

As she placed the bottle next to his tape recorder, he could smell her perfume and see the outline of her bra under her blouse.

Now, if you'd just lift up your skirt and sit on my dick . . .

Certainly, sir.

She slid her tight, black skirt up to her waist revealing her soft, white thighs and suspenders. Then she unzipped his flies and gasped with delight when she saw the size of his prick. Slowly she lowered herself on to it while he unbuttoned her blouse and took out her tits . . .

When he opened his eyes she had gone. He was all alone with a bottle of Scotch, a dud script and an erection.

The whisky didn't help. It gave him a headache. He needed some air and something to eat. Then he would come back and work through the night. He always worked better at night, under pressure.

He put on his jacket and left the room. When he

stepped out of the lift, the barmaid was talking to the receptionist at the desk: probably telling her about the weirdo in Room 10. Cal remembered that he hadn't tipped her, and he approached the two women and gave the barmaid two pound coins, apologizing for his forgetfulness, and explaining that he was writing a film script for a Hollywood producer, and that he had been so wrapped up in his story that he had been miles away, hence his trance-like state when she had come into his room.

The barmaid thanked him, but didn't look too impressed. The receptionist looked interested, though, and Cal hoped that she would still be on duty when he returned.

He took his car out of the hotel garage and drove out of town towards the village. When he reached the open road, he turned on the radio and sang along to a Talking Heads record. Suddenly everything seemed fine, even though the approaching vehicles did seem a bit blurred; and when he looked out across the fields in the direction of Ashwell church and the site of the prisoner-of-war camp, the view was definitely impressionistic.

He drove through the village and parked outside the rec. As he crossed the road towards the gates, he staggered and almost fell. He blamed the road surface. It didn't look as if it had been mended since he was a boy. The rec. didn't look much different either: a bit smaller perhaps, and the swings behind the top goal had been renewed. But the football pitch was just as bare and bumpy as ever. On dry, windy days, it was like playing in the Sahara Desert. When it rained, it turned into a swamp.

As Cal walked unsteadily towards the touchline, he remembered the time when the bottom goalmouth had been flooded after a storm and children were paddling and sailing boats in it as if they were at the seaside. It was so deep that Raymond Deakin had tripped headlong over an old mattress which was floating partially concealed in the muddy water like a basking hippo. He looked towards the other end of the pitch where Colin Marshall, who was playing in goal, had been beaten up by his team-mates for looking up the frocks of the girls on the swings behind him when Roy Campbell had headed past him for the winning goal. And the time when Alan Turner's dog had burst the ball . . .

Cal stood looking across the pitch with tears in his eyes. The emotional turmoil of the day, followed by half a bottle of whisky, had made him mawkish. He started to walk along the touchline. This was where he used to play, out on the wing, out of the way, one of the last to be selected when the teams were picked. He used to run up and down the line in his black pumps, repeatedly pushing his glasses up his nose as he waited for a pass. It used to get cold, out here, out of the thick of the game. And when it rained, his glasses steamed up, and he couldn't see the ball properly when it came towards him, and he would fail to control it and it would run out of play. (He would have failed to control it now, but it wouldn't be due to the rain.) Then they would abuse him and call him specky-four-eyes and professor and a useless, swotty bastard. But he wasn't. They were wrong. School was easy. He couldn't help it. He would have swapped every brain cell in his head to have been able to play like Jack Clayton, who had been for a trial with Manchester United. He thought of Tommy and Charlie and Joe. They had all played here, shouting and cursing as they charged up and down the pitch before leaving school and going to work at Foxmoor pit.

Cal looked across the empty pitch towards the council estate where they had all lived, and in the distance, above the roofs of the houses, the rusting, winding wheels of the colliery were just visible in the fading evening light.

Bernardo had played here too. But there had been no council estate then: just the old village and a walk across open fields to the pit. He played on the wing too. He had run up and down this same strip of ground. But only once. Just the one fateful game. But that had been enough for his mother, who was standing in the crowd. Where had she stood? On the halfway line where he was standing now? Or further down, near the corner?

Cal laughed when he remembered the corners, which retained the only patches of grass on the pitch and usually concealed piles of dog shit. He wondered if Bernardo had got any on his boots during the game against the locals. Cal had trod in it regularly and was always lifting up his feet like a horse being shod, to see if any of the evil-smelling stuff was stuck in the grooved soles of his pumps.

Had Bernardo scored in the match? His mother said he was a good player: tricky . . . Had she said that? Or was he making it up? Cal saw Bernardo control the ball on the edge of the penalty area, avoid a clumsy tackle, then curl a delicate shot into the top corner of the net: 0–1 to Italy! Cal applauded the goal. He was alone in the rec. Anyone watching him from the street would have thought he was crazy. He felt crazy. He saw Bernardo being congratulated by his team-mates: slapping him on the back and ruffling his hair. He trotted back to his position on the touchline, smiling. Cal walked out on to the pitch and trotted back to the touchline smiling, as if he too had just scored a goal. Was this when Bernardo had caught his mother's eye? Had she blushed when she realized that he was smiling at her? Who won? Had the Italians bamboozled the village team with their subtle skills? Or had they contrived a tactful defeat to assuage the home crowd? His mother had left before the end, so he would never know. And Bernardo, where was he now? Did he ever think of that match? Did he remember the final score? Or his mother – did he ever think of her?

Cal turned away and walked unsteadily back to the car. He tried to compose himself by naming the families who had lived in the demolished houses opposite the rec. where the vacant factory units now stood. Top house, Mr and Mrs Betts. Next, old Mr Curtis and his two dogs, Monty and Patch. Then Mrs Ellis, whose husband had been killed down the pit . . . What had happened to them? What had happened to the other families in the row? Many of the parents would be dead now, of course. But the children, the grown-up children like himself – where were they, and what were they doing now? They would be on the dole, mainly, or doing a bit of this and that like Charlie and Tommy, or would have left the district like Joe. Cal started the engine. It was all over, finished, *finito* as Bernardo would have said. The place was dead on its feet.

He drove out of the village along the same road that he had travelled with his mother earlier in the day; but instead of taking the road which led to the church and the site of the prisoner-of-war camp, he took an earlier turning down a lane which led to the derelict Foxmoor colliery. The road surface was riddled with potholes, and even though Cal drove slowly trying to cushion the shock, his head was thumping and he felt sick by the time he reached the entrance. He needed a drink. He wished he had brought the bottle of whisky from his room. The gate was padlocked, and a notice fastened to the wire read:

PRIVATE
KEEP OUT
GUARD DOGS OPERATING

On whom? Cal wondered, as he scanned the deserted pit yard through the windscreen. He got out of the car and slammed the door, hoping to flush out any lurking Rottweilers from behind the pile of rusting coal tubs or the partially demolished office block; or at least provoke a few barks. But there wasn't a sound, and nothing stirred, not even a rabbit or a bird from amongst the ruined buildings. Cal looked up at the NCB board beside the gate. The paint had faded but the name of the colliery was still visible through the thick layer of dust. For some reason he felt proud when he read it: it was his father's pit.

As Cal looked through the gate into the pit yard, he remembered incidents from the strike which people had described to him when he had interviewed them about his father's arrest. This is where the pickets would have gathered: right here, outside the gate. And their cabin would have been here somewhere. He searched the grass verges for signs of their year-long occupation of the site, but the only thing he found was a rusty bicycle frame which could have been dumped there at any time. But Cal was convinced that it had been used to carry sacks of coal, courageously picked from the muck-stack during the long, harsh winter.

Then as he was turning away he noticed the oil drum in the hedge bottom. It was partly concealed in the undergrowth, but he could still see the holes punched in the side. As he hauled it out into the open, nettles stung his hands and spiky, bramble tentacles stripped away sheets of rust from the corroded metal. He stood it up outside the gate and laughed with delight. It was the brazier at which the pickets had warmed themselves during the strike. And even if it wasn't, he was determined that it was going to be.

He set it up on two bricks just as the pickets would have done, then ran to the car and found the book of matches in the glove compartment which he had picked up in the Italian restaurant on his first night out with Christine. He gathered up a pile of old newspapers and magazines from the back seat, collected a pile of dry wood from the hedge, and quickly had a fire blazing in the brazier.

He spread his hands over the shimmering heat as

his father and Joe and Charlie and Tommy and the others had done before him during the long strike. Perhaps it was the whisky taking effect after the emotional events of the day, but Cal felt greatly moved and privileged standing here before the fire, like a boy who had been allowed to join the company of men.

This is where they were standing when the police surprised them and drove the scab back to work. This is where the Land-Rover smashed through the barricade and mounted police pursued the pickets through the village. This is where the pickets built the snowman round the bollard, and this, of all places – he walked across to the gate and stared into the pit yard – was where his father had met his mother.

Cal squeezed through a hole in the rusty wire and walked towards the derelict colliery buildings along the same road that the miners and their families had walked on that momentous January morning in 1947. They had travelled from miles around, his mother had told him as they left the churchyard and drove back to the village . . .

. . . It was like a street party, Karl. There were buntings on the gate and flower tubs along the road that led up to the offices. My dad wasn't fit to go really: his chest had got so bad that he'd a job to breathe, but he insisted. He said he was going to the ceremony even if it killed him, so I decided I'd better go with him just to make sure he was all right.

He wasn't a political man, my dad. Politics were never mentioned at home. It was all religion in our house. But when he saw that new sign outside the gate – THIS COLLIERY IS NOW MANAGED BY THE NATIONAL COAL BOARD ON BEHALF OF THE PEOPLE – I could see how important it was to him. If I'd got a camera, I'd take a photo of it, he said. It was a grand occasion, Karl. There was a brass band playing and a little stage had been set up outside the offices for the officials and union men. There were one or two speeches, then the pit manager unfurled the new NCB flag and ran it up the pole. Well, there was such a cheer went up; I've never heard anything like it in my life. Men threw their caps in the air. They were cheering and waving and shaking hands – I've never known such excitement. I'll never forget my dad's face. He just stood there looking up at the flag with tears in his eyes. I was a bit embarrassed really. He was a dry old stick my dad, not given to showing emotion, but I knew it must be important if he was shedding a tear or two.

And that's when I met your dad. He came across to say hello to my dad. They worked together, and as my dad had been off sick for a while, he came over to see how he was. My dad liked him, I could tell. A bit of a hothead, my dad said when we got home, but a good worker. He started teasing my dad, hoping that he'd thanked God now that they'd been delivered out of the hands of private ownership: that sort of thing. I was surprised how well my dad took it, as I knew how serious he was about blasphemy, but he wasn't in the least offended. I think he quite enjoyed it really. He warned your dad not to be so cocky, and your dad asked him to pray for the Labour Party to make sure they stayed on the straight and narrow. They were an unlikely combination, but they got on really well together, you could tell. It really hurt when I thought about what he'd been like with Bernardo . . .

Cal glanced in through the shattered windows of the office building, then turned round and stared across the pit yard. It was difficult to reconcile the destruction around him with the scene his mother had described earlier in the day. There was no cheering and flag flying now: just silence and long shadows, thrown down across the rubble by the rusty winding gear . . .

*

. . . They must have been chewing the fat a good five minutes before my dad introduced me. I think he'd forgotten all about me in the excitement. Not that your dad took much notice of me either. I think he was more interested in politics than women, even at that time.

It wasn't love across a crowded pit yard then?

She laughed and shook her head. No.

Not like Bernardo?

No. Not like Bernardo. It wasn't like that at all. Perhaps I was wiser and more wary after what had happened before. But I didn't fall for your dad, if that's what you mean. It happened gradually. When my dad became too ill to work, your dad used to come over to see him sometimes. He'd bring him a book to read, or half a dozen new-laid eggs from his allotment: something to try to cheer him up. My dad was in a really bad way then with his lungs – he'd a job to breathe. It was pitiful watching him sit there gasping for breath. Your dad used to sit and talk to him. He'd tell him about what was happening at the pit: technical stuff that I didn't understand. And stories about the war: how he'd escaped from a burning tank in the North African desert. It was funny hearing him talk about the Italians. It was hard for me to think of them as the enemy.

Did it make you feel guilty?

No, not really. Bernardo was fighting for his country; you couldn't blame him for that. As time went by, it seemed like a dream, as if it hadn't really happened. Does that make sense?

They had arrived back at the house by this time, but Maisie made no attempt to get out of the car. Once she opened the door, the link with the past would be broken, and she was determined to finish the story before she went inside. She smiled at her adopted stray cat, which was sitting waiting for her on the wall by the gate.

I loved listening to your dad talking. He was so passionate about things. He always said the Army was his university. That's when he got interested in politics and he joined the Communist Party as soon as he was demobbed. It's hard to explain what things were like then, Karl, just after the war. There were terrible shortages and rationing and that, but there was tremendous optimism about. The Labour Party had won the 1945 election against all expectations and it looked as if people like us were going to have a fair crack of the whip for the first time. I didn't know much about politics at that time, but your dad was full of it. He got involved with the union as soon as he went back down the pit. It didn't last long, of course. Things soon turned sour. The Labour Party was voted out at the next election. But for a bit, just for a year or two, there was real hope in the air, as if things were really going to change. Not like today with unemployment and depression everywhere.

The cat jumped up the car bonnet and miaowed through the windscreen.

Did you ever regret not telling my dad about Bernardo?

Maisie tapped the windscreen in front of the cat's face. Yes. I should have told him at the start, before we got married.

We've all got 20/20 hindsight as they say.

I always felt guilty about it and in the end I don't think it did us any good. I was too passive; I became a martyr. I felt I had to suffer for my sins.

I think we've all suffered in one way or another.

The cat leapt on to the car roof in one long stretch, revealing its pale underparts.

Not as much as your dad, though. All his hopes were dashed when Soviet Communism collapsed. He felt he'd spent a lifetime of struggle for nothing. But he's a fighter, your dad. That's why he was disappointed in you. He expected you to pick up the torch and carry on where he left off.

He expected too much.

I know that. But he was proud of you, Karl. You were clever. You'd been to university. He thought somehow you might succeed where he'd failed.

He thought wrong. He turned me off politics and he won't forgive me for it.

It's not too late.

What do you mean?

Can you remember what he said to you when you arrived?

Cal glanced up. The patter of the cat's paws on the car roof sounded like rain.

How can I forget? Why don't you write something that matters? He laughed. A typical greeting from him, I might add.

Why don't you, then? It'd please him no end.

Cal was thinking about his mother's question as he walked back across the pit yard towards the gate. Suddenly, a shout from behind made him jump.

Hey! What you doing?

Cal spun round. A policeman with a dog was running towards him out of the gloom. Cal thought about making a run for it, but if he did, and the cop let the dog off the lead, he knew that it would catch him before he had gone ten yards. So, rather than risk a nasty bite, he stayed put and waited for his pursuer to approach.

As he drew near, Cal saw that it wasn't a policeman after all. It was a security guard and he was holding his hat on and cursing the dog as it nearly pulled him off his feet. Cal stared at him. No, it couldn't be . . . Yes! It was! He started to laugh. It was Charlie: Charlie Thomas.

Charlie arrived in a fluster with his jacket flapping open. He was panting heavily and roaring at the barking dog to SIT! and HEEL! and BE QUIET, YOU FUCKING THING! But it took no notice of him, and he was so busy trying to control it that he didn't even look at Cal. As he yanked and kicked the brute into submission, he was furious with the bastard in front of him who seemed to think it was all a joke.

You'll not be laughing if I let it off and it rips your fucking throat out!

This amused Cal even more. It looks as if it's more likely to rip your throat out than mine, Charlie.

Only then did Charlie look at him. Karl? Well, fuck me! What you doing here?

Nothing much. Just having a quiet look round until you appeared on the scene.

Look round? I wouldn't have thought there was much to see.

I just wanted to have a last look, I suppose, before it all disappeared.

You're only just in time. They're bringing the bulldozers in next week. SIT DOWN! He was shouting at the dog, not Cal.

I didn't know you were a security guard.

I wasn't. I only started on Monday. He buttoned up his jacket and straightened his cap. The taxi-driving went for a burton as soon as Kenny came back. They've cut my hours at the hotel, so when this job came up, I thought I'd better take it. Beggars can't be choosers, as they say.

Do you like it?

Like it? Two-fifty an hour and provide your own dog. It's crap.

Cal laughed. Not at the wages, but he enjoyed the detail about the dog.

I borrowed him from my mate, Dave. He looks fierce, but he's as soft as a brush really. If he got anybody down, he'd lick them to death.

Cal put the back of his hand to the dog's nose and it licked him.

That's right, spoil him. He'll be rolling over on his back next to have his belly tickled.

What do they call him?
Rambo.
I've got a dog at home.
I have: a Yorkshire terrier. It wouldn't be much good on this job, though.
Cal thought of Bruno stretched out at Hélène's feet in the shade of the olive tree behind the house. They seemed far away: a fading memory, like Bernardo and Gerald.
It's a sad story, Karl . . .
Cal looked at him sharply. Was Charlie a clairvoyant too?
Charlie swept his arm around the pit yard and shook his head.
Who'd have thought it'd have come to this? I worked here all my life from leaving school until it shut down. I didn't have four jobs then. One was enough. One job and a decent wage is enough for anybody.
He took out a packet of cigarettes and offered one to Cal.
No thanks.
It's a funny place, the pit, Karl.
He lit a cigarette then flicked away the lighted match. The dog watched it keenly until it went out.
You love it and hate it at the same time. The work's a bastard, but your mates and the comradeship make up for it. Everybody pulls together. That's what the government hated during the strike: solidarity. It scared them. They knew that if they could beat us, they could beat anybody. They were right as well. Since we went down, they've taken the unions apart. The coal industry's dead on its feet, Karl. There's only two pits round here still working, and they're both under threat of closure.
Charlie inhaled deeply on his cigarette and the upward glow lit up the tears in his eyes. The silence between them lengthened, and it was only when Cal

started to talk to the dog that Charlie came out of his reverie.

I was just thinking, Karl, about that day we marched back after the strike. I'll never forget it as long as I live. The pit yard wasn't like a graveyard then. Even though we'd lost, we still kept our pride and there was no way we were going back with our tails between our legs like whipped dogs. We'd come out together, and we were going back together with our heads held high. Charlie lifted his chin as he said it and straightened himself up. We assembled in the rec. in the village. The whole pit was there. Except for the scabs, of course. They daren't show their faces or they'd have been lynched. There was a massive roar when the union banner was unfurled, just as if somebody had scored a goal. Then the colliery band led us out of the gates. It was a moving experience, Karl . . .

He patted his pockets, then took out a handkerchief. Cal stroked the dog and kept his head down while Charlie blew his nose and wiped his eyes.

When we marched through the village, there were people standing at their doors, cheering and clapping every inch of the way. It made me feel proud, I can tell you. Do you remember that time I saw you outside the bookie's when I was driving the taxi? We marched past there.

Mr Peters the newsagent was out on the pavement clapping, and funnily enough, Jack Collins, who's the manager of the supermarket now, he was playing in the band that day. Your dad and Joe were up at the front. I think your Joe was helping to carry the banner. And your dad, well, he was a fucking hero, there's no other word for it. We all used to think he was a bit of an extremist when he used to go on about capitalism and that. But all his warnings about pit closures came true, even though nobody believed him at the time.

It was Cal's turn to feel for his handkerchief now.

When we left the village, we marched out here

behind the banner, with the band playing in front. It was an emotional occasion, I can tell you, Karl. There used to be a chant during the strike – it went: The miners united, will never be defeated. And I know that I didn't feel defeated when I was marching along that road to the pit. We might have lost the battle but we won the arguments, and this bloody pit and dozens like it are proof of that!

His anguished cry echoed amongst the derelict buildings and flushed a roosting pigeon from the roof of the engine shed.

But the most moving thing of all, Karl, was when we reached the pit gate and the women in the support group were waiting for us.

Instinctively, they both turned towards the gate. Cal saw the brass band leading the procession, followed by his father walking underneath the banner and Joe grasping one of the poles . . .

They were singing and applauding as we walked past. Your mother was there, and Joe's wife, Christine. It was bloody marvellous, the work they did during the strike: fund-raising, organizing the food kitchens and that. Your mother went fund-raising abroad somewhere, didn't she?

She went to Germany.

And let's face it, she was no spring chicken, was she? It took some guts to do a thing like that. We wouldn't have held out half as long if it hadn't have been for the women. In fact they got more determined as the strike went on. If it had been left to them, I think we'd have still been out today.

Charlie looked at his watch.

I'd better be off, I'm late. I've to go up to Clifton Industrial Park next. Mind you, what with all the fucking grass that's growing on it, it's more park than industry. Most of the units have been empty since it was built.

And what's going to happen here then – are there any plans?

There's talk of building a new shopping centre, but it's only rumours.

Charlie dropped his cigarette end into a puddle and looked towards the mine shaft.

This is where we used to stand and have a last smoke, before we walked across to the cage.

EXT. PROF. KNUTT'S HOUSE. DAY.

A police car pulls up in front of the house and DETECTIVES GOODING and CARDARELLI get out. The house is shabby and needs painting and the yard is full of wrecked cars and machine parts etc. DET. GOODING rings the doorbell. Then, instead of the usual chimes we hear a blast of 'The Ride of the Valkyries'. GOODING and CARDARELLI shake their heads and raise their eyes in world-weary fashion. The guy is obviously some kind of screwball.

Cal read it through. The scene hadn't improved while he'd been away. There had been a message for him at the desk when he returned to the hotel. He leaned over the counter and looked at the receptionist's legs when she turned round and reached into the pigeonhole. He wondered what she would say if he invited her up to his room for a drink? He still had half a bottle of Scotch left. But he forgot all about the receptionist's legs (and her other parts as well) when he read the note. It was from Christine. She would call round at eight o'clock tomorrow evening. He couldn't wait. He wished that she was here now. He cleared the screen and began to type.

INT. HOTEL BEDROOM. NIGHT.

There is a knock on the door.

CAL

(sitting at his word processor)

Come in!

The door opens and CHRISTINE enters. CAL is working hard on his script and there is a pause before he turns round. He is amazed and delighted when he sees who it is.

CAL

Christine! What are you doing here?

CHRISTINE

I've been waiting for you all evening. I just had to see you.

CAL stands up and CHRISTINE crosses the room towards him. She is wearing a tight dress which shows off her figure. They embrace hungrily, then CHRISTINE sits on the bed.

CAL

(indicating the bottle of whisky)

Would you like a drink?

CHRISTINE

No. Not now. I want you. Quickly . . .

She holds out her arms and CAL walks across to the bed.

It was trite stuff, but he still got a hard-on, thinking about what happened next . . .

He cleared the screen again and imagined himself settling down at his trusty old Remington in a Los Angeles hotel room. Then, after a few false starts (cut to screwed-up sheets of paper in the wastebin), he hits his stride. Hour after relentless hour through the night (he was glad he wasn't in the next room) with the pages mounting steadily beside the typewriter. Then, in the morning, he wakes up bleary-eyed and unshaven with his head on the typewriter, wondering where the hell he is. He notices the completed script (about two inches thick), and starts to read it. After a few pages, he sits back and smiles. It's a masterpiece . . .

Cal couldn't make out the title on the top page, but it didn't look like *It's a Dog's Life*. But masterpiece or not, he had to get on with it. He recovered the scene on his word processor where the TWO DETECTIVES are standing at PROFESSOR KNUTT's door, read it through again, then began to type . . .

Charlie Thomas. Can you remember him, Dad?

Harry Rickards nodded.

I met him out at Foxmoor pit last night.

Cal was exercising his father by walking him around the room.

Charlie-worked-with-our-Joe.

Cal mouthed the words with him as he struggled to get them out.

That's right. They were big mates when they were at school.

What were you doing at Foxmoor?

Cal looked across at his mother who was ironing by the window.

When I got back to the hotel I had a headache, so I went out for a bit of fresh air. I drove around for a while, then I finished up at the pit. I thought I'd have a last look before they demolish it.

Well, it'll not be here the next time you come, there's no doubt about that. Put him down now, Karl, I think he's had enough.

Cal carefully lowered his father into the armchair by the fire.

There you are, Dad. You'll soon be doing aerobics.

Maisie laughed. That'd be a sight for sore eyes. She took a shirt out of the clothes basket and spread it out on the ironing board. It sounds as if you're getting ready to go back to France.

Cal watched her guide the iron across the shirt front and round the buttons. What makes you say that?

Well, having a last look round and that.

Cal remembered his white school shirts, and how jealous he used to be of Joe because he could wear shirts of any colour at his school.

I suppose it's time I made a move.

I'm surprised you've stayed so long. I thought you'd have gone back as soon as you saw your dad was on the mend.

Yeah, so did I.

So what kept you?

Cal glanced across at her, but he couldn't interpret her expression because she had her head down over the ironing board.

Oh, this and that.

He turned back to his father to prevent further questioning.

Charlie was telling me about when you marched back to work after the strike, and how the women's group were waiting for you when you reached the pit.

He paused when he saw that his father was working himself up to speak. In the silence, he realized that the bump and swish of the iron had stopped. He glanced across at his mother who was standing motionless behind the ironing board with tears running down her face as she relived the events of that crucial day.

Your mother started the women's group, Karl. They went all over the country raising money. His slurred voice sounded like a record being played at the wrong speed. Your mother went to Germany. Where was it, Maisie? Where did you go?

Cal answered for her. Freiburg.

She brought some photos back. They're in the box upstairs.

Cal nodded. Yes. I've seen them.

Cal found himself rocking slightly on the edge of the settee as he leaned forward trying to draw out his father's words. If Harry had been a racehorse, Cal would have applied the whip.

Some families went to France on free holidays, organ . . . organized by French trade unionists . . .

Suddenly Cal remembered the photograph of the farmhouse in Italy amongst the family snaps, and how his mother had snatched it from him and hidden it in her pinafore when he asked her what it was.

. . . They didn't starve us back to work like in 1926, Karl. We went back with pride and dignity and we showed wha . . . what can be done when working people stick together.

Cal smiled and looked across at his mother. You can tell he's getting better.

He's going to get excited, though. He'll be having a relapse if he's not careful.

Cal glanced at his watch. He hoped not; he was meeting Christine in an hour. There was just time for a quick shower and change of clothes. He felt a stir of anticipation.

Maisie walked across to the hearth and gently sat her husband back in the chair.

Have a rest now, Harry, or you'll be wearing yourself out.

Cal stood up and put on his jacket.

Aren't you stopping for something to eat?

He could see that his mother was disappointed because he was leaving. No, I've got some work to do. It's urgent. They're breathing down my neck for the script.

On his way out, Cal went upstairs to the lavatory, then went into the spare bedroom. He took out the shoe-box from the bottom drawer and placed it on top of the chest next to the 'Evils of Capitalism' bronze. After all the hardship stories he had heard about the miners' strike, and the subsequent decimation of the coal industry, Cal was convinced that the top-hatted figure looked more bloated than ever.

He took the lid of the box and flicked through the collection of snapshots inside . . . No, it wasn't there. The Italian photograph was missing.

Cal had arranged to meet Christine in the hotel bar. When she arrived, he was disappointed to see that she was wearing trousers. He had been anticipating watching her cross her legs when she sat down, then secretly stroking her thighs under the table.

He stepped down from the bar stool. I thought you'd left the country.

I've been busy.

What would you like to drink?

Dry white wine, please.

They watched the barman fill the glass.

Isn't Charlie on tonight?

It must be his night off.

Cal imagined Charlie and his dog Rambo patrolling some godforsaken industrial estate.

Have we to sit down?

As they crossed the room, two men standing at the bar turned round and watched Christine. Dirty bastards, Cal thought as he led her to a table in the corner. They sat down under the photograph of Humphrey Bogart, one of the Hollywood legends ranged around the walls.

Cal leaned forward and kissed Christine on the lips. I've missed you.

Christine looked up at the photograph and laughed. My mother used to be mad about Humphrey Bogart. My dad used to get ever so jealous. Silly, isn't it?

Jealousy often is irrational.

I know, but he was hardly going to walk down our street and carry my mother away, was he?

The hotel receptionist appeared in the doorway and looked round the bar. When she saw Cal sitting in the corner, she crossed the room towards him. Cal watched her approach, her tight, black skirt restricting her stride. The two men at the bar turned round a second time.

Excuse me, sir, there's a telephone call for you.

Cal stared at her scarlet lips then stood up, quickly. I bet it's my dad. Excuse me, Christine.

He was so fearful of hearing his mother's voice that he didn't even notice the swing of the receptionist's hips as he followed her across the bar and into the foyer.

Would you like to take it here, sir? Or shall I put it through to your room?

Cal couldn't wait that long. I'll take it here.

As the receptionist handed him the receiver, the uncurling flex reminded him of the rusty chest expanders which Joe had found on a rubbish tip when he was a boy. He remembered how resistant they were, and how the only way he could stretch the springs was by holding the left-hand grip rigid, then pulling with his right arm. But even then he could only extend them halfway. And then his father would pick them up and pretend he was playing an accordion.

Hello . . .

He relaxed and smiled with relief when he heard the voice on the other end of the line. The receptionist thought he was smiling at her and looked away.

. . . Fine. Yes, he's improving fast. He should be able to get about on his own soon . . . Miss you too . . .

He said it softly, feigning intimacy and turning his back on the receptionist, hoping she wouldn't hear.

. . . I can't wait. We'll have a few weeks together before you leave for Berlin . . . Why? . . . So when are you going? . . . Next week! . . . What, here? . . . Of course I do. I'm just surprised, that's all . . . So when will you arrive? . . . Fine. Yes. That's fine. I'll meet you at the airport . . . What? It's fifty miles! Still, I suppose that's the sort of extravagant thing film stars do . . . Yes, I'll be here, waiting . . . Me too. I've got to go now. I'm going to babysit my father while my mother goes to the bingo. It'll do her good to get out for a change . . . Bye. I'll ring you tomorrow.

Cal was so preoccupied with Hélène's call that he didn't even glance at the receptionist as he crossed the foyer and entered the bar. Still, it could have been worse: Hélène could have arrived unexpectedly and been due at the hotel in an hour.

Sorry about that. Cal sat down and finished his drink. He wondered if the call had left him looking anxious or flushed. It was my agent. About the script. It's overdue and the producer's going nuts.

What's it about?

Nothing much.

Why can't you finish it then?

Cal couldn't tell if she meant it seriously, or as a joke. Because I've lost interest in it. It's crap.

But that had never stopped him delivering on time before. In fact it had often had the opposite effect. The more banal the material, the greater the incentive to finish it.

Would you like another drink?

Christine shook her head. No thanks.

Cal remained in his seat and stared at his empty glass.

Don't worry about it. Christine placed her hand over his on the table. You'll be going back to France soon. Once you're back there and you don't have to worry about your dad and that, you'll be able to concentrate on it again.

I know. That's what I'm afraid of.

He raised Christine's hand on his and kissed it. Anyway, bugger Toby, let's go and have something to eat.

Who's Toby?

The boy in the script who turns into a dog and then into a nightmare. Where would you like to eat? In the hotel, or have we to go out somewhere? I discovered a nice place when I took my mother for a drive yesterday. It's the converted rectory at Ashwell church. Do you know it?

I'm sorry, Cal, I can't stay.

What do you mean?

She glanced at her watch. I've got to go soon.

Why? People glanced round from adjacent tables. Cal lowered his voice. I thought . . . Well, you know.

Yes, I know you did. But I'm going out.

Who with?

It's none of your business.

With a man, I suppose.

Christine laughed.

What's funny?

You. Men.

I'm disappointed, that's all. I was looking forward to seeing you. He reached under the table and placed his hand on her knee. Can't you put this – this other person off?

He smiled, expecting her to give in. Christine smiled back at him and shook her head.

Just this once?

I can't.

Cal stroked her knee. Why not?

Christine moved her leg, making his hand fall limply against the chair. Because I'm going to marry him.

Cal stared at her. Marry him? Marry who?

Someone at the next table laughed. Christine blushed, angrily. There's no need to make a public announcement.

I didn't even know you were going out with anybody.

You didn't ask.

Are you sure you wouldn't like another drink?

Positive. I won't be seeing you again, Cal.

He glanced up at the portrait of Humphrey Bogart on the wall. His expression had changed. He was laughing at him.

Who is he then, your *fiancé*?

Christine kicked him under the table. Don't be sarcastic.

Why not? It's all I've got left.

They call him Alan. We've known each other for years in a semi-serious sort of way.

What does he do?

He's an engineer.

An engineer!?

He didn't say it like that. That was how he thought it. He confined himself to a few non-committal nods, and anyhow what had he to sneer about? At least engineers did something useful. They built houses, hospitals, bridges. They produced architectural masterpieces: Nôtre Dame, St Paul's, the Sydney Opera House, to name but three. Cal put up three of his own masterpieces for comparison: *A Stitch in Time*, *Hook Line and Sinker* and *Wowee!* OK, he was being unfair to himself; he realized that. How could the work of one person compare with the cream of centuries? But he didn't feel like being fair to himself. He was trying to be honest with himself for a change. But even so, he did feel diminished by the comparison and he tried to restore a modicum of dignity by selecting his best three. He didn't have a best three. They were all as bad as each other; and while Christine narrated the history of her friendship with Alan, Cal engineered the next scene of *It's a Dog's Life*, to prove it . . .

PROF. KNUTT

Sure I remember him! A damned
nuisance he was too. He was always
teasing my dog. I sure cured him
of that, though. Haven't seen hide
or hair of him since!

(he laughs fiendishly)

DET. CARDARELLI

What do you mean, cured him?

PROF. KNUTT

I gave him a taste of his own medicine.

(he points to the Transformation Chamber)

I shut him in there for a while.

DET. GOODING

What is it?

PROF. KNUTT

I've been working on it for years. Kind of Jekyll and Hyde stuff only a step further. Instead of changing a person into a different kind of person, you can go the whole hog and change a person into anything you want.

CARDARELLI and GOODING glance at each other. This guy is weird. Could be dangerous too.

PROF. KNUTT

So I tried it on the boy. Worked a treat. He sure came out barking. Not a bad-looking little mutt either. Nice black patch over one eye.

DET. GOODING

(incredulously)

Are you trying to tell us you changed the boy into a dog?

PROF. KNUTT

Sure did. Kicked him out then. I thought it might stop him being

cruel if he saw things from a dog's
point of view. I calculated that the
dose from the machine would last
an hour. Then he'd change back
and run home to his mum and dad.

DET. CARDARELLI

Well, he didn't run home. He's still
missing.

PROF. KNUTT scratches his head and walks across to the Transformation Chamber. He studies the dials, then turns round in alarm.

PROF. KNUTT

Holy Jesus! I gave him the wrong
dose. I read days for minutes.
(pause working it out)
That means he hasn't changed
back yet. He's still a dog!

It was High Art; there was no doubt about it. How could a mere engineer compete with the author of a masterpiece like that?

So when are you getting married?

In the autumn. October probably.

Does Colin know about me?

Alan.

Sorry, Alan.

Of course not. Why should he?

What would you say if I asked you to marry me?

Ask me.

Will you marry me?

Yes.

Cal turned pale.

Christine laughed and sat back in triumph. There you are! You nearly had a heart attack at the thought of it!

She was exaggerating somewhat. But it was a nasty

shock, and Cal could feel the sweat breaking out under his arms.

You've no intention of marrying me. You're just miffed, that's all, because I won't go upstairs with you.

He couldn't deny it. But he tried. No. It's more than that. I've grown really fond of you.

Christine leaned forward and lowered her voice. You mean you're fond of me in bed. Would you be as fond of me wheeling a trolley round the supermarket? Or when I'd been up all night with a crying baby?

Baby? What baby?

Christine stared at him, then slowly shook her head in disbelief. You're incredible.

What do you mean?

You thought I was pregnant, didn't you, and you might be the father?

Cal blushed at being caught out so blatantly. Well, what did you mean then?

I meant that I'd like to have children, that's all. I've been on my own for ten years now and I want to marry somebody who loves me and cares about me, and not only in bed. That part of it's important, I know that. But it's not everything, and if that's all it depends on, I can't see how it can last.

Cal didn't know whether to shake his head or nod.

I know it's not what you want, Cal.

I wouldn't count on it.

He laid his hand on her arm. I shall miss you.

Yes, but not for long.

She was right again. Two or three postcards with views of the Côte d'Azur and a few telephone calls . . . But that was in the future, and it did nothing to diminish the disappointment, the pain even, that he was feeling now. He sat up and turned towards the bar.

I think we should celebrate. How about a bottle of champagne?

Christine shook her head and grasped his sleeve. No, Cal. Honestly. I've got to go now.

Pity. He raised his empty glass. Anyway, congratulations. I hope you're both very happy.

Thank you.

Perhaps you'll invite me to the wedding?

Christine laughed and stood up. Not likely!

Tommy Johnson was assembling the aquarium when Cal visited his parents' house the following day. A lot had happened since the last time he had been there.

After Christine had said goodbye, he went straight up to his room determined to get drunk. But even as he poured his first drink, he knew he was deceiving himself. He wasn't *really* brokenhearted. He wasn't going to hurl himself out of a window, or slit his wrists and sit in the bath. He was sulking, that's all, and using their break-up as an excuse to postpone writing. And in the morning, his hangover would be another good excuse to postpone writing again.

But he knew that the best way to forget Christine was not to get drunk, but to work. He had to sit down at his word processor and write. Anything would do, no matter how trite. (He could always revise it later.) Anything to get him moving again.

So he did. He rinsed his glass and replaced the bottle of whisky in the bedside cupboard. (If he had been writing the scene in a script, the writer would have emptied the bottle down the sink. It was the sort of cliché that came naturally to him.) Then he sat down and finished the scene in which the TWO DETECTIVES are questioning PROFESSOR KNUTT about the missing boy. After he has told them about his miscalculation with the Transformation Chamber, and that TOBY is still a dog, the PROFESSOR manages to give them a description, and an alert goes out throughout the city to be on the look-out for a small black and white mongrel with floppy ears.

Cal sat tight, forcing it out. He worked into the

night, slept for a few hours, then resumed early next morning and worked through until lunchtime. It was his most sustained spell of writing for weeks. They hadn't found TOBY yet; they were searching the city dog pounds before it was too late. But the end was in sight. Not for TOBY – a happy end was obligatory – but for the script; and Cal was in a relaxed mood when he walked into his parents' house and saw Tommy Johnson assembling the aquarium.

He laughed when he saw the rocks and plastic bags of gravel and aquatic plants spread out on the table.

It looks like the set of *Jaws*.

Tommy looked round from the corner of the room where he was setting up the aquarium stand next to Harry's chair. I got some jaw when I came in, I can tell you. I thought your mother was going to bite my head off.

Don't exaggerate, Tommy. I was a bit surprised, that's all.

Cal sat down on the sofa next to his father. That was the idea. It's a surprise for my dad. Cal turned to face him. I thought they might help your recovery as well as give you some pleasure. They're supposed to be therapeutic, aren't they, Tommy?

Definitely. It's a scientific fact. Doctors recommend fish-keeping to relieve tension and help you relax.

Maisie examined the aquatic plants on the table. I thought it would look better under the window, but Tommy says it's too light.

It'd be in direct sunlight. If the water gets too hot it can kill the fish and the plants. This is the best place, right next to Harry's chair. He'll not need the telly on once I've got this set up for him. You'll have to draw a curtain across it to stop him watching.

Tommy picked up the bag of gravel from the table.

I'll just go and rinse this through before I put it in the tank. It's supposed to be washed, but there's usually some muck in it.

Maisie took it from him. I'll do that if you like. You stop here and talk to Harry, he'll enjoy that. It's good for him, a change of company.

Tommy picked up an ornamental treasure chest and a mermaid from the table and showed them to Harry. If you don't like these, I've got some more at home: sunken galleons and pagodas and that.

Harry took the treasure chest from him and held it clumsily in his shaking fingers.

You'll-not-get-much-treasure-in-that-Tommy.

No, but it's big enough to get my dole money in, though, Harry, I can tell you that.

They were joking about the mermaid when Cal followed his mother into the kitchen. Maisie had poured the gravel into the washing bowl and was shaking it about under the tap as if she was panning for gold. She turned round and smiled at Cal.

It's nice to hear your dad laughing again. He likes Tommy. I think he was under your dad's supervision when he went to work on the coal face.

I used to sit with him in primary school.

I can remember. You said he used to copy your sums.

He was brilliant at drawing. He used to draw little figures in the top corner of his exercise books, then flick the pages so that it looked as if they were running. Cal looked at the field of lavender on the calendar on the wall. He seems to have had a rough time these last few years.

He's not the only one round here.

It seemed to be a good way of helping him out, buying the aquarium. It'll do my dad good as well. Therapeutic, as Tommy says.

It's a nice thought. I'm sure your dad appreciates it.

Do you think so?

Of course he does. He's appreciated you staying on as well. I think he expected you to fly straight back as soon as you'd seen him.

He always did think the worst of me.

He thought the world of you, Karl.

Until I opposed him. I wanted to go my own way, not his.

He thought you sold out.

It was a difficult charge to refute. Cal didn't even try.

Do you know what he said when he read your book?

I didn't even know he'd read it.

He did, eventually. I thought he was going to throw it on the fire when he saw you'd changed your name. He took it personally.

That was the intention. I was trying to get my own back. He picked up a handful of gravel out of the bowl and watched the water drain through his fingers. What did he say about it?

He tried to sound casual, but even after its publication fifteen years ago, Cal was still eager to discover his father's opinion of his long-forgotten novel.

He wasn't wild about it, as you can imagine. It was a bit too near home and I could see what he meant. But in spite of that, he said you'd got the makings and you might write a decent book some day now that you'd got that one off your chest.

Cal felt an unexpected surge of pride and gratitude even though the verdict endorsed his father's accusation of selling out.

I was surprised that you never mentioned it whenever you came home. Were you ashamed of it or something?

I wasn't ashamed. I was humiliated.

Why, because you thought it was bad?

No, because nobody bought it.

Maisie swirled the gravel around in the bowl. Some of the description was good.

Cal laughed. You can read travel books for description.

I didn't like the main character very much, though. Always going on about not knowing what he wanted to do with his life and not knowing where he belonged.

It's called alienation.

He got on my nerves. And all them different jobs he had. He was never satisfied.

Cal wasn't sure whether her criticism of the book was meant as implied criticism of himself.

It's a good job he wasn't looking for a job today, Karl, or he'd have something to grumble about. Ask Tommy. He didn't know how lucky he was.

Cal would have liked to discuss the book further with his mother – especially the female characters – but when she began to pour the water from the bowl, he changed his mind. He had something more important to ask her before they returned to the living-room.

You know when you told me about Bernardo and Gerald the other day?

What about it?

You didn't finish the story, did you?

What do you mean?

He trickled the handful of gravel back into the bowl. Can you remember when I arrived, and you got the old photo box out to find my dad's prison letters.

I'd forgotten about that. Don't forget to let me have them letters back before you leave, will you?

Well, in among the family photos, there was a photograph of a farmhouse on a hillside . . .

In the living-room, Tommy said something which made Harry laugh.

It looked like Italy. You took it off me when I asked you about it.

Maisie slowly drained the water from the bowl, then placed her hand across the rim to prevent a landslide of gravel.

I'd better take this in for Tommy.

Wait a minute . . .

But she ignored him and left the kitchen. Cal waited a few moments, then followed her into the living-room, where Tommy was standing at the table sifting the gravel through his fingers.

You've been long enough, haven't you? I thought you'd been digging the bloody stuff – I don't know about washing it.

Our Karl was telling me about the new book he's writing. It's about a young woman who falls in love with an American air force pilot during the war, then, years later, goes to America to try to find him.

Tommy turned to Cal. Does she have a baby?

Cal looked at his mother. Yes.

I thought so. It happened all the time. They had the time of their lives over here, them Yanks.

Tommy tipped the wet gravel into the tank. Does she find him?

I don't know. I haven't worked it out yet.

Tommy began to spread the gravel. I don't think there were any Americans round here, but there was an Italian prisoner-of-war camp up near Highfields. Did you know that, Harry?

Harry Rickards shook his head in a series of jerks.

I-nearly-got-captured-by-the-Italians-in-North-Africa.

My dad told me that they once played football against a team of local lads in the rec.

Maisie appeared not to be listening. She was so attentively watching Tommy landscape the gravel, that she looked as if she was attending a class on Fish-keeping for Beginners.

As Maisie stepped off the bus in the village square, she was stunned by the fierce heat and sudden glare. She closed her eyes and staggered. She thought she was going to faint. She felt a steadying hand on her arm and when she opened her eyes the young man who had followed her off the bus was staring at her anxiously.

Non sta bene, signora?

Yes, thank you. Thank you very much.

She felt embarrassed. People were beginning to stare. She walked across to the fountain in front of the church and rested against the cool, granite wall. She looked round. She needed to sit down in the shade with a drink and work out her next move. A pigeon landed on the lip of the fountain, ducked down and scooped up a beakful of water. As she watched it fly off, Maisie suddenly felt desperately homesick. She could have cried. What was she doing here? What did she expect to find? But before she could decide anything, she had to get out of the sun.

She picked up her bag, then walked across the square to a bar and sat down at a table under the striped awning. The only other customers were four workmen in stained vests playing cards at a nearby table, and a boy, lit erratically as if by lightning, playing the pinball machine in the gloomy interior.

The proprietor walked out of the bar and approached Maisie's table.

Buon giorno, signora. He wiped the table with a cloth. *Desidera?*

Maisie was able to guess his question. A cup of tea please.

The proprietor guessed her answer. *Tè. Si. Al limone?*

She couldn't guess that one. She looked up at him, embarrassed. However was she going to make anybody understand why she was here, if she couldn't even order a cup of tea?

Sorry.

The proprietor looked to the skies as if appealing for help . . . He got it!

Limone . . . Limon! Limon!

Oh! Lemon. No thank you. Maisie shook her head

emphatically. Tea with *lemon*? No thank you. With milk.

She tried to help him with a tipping motion, as if she was pouring it from a jug.

The proprietor shook his head. He was growing impatient. *Scusi, signora. Non capisco.*

Then it came back to her. She remembered carrying the milk pail from the farm across the fields to the camp with Bernardo. She could hear his voice. Hear him laughing as she repeated it . . .

Latte.

The proprietor looked at her in surprise. He smiled. *Latte. Tè al latte. Si, signora.*

He went back inside, pausing for a moment to check the boy's score on the pinball machine. Maisie sat back and dabbed her face with her handkerchief. That was another obstacle overcome. If she had realized all the difficulties before setting out, she doubted if she would have undertaken the journey.

Manfred and Lotte Krabbe, with whom she had been staying in Freiburg on her fund-raising tour, had planned her itinerary meticulously. They had put her on the train to Munich with written directions to change at Florence for Perugia. From there she would catch a bus to the village, and if she had any difficulties, don't hesitate to phone them.

But it had been nerve-wracking all the same. She couldn't understand the announcements on the stations. Was she on the right platform? Was this the right train? And she had been in such a panic about dropping off to sleep and going past her stop that she stared through the window in a daze, barely noticing the passing scenery. But now that she had started, she was determined to carry on. She would never be this close again. If she didn't find out now, she never would.

It was dark by the time she reached Perugia, so she found a cheap hotel by the station and took a room for the night. As she lay in bed in the sparse room, she thought of the hotel in Liverpool where she had stayed with Gerald and Bernardo and his mother, before they sailed back to Italy the following day . . . And now she had arrived, almost forty years later, nearing her destination after a tiring bus journey through the hills from Perugia.

While she waited for her tea to arrive, Maisie watched the card-players at the next table. Their discussions at the end of each hand were so animated that they appeared to be arguing. It was like listening to Bernardo when he lost patience with his broken English and reverted to a rush of Italian to relieve his frustration. She looked at the four men in turn. Two of them were middle-aged. The other two, including the one with his back to her with the thick, shoulder-length hair and narrow waist, were much younger. Maisie concentrated on the older pair. Could one of them be Gerald? Who had he taken after – Bernardo or herself? She couldn't make out any similarities in either of them and it would have been a remarkable coincidence if one of these men had been her son. She wondered if she would recognize him instinctively? Would something tell her – a feeling perhaps? Probably not, and on the pretext of wiping the sweat from her face, she cried at the loss of the child she had never known.

Anyway – she composed herself and put away her handkerchief as she saw the proprietor approaching with her tea – he was probably married now with grown-up children of his own. And Bernardo: did he get married? And did he grieve for her when he received that final, fateful letter? Yes. Yes. She knew he did. He had loved her so much and the thought of him, bereft and inconsolable, awoke her love for him too. She had come to join him as promised. At any moment he would enter the square with Gerald in his arms. They would see each other and she would stand up and run to greet them . . .

Tè al latte, signora.

The proprietor unloaded his tray, then tucked the bill under the saucer.

Maisie looked up at him, dazed and disappointed. Thank you.

As she sipped her tea, she looked across the square, where a panting dog lay, almost invisible in the deep shadow of the church. This is where she would have done her shopping with Gerald . . . with Geraldo, holding his hand. Buying him little treats: a cake from the baker's over there, or a peach from the trays outside the fruit shop. They would have sat at this bar and she would have ordered tea – in Italian – and an ice cream for Geraldo. Or a coffee sometimes. Black coffee in little cups like the card-players at the next table. And she would know their names, and the name of the proprietor too. And gradually, as the years passed, she would have become more Italian than English. She worked it out. She would have lived here nearly forty years. She would have become one of them.

When she paid the bill, Maisie handed the proprietor a sheet of notepaper with a name and address printed on it.

He read it, then stared at her. *Bernardo. Conosce Bernardo Rossi?*

Maisie smiled and nodded. She didn't understand the language but she understood the question. Yes, and his son Gerald . . . A long time ago.

Si, Geraldo.

At the mention of Bernardo and Geraldo, the card-players looked up from their cards, and Maisie heard their names repeated many times when the proprietor showed them the sheet of notepaper.

Aspetti un attimo!

He held up his hand, then turned abruptly and disappeared into the bar, this time ignoring the boy on the pinball machine as if he wasn't there. The card-players resumed their game, but in a desultory manner. Their attention had been diverted by Maisie's arrival and they played the hand slowly, while they waited for the proprietor to reappear.

Maisie wondered if the men had guessed who she was. She wondered if Gerald knew who his mother was. Or had Bernardo been so embittered by her betrayal that he had withheld her identity?

The proprietor emerged from the bar wiping a framed photograph on his apron. He placed it on the table in front of Maisie. It showed a group of adults and children assembled outside the church in the village square. They were dressed in their best clothes, with the adults standing at the back and the children seated on chairs and cross-legged on the floor.

La Prima Comunione.

Maisie nodded, but did not understand as she bent closer to look at the photograph.

La Prima Comunione.

Of course! *Comunione.* Confirmation. It had been taken after a confirmation ceremony; with the boys dressed in their best suits, the girls in white dresses and their proud parents standing behind them. There was a similar photograph in the old shoe-box at home taken after her own confirmation.

The proprietor pointed to a boy sitting up straight with his arms folded like a footballer. *Questo sono io. . .* He laughed. *E questo è Bernardo.*

The proprietor didn't have to point him out. Maisie had found him straight away. He was standing in the middle of the row of adults behind the chairs. He was older now and he had broadened out. How handsome he looked in his dark suit with his hair slicked back. Maisie fell in love with him all over again. The camera had caught him turning towards a woman standing beside him. They were smiling at each other. The woman had a baby in her arms and Bernardo had his arm around her waist.

E questo è Geraldo, il figlio di Bernardo.

The proprietor touched the boy sitting on a chair directly in front of Bernardo.

Geraldo era il mio migliore amico. Andavamo a scuola assieme. Durante il raccolto gli aiutavo al podere . . .

Maisie wasn't listening. She was staring at the boy. How old was he? Seven? Eight? How nice he looked in his little suit with his hair parted. Geraldo . . . Gerald. Her son. She looked for resemblances. Who was he like? Whose nose had he got? Whose eyes? But the figure was too small to distinguish that kind of detail. But nevertheless, Maisie was determined to see something of herself in him. Perhaps his hair was fairer than the others? Or his skin lighter? But no, she had to admit it as she scrutinized the row of seated children: there was nothing that made him stand out from the rest. He was an Italian boy. He would have spoken the Italian language and probably he never knew that he had an English mother.

By this time, the card-players had suspended their game and were gathered around Maisie looking at the photograph on the table. They kept pointing and laughing and making fun of the outdated fashions and changed appearances of people they knew. But Maisie didn't hear them, and the other sitters became blurred as she focused on the family group at the centre of the photograph: Geraldo, Bernardo, and the pretty young woman by his side nursing the baby.

Marco – the youngest of the card-players with the shoulder-length hair – stopped his van at the bottom of the track and pointed up the hillside.

E' quella lassù.

Maisie looked up and there, surrounded by vineyards and fields of sunflowers, stood the old farmhouse she knew so well from the creased photograph in her bag.

Marco leaned across the passenger seat.

Vuole che l'aspetto?

Maisie smiled apologetically for not understanding. Sorry . . .

Marco frowned, seeking the translation. Me . . . Jabbing his chest, then pointing emphatically downwards. Stop for you here.

Maisie shook her head, anxious not to inconvenience him further, and her rapid hand movements looked as if she was cleaning a chalkboard. No. No. Thank you very much. I'll make my own way back.

Marco pointed at the sun and wiped his brow. *E' una lunga camminata dal villaggio* . . .

He was about to add, *for una signora anziana*, but he didn't want to insult her, even though she wouldn't have understood what he said. But he wasn't too worried about leaving her as he pulled shut the van door. If she had managed to travel all the way from England on her own, she was certainly capable of making her own way back to the village, even in this heat.

OK. Arrivederci. E buona fortuna.

Maisie smiled at him. He was about the same age as Bernardo, when they had been together. Thank you . . . *Arrivederci.*

She blushed as she uttered the once familiar word . . . *Arrivederci, Bernardo*, she used to whisper as they embraced before he returned to the camp.

Maisie waved the van out of sight; then she was alone on the quiet road which ran through the valley. Before starting the long climb up to the house, she opened her bag and took out a folded, embroidered handkerchief which she had kept since she was a girl. She unwrapped it carefully in her palm, revealing the sunflower brooch which Bernardo had fashioned for her out of a flattened corned beef tin. He had cut out a circle the size of a half crown, then, using a penknife, engraved petals around the edge and heavily scored the centre with dashes and dots. Maisie polished it lovingly on the handkerchief before fastening it to her dress with the safety pin which Bernardo had soldered on to the back. Tearfully, she looked up the hillside, then set off up the track towards the house.

The road was unmade, but she could tell that it was still in use by the tyre tracks in the dust and the loads of rubble which had been tipped into the potholes. She passed a vineyard – she had never seen grapes growing before – then reached a field of sunflowers, their heavy heads bowed towards the sun, growing right up to the edge of the track.

Maisie touched her brooch . . . They were sitting by the hedgerow in a field when Bernardo had given it to her. He pinned it to her dress, then demonstrated with his hands the size of real sunflower heads in the fields at home. Maisie picked poppies and buttercups and taught him their names in English, then she reached up and picked a wild rose from the hedge.

Rose.

Sì! Rosa anche in italiano.

They laughed, then Bernardo felt the petals between his fingers and stroked Maisie's cheek.

Soffice . . . Soft. *Soffice come una rosa.*

And then they made love, flattening a patch in the long grass and sweet-smelling clover by the wild rose bush. And it was so wonderful, and Maisie was so much in love, that afterwards she convinced herself that that was when it happened. That was when Gerald was conceived. And now, wearing Bernardo's brooch, staring up at the dark golden heads which Bernardo had described so passionately, she was convinced of it.

As Maisie approached the house, she could hear shouting and splashing from behind the high wall. She was exhausted after the long, steep climb in the afternoon sun. Her dress was sticking to her back and the blue flowers in the material had turned black with sweat. She stumbled on the rough track, puffing up the dust, rested for a moment, then walked the last few yards to the gateway.

The new wrought-iron gates stood open and a Range Rover was parked on the drive. Two children were squabbling over a waterbed in the swimming pool and a young woman was reclining on a lounger reading a magazine. Maisie took all this in at a glance and without much interest. It was the house she had travelled all this way to see. The house where Bernardo and Gerald had lived. The house she would have lived in if she had kept her promise and followed them here. It was just as he had described it, except for the bright new roof and shutters. Maisie raised her hand to her face to exclude the Range Rover and swimming pool, then half closed her eyes and looked at the house in dimmed, soft focus . . . Yes, that was how it would have looked then, a working farmhouse with a yard full of animals and machines . . .

Excuse me? Can I help you?

Maisie opened her eyes. The woman had got up from the lounger and was standing by her side. She was wearing a bikini and a red baseball cap. She raised her sunglasses and looked at Maisie as if she was an old gypsy selling lucky heather and clothes pegs.

Sorry . . . If Maisie had not been flushed already, she would have been seen to be blushing.

Are you looking for someone?

No . . . I'm looking at the house . . . I knew the family who lived here.

Here! Surely not. The place was a total wreck when we bought it, and had been for years, judging by the state of it.

Before that. When it was a farm.

Oh, I see. But she still sounded doubtful. It must have been some considerable time ago.

Yes. It was just after the war.

The war! She made it sound as distant as the Norman Conquest. Before my time, I'm afraid. It must be quite a shock seeing it now with the swimming pool, etc.

Yes . . .

We've had a tennis court laid round the back where an old barn used to stand. We were planning to convert it into an apartment but decided against it in the end. The place had cost an arm and a leg as it was, what with the new roof and having to redesign the interior. It was like a maze – lots of little rooms built on over the centuries. We opened the whole place out to let in more light.

What have you done with the stables?

That shut her up.

The stables?

Underneath the house.

We converted them into a playroom for the children. She answered slowly, paying full attention to Maisie for the first time. You obviously know the house well.

Maisie nodded. Yes, I used to live here.

Live here! In this house? I thought you said . . .

It was my husband's family home. I met him in England. After the war. Then his father became ill and he returned to run the farm. I followed him later. We were married in the village church down the road . . .

Golly. How romantic!

One of the children called to her from the pool, but she took no notice of him.

. . . It was wonderful. Everybody made me feel welcome. They treated me like one of the family . . .

She tailed off and gazed at the house. The woman waited. She wanted Maisie to continue her story. A fascinating conversation piece was unfolding for her next dinner party when she returned to England at the end of the summer . . . *I was lying by the pool when I looked up and saw this old lady standing by the gate. I thought she must have got lost or something. She looked exhausted, poor dear. A most unlikely person to have turning up at one's house in the middle of the afternoon, I must say.*

... But in the end, we couldn't make a living, and when Bernardo's father died – that was my husband, Bernardo – we left and went to Turin, where Bernardo and our son Geraldo went to work in a car factory. Bernardo hated the city after living here.

The woman looked across the valley towards the distant hills. Yes. I can well imagine. We considered several derelict properties before settling on this one. There was a house further up the hillside with enormous potential.

She pointed up the slope towards a ruined building partly concealed amongst olive trees.

Maisie nodded. Yes. The Baggio family lived there. They had a daughter who became a famous opera singer ... *Baggio. Conte. Sivori ... Bernardo pointed to the names on the rough map he had drawn of the valley. Then, in broken English supplemented by vigorous mime, he told her stories about the families who owned the farms. Maisie enjoyed the sound of their names so much that she learned them off by heart, like the capital cities of the world in Geography at school* ... The Baggios were sheep farmers. You could hear the bells round the sheep's necks all over the valley.

Yes, we've occasionally seen sheep with bells around their necks. No idea who they belong to, though. Don't have much to do with the locals, I'm ashamed to say.

But Maisie wasn't listening. She was gazing up the hillside at the Baggios' derelict farmhouse.

One of the other daughters married a good friend of mine.

The woman touched Maisie on the arm. Her attitude towards her visitor had changed considerably during the few minutes they had spent together. Would you like to see the house? We've made extensive alterations since your day, of course, but we have managed to retain some of the original features.

No thank you. It's very kind of you, but I think I'd like to remember it as it was.

Yes. That's understandable. Well, how about a cool drink and a rest by the pool before you leave? You must be exhausted after that long trek up the hill.

No. I'd better go, thank you. My son'll wonder where I am. He's waiting for me in the car at the bottom of the hill. He couldn't bear to come up and see the house. Too many memories. He said he'd have been too upset.

Cal watched the bubbles rising in the fish tank. Before leaving the house, Tommy had equipped it with plants and rocks and the treasure chest embedded in the gravel, but he said it needed to settle down for a few days before he introduced the fish. The excitement of Tommy's visit had exhausted Harry and he had fallen asleep on his bed by the wall.

Cal looked across at his mother. What did you do, then?

I came home.

Did you think of going to Turin to try to find them?

No. That was the end of the journey as far as I was concerned. Once I'd seen the house I was satisfied. Even when the men at the bar told me that Bernardo and his family had left years ago. I still wanted to see it. It was a kind of pilgrimage. Do you understand?

Cal thought of his own painful journey when he went to find Becky. Of course I do . . .

It was as if a weight had been lifted off my shoulders.

When you came home, did you regret it? Did you wish you'd married Bernardo and made your life there?

Maisie laughed. You wouldn't be here asking me if I had.

But Cal refused to be deflected. Did you, though? It must have been really important to you, making a journey like that after all those years.

Maisie stared into the aquarium as if it was already

stocked with fish. I don't know, Karl. I honestly don't know. I could have had a good life there, but then . . . She switched her gaze to her sleeping husband but did not complete the sentence.

Can I have a look at the sunflower brooch? I'd like to see it.

Maisie walked across to the bed and wiped a dribble of saliva from Harry's chin. I haven't got it any more. I buried it in the field of sunflowers on my way back down the hill.

When Cal arrived back at the hotel, Joe was waiting for him in the foyer. They hadn't seen each other since meeting at their parents' home soon after Cal arrived from France. After that, their visits never seemed to coincide. Maisie never failed to remark on it. As soon as he walked into the house she said, You've just missed Joe. It was a good title. Perhaps he could work on it.

Cal was pleased to see him. He had been going to visit him in Manchester, but somehow, what with one thing and another, he had never got round to it. But he could stop worrying about it now that Joe had come to see him. This could be the last time they would see each other for ages. Joe!

Joe looked up. He was sitting on a shiny, leather chesterfield reading a magazine. As he stood up, Cal was struck by his shabby appearance. In his worn jeans and jumper, he looked more like a workman than a visitor. Joe replaced the magazine on the coffee table. Cal wondered if they would allow him into the dining-room without a jacket. A jacket! He wasn't even wearing a shirt. But business was bad. They would probably have allowed him in wearing swimming trunks. They would go into the bar first, have a few drinks, then decide where to eat later. It was a pity that Charlie was no longer working at the hotel – they could have had a good laugh together. Joe looked as if he needed a laugh. Cal wondered if he had brought bad news.

Hello, Joe. What a nice surprise.

Joe stepped forward and punched him in the face. Cal went down, scattering magazines and onyx ashtrays from the coffee table. The receptionist and two guests formed a tableau of alarm as they spun round from the desk. They looked as if they had been caught reading salacious material, rather than a leaflet for the local mining museum.

Cal looked up from the carpet tiles. He wasn't unconscious, but he stayed down long enough for Joe to have counted him out.

What was that for?

You know!

He stabbed his finger at Cal, then turned abruptly and left the hotel. Cal raised himself on one elbow and watched him go. The doors were revolving so fast after his departure that an incoming guest had to wait a few moments before he could enter in safety.

Cal touched his mouth. He could feel the split in his bottom lip. Joe was right. Cal did know why Joe had thumped him, even though it might be illogical. Perhaps Christine was the excuse he was looking for. Perhaps he had been waiting to get his own back all his life.

The receptionist hurried out from behind the desk and crouched down beside him. Are you all right, sir? Have I to call the police?

Cal shook his head slowly. No. No. I'm OK . . .

But he was too shocked to even notice that the receptionist's skirt had slid above her knees, giving him a thrilling view of her thighs. She supported him on one arm and dabbed his face with a tissue. Would you like me to call an ambulance?

No thanks. I'll be all right in a minute . . .

Cal inhaled her perfume as she leaned over him, and the sight of her cleavage, inches from his face, revived him considerably.

Would you like a drink of water?

Cal shook his head. No thanks.

Is there anything else I can do for you?

A crowd of onlookers had gathered and Cal began to feel foolish. He imagined the latecomers thinking that he must have had a fit or something and banged his face when he fell. He started to get up.

Careful . . .

The receptionist helped him on to the chesterfield then began to pick up the magazines.

I thought he looked a bit dodgy, a bit scruffy like, when he came in. We don't usually get that type in here. I was surprised he asked for you by name.

Realizing that the excitement was over, the crowd began to disperse. The couple who had been enquiring about the mining museum left the hotel holding their leaflets. When they arrived there, Charlie would probably be one of the guides.

The receptionist continued to fuss over Cal, and now that he had explored his face with his fingers and realized that his nose wasn't broken and none of his teeth were missing, he began to enjoy his condition. If he played his cards right . . .

I still think we should call the police.

No. Forget it. It was just an argument, that's all.

Did you know him then?

Cal could see her knicker-line as she bent over to pick up an ashtray. Vaguely. A long time ago.

INT. HOTEL ROOM. NIGHT.

The door opens and AL enters with the RECEPTIONIST who is supporting him and looking concerned. AL is dabbing his mouth with a handkerchief and his face is bruised.

RECEPTIONIST

You'd better lie down.

AL

I'll be OK.

He sits on the bed.

RECEPTIONIST

Can I get you anything?

AL

Yeah. There's a bottle of Scotch in the drawer over there.

The RECEPTIONIST crosses the room, opens the drawer and takes out the bottle of Scotch. She then goes into the bathroom, returns with a glass and pours AL a drink.

RECEPTIONIST

Anything with it?

AL

No thanks. That's fine.

The receptionist walks across to the bed and hands the glass to AL.

AL

Thanks. Why don't you join me?

RECEPTIONIST

(pause)

Sorry. I'm on duty.

AL

The other girl can hold the fort, can't she? Let's face it, you're hardly overrun with customers down there.

RECEPTIONIST

(laughing)

OK. Just a quickie.

She disappears into the bathroom, returns with another glass and pours herself a drink.

RECEPTIONIST

Cheers.

They drink a toast. The RECEPTIONIST sits on the edge of the bed.

RECEPTIONIST

It was awfully brave what you just did down there. I thought he was going to get clean away.

AL

(modestly, feeling his bruised face)
Yeah, well . . . I just couldn't stand around and do nothing, could I?

RECEPTIONIST

You were brilliant. It's the first time we've had an armed robbery. I was petrified.

She gazes at him admiringly and their eyes meet.

RECEPTIONIST (cont.)

If there anything else I can do for you, before I go?

Cal stood up and examined his face in the mirror on the wardrobe door. How was he going to explain his split lip to Hélène? Would he tell her that he'd been assaulted by a gunman in reception? Or that Joe had flattened him for having an affair with his ex-wife? Neither explanation was acceptable. He would have to think up something more prosaic between the two extremes.

He sat down again at his word processor, read through the hotel-room scene, then reluctantly wiped it. He was much more interested in what was about to happen between AL and the RECEPTIONIST (definitely porno-movie material) than in TOBY, who was about to be captured by the stray dog patrol . . . Perhaps he could act out the scene with Hélène when she arrived. She might be ready for a spot of sexual excess after their long separation. He shook his head. He couldn't see it. Christine would, when she was in the mood. But not Hélène. She didn't go in for that kind of thing. Except in front of the camera.

> EXT. BACK ALLEY. DAY.
>
> Two DOG WARDENS have got TOBY trapped at the end of the alley. He snarls and barks at them as they approach him warily holding out their dog catchers . . .

Cal had worked until the early hours, slept late, then started again after a late breakfast in his room. He was sitting at his word processor studying the pattern on the wallpaper, while he considered when to change TOBY back into a boy. Should it be before his family found him or after? There was also the problem of the scene where DETECTIVES CARDARELLI and GOODING accompany PROFESSOR KNUTT to the dog pound looking for TOBY. Surely the professor would recognize him? But if he did, it would ruin the plot . . . Perhaps he misses seeing TOBY somehow. Or perhaps he's forgotten what TOBY looks like. After all, mad professors are always absent-minded in films. It's an essential part of their character.

While he was trying to work it out, he forgetfully tapped his bottom lip. He winced. It was sore. Swollen too. When he looked down, he could see it sticking out . . . Why hadn't he hit Joe back, instead of just lying there at his feet? He hadn't been unconscious. He wasn't even badly hurt. No, but he was shocked. He hadn't been expecting it. He was too shocked to move . . .

He was still trying to excuse his cowardice when there was a knock on the door.

Come in!

. . . He could understand it in a way: successful older brother, jealousy, in and out of work . . . He'd probably had a drink or two and started brooding. Poor old Joe. Anyway, it would have been absurd, the two of them slugging it out in reception.

He turned round. There was a woman standing in the doorway. Cal stared at her, and for an instant, preoccupied with Joe and taken by surprise, he failed to recognize her. It was Hélène! He jumped up. Hélène dropped her travel bag, then ran across the room into his arms. Cal inhaled the familiar perfume as he kissed her neck. It was understated and expensive, in marked contrast to the overpowering smell of the receptionist's perfume which had revived him like smelling salts the previous day. Hélène pulled away to kiss him, then noticed his split lip and bruises.

Darling, what happened to you?

What? Oh, that – feigning indifference as if he was a regular hard man. I tackled two youths who were mugging an old woman in town.

He had intended to say that he'd walked into a door, or something obvious like that. But a late flash of inspiration had saved him from the banal and transformed his feeble submission into an act of reckless courage.

That was a brave thing to do.

Yeah. I managed to save her handbag, but unfortunately they got away.

Hélène raised her mouth and gently touched his lips with her tongue. Cal felt like a hero. He held her at arm's length and looked her up and down. She was wearing a beige linen dress with a short skirt and low neckline. Cal imagined the glances when she entered the foyer and the look on the receptionist's face when she asked for him at the desk. It served her right. She should have taken advantage of the situation while she had the chance.

You look beautiful.

She smiled. She was wearing an antique silver necklace which he hadn't seen before.

I thought you were arriving on Thursday. Or did I get the day wrong? I've been working so hard that I've lost all track of time.

No. They've brought the film schedule forward so I had to come soon.

You should have let me know.

I phoned yesterday but you weren't here. Then I decided to come by surprise.

Cal laughed. You should try an aeroplane next time.

Sorry?

Nothing. I'd have picked you up at the airport if I'd known. Is the rest of your luggage downstairs?

No. That is all I have brought with me.

This?

He held up the bag. He could tell by its weight that there wasn't much in it. Hélène bent forward and read the scene on the word processor.

How is the script coming along?

Fine.

When he placed the bag on the bed it sagged like a collapsed tent.

How long are you staying?

Hélène turned round and walked towards him. Only for one night, I'm afraid.

What?

I know. I'm sorry, but I have to get back. Rehearsals start next week, and I have so much to do.

One night? It's hardly worth coming for.

But I wanted to see you before I leave for Berlin.

Why didn't you come earlier then?

It was impossible to get away. You know what it is like before a film begins, with all the meetings and everything.

Cal nodded, but he still wasn't convinced.

The script has been a nightmare. I would learn my lines, then the scene would be cut and a new scene faxed to me next day. Finally, I had to go to Paris to meet Roland to discuss our relationship.

Your relationship?

In the film. There were so many script changes that the meaning . . . the emphasis between our characters had changed too. We had to talk about it.

You never said anything about Paris when we spoke on the phone.

I telephoned you from Paris but you weren't in. I telephoned you many times but you were not in.

And what about the times I phoned you and you weren't in either? he almost added. But he realized that he was in danger of spoiling her arrival, so he put his arms around her instead. I've missed you.

She rested her cheek on his shoulder and he stroked her hair.

Why were you away so long, Cal?

He continued to stroke her hair. It's difficult to explain . . . I got involved.

She pulled away and looked up at him in surprise. Involved? What do you mean?

It's hard to explain . . . family . . . the past. He turned away from her and stood behind the chair staring down at his word processor. The scene read no better standing up than sitting down. I suppose I've been trying to make amends.

Hélène came up behind him. I'm afraid I do not understand.

No, I don't suppose you do. I've had a lot of trouble understanding it myself.

How is your father? Is he recovering well?

Yes, he's much better. He can hobble around a bit now and he's gradually recovering his speech.
I would like to meet him.
Cal laughed and turned round. Meet my dad?
Of course! Why not? And your mother too. And I would like you to show me the sights before I leave.
The sights! The notion amused him. It's a sight for sore eyes round here, I can tell you.
Hélène frowned and looked at him, bemused. Sore eyes?
Forget it.
He kissed her and felt up her dress. But when he pulled it up round her waist and pushed her on to the bed, she insisted on taking it off first and hanging it up. Linen creases very badly, she said.

Hélène changed into a pair of jeans and a silk shirt before they drove out to the village. Cal had telephoned his mother first to let her know they were coming and to give her time to tidy up. Not that the house needed tidying, but she would have been put out if they had arrived without warning, and she would have started plumping the cushions as they entered the house.
As they drove through the village, Cal showed Hélène the primary school which he had attended as a boy; the site of the demolished houses where he had been born; and the rec., the venue of those epic football matches.
The wreck? Hélène scanned the deserted football field in vain. Where? I can't see it.
See what?
The wreck.
Can't see it? It's there! Over the wall!
Hélène looked again. She shook her head. I still can't see what is wrecked. All I can see is a football pitch and some swings.
Cal stared at her. Then the penny dropped and he

laughed at the misunderstanding. I didn't mean wreck as in shipwreck. I meant rec. as in recreation ground. He started the car. I'll show you a real wreck if you want to see one.

They turned off the main road and drove around the council estate: street after street of shabby houses, some bricked up, some burnt out. An abandoned car. A police car. A gang of youths running away, A toddler in a vest paddling in a pothole. A pack of dogs snarling round the car when Cal slowed down to avoid a plundered cigarette machine lying in the road.

As they drove past the shops, Cal pointed out the scab's house and told Hélène that this was where his father had been arrested, during the strike. He translated scab into blackleg for her, but when he said they were lower than lino, Hélène was totally bemused. She sat slumped in her seat, stunned by the squalor around her. She knew that Cal came from a mining family, but he rarely spoke of his background and she was totally unprepared for this. It was like driving through a war zone.

Cal pulled up outside his parents' house and they sat silently for a few moments reflecting on what they had just seen.

It wasn't always like this, you know. It was a decent estate at one time, a nice place to live. My mother thought it was marvellous when we moved here. A new house with a bathroom and all mod cons. She was thrilled to bits with it. But things were different then. Everybody had jobs. It's lack of work, lack of money, lack of hope. That's what's caused this.

As they got out of the car, two women passing by stopped talking and stared at Hélène as if they recognized her. They kept glancing back. Isn't she on the telly? Wasn't she in such and such? It was unlikely that they would have seen any of the films in which Hélène had appeared on television, but their confusion was understandable. She *looked* like somebody on television. She looked different from them and she hadn't got that tan in Skegness either. Standing outside the Rickards' council house, she was too glamorous for the setting. She looked like an actress visiting the location of a film for which she had been ludicrously miscast.

But Cal wasn't ashamed of the location. Not like he was when he was at university and had occasionally brought Laura to the house. He was proud of his roots now, and he was proud of his parents when he introduced them to Hélène. He was even proud to introduce Tommy, when he arrived unexpectedly to check the aquarium.

Pleased to meet you, love, he said, shaking hands. I once went to France on a day trip. I've got a photo somewhere with a string of onions round my neck.

He spoke so quickly, and his accent was so broad, that Hélène could not understand a word he said. But she laughed along with the others, and she could tell that Tommy was thrilled to meet her.

Watching his mother smooth down his father's hair with her hand, Cal felt more at home now than at any time since his childhood.

That evening, they drove to the Old Rectory for dinner. Instead of the planned last night out with Christine, Cal was here with Hélène, and she was the one leaving for France the following day, not him. He noticed the waiters admiring Hélène as she crossed the dining-room. They wouldn't have looked at Christine so covetously, but he still felt a pang when he thought about her, and what they would have got up to, back at the hotel afterwards.

They sat at a table by the large, bay window with a view of the church through the trees. Hélène touched the starched cloth and heavy cutlery.

Have you been here before?

Cal shook his head, wistfully. No . . . Unfortunately.

That makes you sad?

Only because I discovered it a few days ago when I drove by with my mother. It's not exactly a gourmet's paradise around here, you know. He reached across the table and took her hand. Of course I'm not sad. Why should I be?

Hélène smiled and glanced around the room. I like it here. It is very English.

Yes. They've made a good job of it.

The two main downstairs rooms had been converted into a dining-room by removing the double doors between them. The floorboards had been sanded and polished, and except for the new wall lights illuminating a set of sporting prints, all the fixtures were original.

Cal looked across the room and out of the back window which framed a few old apple trees growing behind the car park. Were they the same trees from which Bernardo had stolen apples for Maisie?

Cal pointed towards them. You see those apple trees through there?

Hélène nodded.

When I was a boy, I used to sneak through the hedge with my mates and steal apples from them.

Hélène frowned. Mates? You mean girls?

Cal laughed. No, not that kind of mate: pals, friends, chums. I used to come with Tommy and Charlie.

If his story had been true, Tommy and Charlie would have done the stealing, while he kept watch outside.

Charlie? Is he another friend?

That's right. You haven't met him.

Although there was still time. Cal wouldn't have been at all surprised to see him emerge from the kitchen balancing a plate on each hand.

It was a pity I did not meet your brother, Joe. I would have enjoyed to meet him.

Yes . . . Well . . . We'll arrange it next time you come over.

What do you mean? Are you staying here in England?

No. Of course not. Although I would like to come home a bit more often. My mother and dad are getting old now and I feel I've neglected them.

I thought your home was with me, in France.

It is. But you always call it home where you were brought up, don't you?

You never called it anything before. You never even talked about it.

The waiter arrived. It wasn't Charlie. He lit the candle on the table then handed them the menus. As Cal opened the leatherbound covers, he pretended to drop it to exaggerate its weight.

You could do with a lectern to hold this up. I wonder if there's a spare one stored in the attic?

Hélène didn't get the joke and Cal didn't try to explain it. As he read through the starters, he began to laugh.

What's funny?

This. Yorkshire pudding in onion gravy. In French.

What's so funny about that?

It's ridiculous. You're probably the only French person who's ever been here.

Maybe they knew I was coming.

Maybe they've baked you a cake.

She didn't get that either, so Cal laughed at his own joke.

Why don't you try it? *C'est une spécialité de la région.*

She chose the fish soup instead.

Cal studied the wine list. How about a bottle of champagne to celebrate our reunion?

Hélène smiled. She had tears in her eyes.

The other diners looked impressed as the waiter wheeled the ice bucket across the room and opened the bottle at their table.

A ta santé.

They touched glasses.

And to your new film.

Thank you. And to your family too and your father's good recovery.

They liked you. They don't say a lot, but I could tell.

When their starters arrived, Cal tasted Hélène's soup. Not bad. Considering it's out of a can. When you get back from Berlin we'll go to the Dolphin and have real fish soup.

Hélène paused with her spoon at her lips. Do you remember the time we went there with Roland?

Cal didn't want to hear anything about Roland, especially as Hélène would be on location with him for the next two months. He glanced up at the hunting print on the wall and thought of Bruno putting up hares on their walks together. Except for the dog, there seemed little to go back for.

I'm looking forward to seeing Bruno again.

He will have forgotten you.

What, after a few weeks? Don't be ridiculous!

It came out sharper than he intended and Hélène bowed her head and concentrated on her soup.

I'm sorry.

She ignored him and he realized that it was something more serious than his rebuke.

What's the matter?

Slowly, she raised her head and, her tears reflecting the candlelight, achieved a strikingly poignant effect. A cameraman couldn't have lit her more sympathetically. We have drifted apart, Cal.

Like ships in the night, he said to himself, unable to resist a cliché even though he was becoming fearful of what Hélène might be leading up to.

He refilled their glasses. It was just bad luck, that's all, me being over here and you being wrapped up in your new film. I suppose I could have asked my dad to postpone his stroke to fit in with your schedule.

He wasn't sure if she understood the sarcasm, but the arrival of the waiter delayed her response, and by the time he had removed their dishes, the moment had passed.

I couldn't feel you, Cal.

What do you mean?

When we've been apart before you've been with me. But this time it was different.

But I phoned every day.

Yes. Yes. I know . . .

You were never there. The only reply I ever got was myself on the answerphone. He put on his answerphone voice. Hello. Sorry we are not in. However, if you would like to leave a message . . . I felt like saying, No, I know you're not in, you silly cunt, you're here! But where the fuck are *you*?

Hélène was taken aback by his outburst, but the woman at the next table turned and looked at him with some interest.

I was busy, Cal.

Yes, I know you were. Perhaps that's why you couldn't feel me. Perhaps you were too busy feeling . . . He just managed to stop himself in time and to reconstruct the sentence more ambiguously . . . Perhaps you had other things on your mind.

I missed you, Cal. You know how nervous I get before a new film. I wanted you there.

I know, but my dad was seriously ill. He nearly died. We might have had our differences in the past, but he's still my father and my place was here.

Yes. I understand. I know that you should be with your parents at such a time.

She reached across the table for his hand. She was trying her best to be sympathetic. But Cal knew her too well. She was ruthless. All she *really* cared about was her work. She chose her scripts carefully, often turning down lucrative but meretricious projects. Cal admired her for it. That was why she was so good and he was only a hack.

Is that why you went to Paris?

What do you mean?

Because you were nervous. Because you didn't want to be on your own.

I went to Paris to discuss the script!

Once again the woman at the next table turned round. First the champagne, then the colourful language and now talk of films and Paris. It sounded much more intriguing than the new barbecue her husband was enthusing about. Cal gave her a quick once-over. That frock did nothing for her at all, but she looked as if she might have a nice pair of tits hidden under all those ruffles. He remembered a film in which two strangers had exchanged glances in a restaurant, then, on the pretext of going to the lavatory, they left the room and fucked in a cubicle in the Ladies, before returning to their tables without speaking, or ever seeing each other again. What was the title? . . .

Hélène lifted the bottle from the ice bucket and topped up their glasses.

Please, Cal, let's not quarrel. Not tonight. Let's enjoy ourself.

They tried. They even ordered another bottle of champagne. But it was too late; the evening was spoiled and they had to work hard to avoid dangerous silences. Cal had been looking forward to telling Hélène about the new project he was planning. But it no longer seemed like the right time, and a growing sense of disquiet prevented him from sharing it with her now.

They tried to make up for it in bed, but there was no joy between them, and afterwards Hélène turned away from Cal and cried. Later, as they lay quietly in each other's arms, Cal willed her to stroke his face as she used to when they first met, and as she had stroked Roland Lafond's on the film he had watched with his mother. But she kept her arms tightly around him and he felt her relax as she went to sleep.

*

They hardly spoke as Cal drove Hélène to the airport. She had protested that it was unnecessary and she could have taken a taxi. But Cal insisted, even though he knew that Hélène was right, and it would have been more sensible to say goodbye at the hotel rather than prolong their misery for another bleak hour on the motorway. He hoped that her flight would be on time. A long, painful wait together would be intolerable. But not as intolerable as an immediate parting and suddenly he wished the flight would be delayed indefinitely.

But it wasn't delayed; it was on time and the departure board instructed passengers for Nice to proceed to passport control. They were both tearful as they hugged each other. Cal said he would be home soon and he would visit her in Berlin as soon as he'd settled in. Hélène reminded him to take Bruno to the vet if his sores didn't improve. And yes, she loved him and he loved her, and when the film was finished they would have a holiday together. Yes. Yes. That would be wonderful – just the two of them together again.

With a final hug and a kiss on the cheek, she left him. She waved as she passed through passport control, then again as she took her bag off the security scan. And then she was gone. Cal looked up at the departure board and the Nice flight was flashing: BOARDING BOARDING BOARDING . . .

Cal took the bottle of whisky out of the drawer, poured himself a drink, then sat on the bed. It was time to make plans. No moping. Think positive. But he couldn't stop thinking about Hélène when she left him at the airport. He could see her walking away with her soft leather travel bag over her shoulder. He touched the spot on the bed where he had placed it the previous day. She was walking fast. (Glad to see the back of him, no doubt!) But the plane was boarding, for Christ's sake! Everybody walks fast when the plane is boarding. But she didn't even wave. Yes she did: twice! Yes, but not at the last corner where he was willing her to turn round. And while he was driving back along the motorway she was flying to Nice and looking forward to Berlin and seeing Roland again. He looked at his watch. She would be almost there now. He could see her looking down across the city as the plane banked over the sea, then walking out through the airport into the glare and the heat . . . While he was still here in this crappy hotel. In this crappy town. Writing a crappy script . . .

He poured himself another drink. Think positive. Calm down. He was angry with himself. He shouldn't have brought up that business about Roland again, not then, as they were leaving the hotel. She was hurt by his accusation. Her lips quivered. She cried when she got in the car. He felt rotten. He apologized. Of course I believe you, he said . . . But she was an award-winning actress, for fuck's sake! And he didn't believe her now, now that she had gone. What a time she was going to have with that slime-ball, bastard frog! And what about him? What had he to look forward to when he got back? An empty house and a mangy fucking dog!

He paced around the room muttering and fuming, consumed by self-pity. He felt rejected: cast off. He decided to telephone the airport and book a flight to Nice. He could leave today, tomorrow at the latest. A quick visit to his parents pleading urgent business and he could be in France tomorrow at this time. He might even catch Hélène before she left for Berlin. The surprise on her face when he walked in! He would tell her how much he loved her, and they would make love and make up and everything would be all right between them again. Yes. Yes. That's what he would do. He picked up the telephone, then paused as he read the screen of his word processor: INT. TOBY'S HOUSE . . .

No, that wasn't the answer; rushing back to France in a panic wouldn't solve anything. He had to hang on and finish *It's a Dog's Life* here. He wanted it behind him before he returned home to start his new novel. He sat on the bed and imagined it. He could see himself sitting at his desk waiting for the first sentence to form . . . But he could not sustain the picture and his thoughts drifted back to Hélène . . . Perhaps it was better that they had parted here on neutral ground, rather than at home with their own things around them. Anyway, he would be going to see her in Berlin in a few weeks' time. Then, when she returned . . . It didn't work. He began to cry, and neither Christine, or the receptionist, or the barmaid, or anyone else in high heels and stockings could have consoled him just then.

Except for daily visits to his parents' house, Cal stayed in the hotel and worked on the script. It was painful, but he forced himself to stick at it. He even booked a flight home to give himself a deadline to work to.

He was reaching the end now, and TOBY's plight was becoming so perilous that occasionally he even became involved in the story and forgot about Hélène for a while.

INT. CITY DOG POUND. DAY.

The camera pans along the row of cages containing the stray dogs which are about to be put down by the vet. We see TOBY in one of the cages.

INT. VET'S SURGERY. CITY DOG POUND. DAY.

The VET is filling his syringe with the lethal solution. He squirts a jet into the air.

VET

(to assistant)

OK, Debbie. Bring the first one in.

DEBBIE leaves the room.

INT. CITY DOG POUND. DAY.

DEBBIE enters the dog pound, opens the first cage and puts the dog on a lead. It wags its tail, pleased to be released.

DEBBIE

(leading the dog away)

There's a good boy.

Cut to TOBY in the next cage, watching the dog being led into the vet's surgery . . .

Cal sat back and looked at his watch. One o'clock: it was later than he expected, which was always a good sign that things were going well. He decided to break for lunch, then visit his parents and continue work when he returned. He phoned reception, ordered sandwiches and coffee to be sent up to his room, then switched on the television for the lunchtime news.

A reporter and an official-looking man in a suit materialized in a pit yard, backed by the winding gear. But there was no sound, and even as Cal pressed the volume control, the reporter returned the viewers to the studio and the latest trade figures.

Something was bothering him. The next scene involved a police car containing DETECTIVES GOODING and CARDARELLI, TOBY'S PARENTS and PROFESSOR KNUTT, speeding dangerously across town with its siren blazing in a frantic effort to reach the dog pound before TOBY is put down. But if PROFESSOR KNUTT hadn't recognized TOBY when he had visited the dog pound earlier, how did he know he was there now? And surely the police would have phoned the dog pound to suspend all killings until they arrived? But the mercy dash across town, with its near misses and screeching round corners, was essential to the approaching climax . . . Cal stopped at a traffic light and he was so engrossed in working out the plot that the car behind had to pip him when the lights changed.

Perhaps he could rewrite the scene where PROFESSOR KNUTT visits the dog pound, only this time TOBY isn't there. OK. But where is he then? And perhaps the line is engaged when they telephone the dog pound and they can't afford to wait? . . . But Cal forgot all about TOBY's problems when he saw the ambulance and the crowd outside his parents' house. He parked the car and people stopped talking and stared at him as he got out. As he hurried down the path, he noticed the cat, coolly washing itself in the front window.

The living-room was crowded. A doctor and two ambulancemen were conferring quietly in the middle of the room, his father was in bed and his mother was sitting in the armchair by the fire, staring into the aquarium.

What's happened?

Without waiting for an answer, he crossed the room to the bed by the wall. He could tell immediately that his father was dead. His muscles had relaxed, restoring his face to normal. He looked calm now, a quality which Cal had never associated with his father. Even when he came home from work exhausted and fell asleep by the fire, he rarely relaxed. He was always twitching and muttering, fighting some cause or another.

Cal felt his eyes start to prickle as he touched his father's cheek.

I'm sorry, Dad.

The doctor and ambulancemen had stopped talking

when Cal entered the room, and they remained silent while he stood over his father and paid his respects. He dabbed his eyes then turned round.

The doctor touched his arm. I'm terribly sorry, Mr Rickards. He had a heart attack. He was dead when I arrived. He appeared to be well on his way to recovery, too.

Cal walked across to his mother and sat on the chair arm.

She turned away from the aquarium and took his hand.

It was that report on the television that caused it.

What do you mean?

About the privatization of the coal industry. It's the last day of nationalization today. He got upset and started shouting. I couldn't calm him down. She looked across the room towards the bed. Everything that he believed in and fought for had been destroyed.

The cat, sensing her distress, jumped down from the window-sill and up on to her knee; and only then, as she stroked it and hugged it to her, did she begin to cry.

They assembled in the rec. to pay their respects: hundreds of them, ex-miners from Foxmoor colliery where Harry Rickards had championed their cause as union branch secretary for twenty-six years. A cheer went up as the colliery banner was raised, cracking like a sail in the wind, and accompanied by a thump on the big drum by Charlie Thomas, who never thought he would wear his band uniform again.

The men lined up on the football pitch behind the band and the banner, and when the cortège drove slowly by, the band struck up and followed it. The procession was so long that the hearse had reached the primary school at the end of the main street before the last of the marchers passed through the rec. gates.

Cal was in the first car with his mother and Joe. When he saw Charlie twirling his drum sticks and

Tommy holding one end of the banner – UNITY IS STRENGTH – he started to cry. Maisie, who had been trying to control herself all morning, broke down too, while Joe, who had ignored Cal since his arrival from Manchester, finally relented and exchanged glances of filial pride.

The whole village had turned out for the funeral, as it had when the miners marched back to work after the strike. But this time there was no cheering or defiant applause from the onlookers lining the pavements, just tears and respectful silence for a man who had given his best on their behalf.

The procession left the village and continued along the main road in the direction of the church. As they passed the ruins of Foxmoor colliery, with its rusting headgear and derelict buildings, the band stopped playing in silent protest; except for Charlie, who kept the column in step with a regular beat on his bass drum. Then, with the mine and their memories behind them, the brass players licked their lips and blasted off with 'The Thin Red Line', followed by other rousing favourites.

They turned down the country lane where Cal had driven his mother on the day she had shown him the site of Bernardo's camp. The unfamiliar noise of the band flushed birds from the hedgerows, startled a horse into a gallop and set off a farm dog howling across the fields. They marched past the Old Rectory and up the rise to the church, where the bandsmen left their instruments and peaked caps in the porch, then respectfully filed inside with the other mourners.

Cal waited outside with his mother and Joe and other close relatives, while the bearers slid the coffin out of the hearse and carried it into the churchyard. Charlie and Tommy were shouldering the front of the coffin with two more of Harry's pit mates supporting the back. They stopped at the porch doorway, then, with Cal and Joe flanking their mother, the vicar led the procession into the church. When Cal saw the size of the congregation gathered inside, he had never felt so proud in all his life. The people standing at the back parted silently to form a gangway, and those crowding the aisles had to squeeze back into the pews to let them through. The Rickards family occupied the front two pews, with Maisie insisting on the aisle seat next to the coffin.

While the vicar was reading the opening prayer, Cal glanced round and noticed Christine sitting a few rows back. She smiled. Perhaps she had been staring at the back of his head, willing him to turn round. He imagined being squashed into the pew next to her with his leg pressed against hers. Perhaps she would tease him by crossing her legs and making her tights swish . . . He glanced down at his crotch, then buttoned up his jacket to hide his erection. He couldn't get used to himself in a dark suit. It was like looking down at a stranger. He didn't like to think about the next time he might be wearing it.

He joined in with the opening verses of Psalm 23, The Lord is My Shepherd, but he soon lost interest and his attention drifted away from the prayer book to the coffin. He couldn't understand why his mother had arranged a Christian burial when his father had been a lifelong Communist. It didn't make sense. I wouldn't be seen dead in church, he used to say. Perhaps he hadn't got round to issuing funeral instructions before he died. Or if he had, perhaps his mother's religious upbringing had prevailed and she had ignored them.

At the end of the psalm, the mourners sat down and the vicar delivered a brief eulogy on Harry Rickards' life. He stressed his loyalty to his family and friends and the community, but he said nothing about his political or trade union work. He could have been talking about anybody. It was a bland, conventional summary spoken without passion or insight, and most of the people listening – including his family – could have given a much more enlightened version.

Jerry Morris could have stood up and told them about the time Harry had won his compensation case for him when he had crushed his hand and the management had claimed that it was his own fault due to negligence. Terry Morgan could have told them about Harry's skill in negotiating contract prices on the amount of coal cut, and how assured he was when presenting cases at medical tribunals. Many of the men present could have told similar stories, and Cal was wondering if he should have prepared an appreciation, when his mother stood up. At first he thought she must be feeling faint and needed to go outside. But when she stopped by the coffin and turned to face the congregation, he realized that she intended to speak. The vicar looked surprised when she appeared beside him, but when she asked him if it would be all right to say a few words, he smiled and nodded his assent. Maisie placed her hand on the coffin lid and composed herself for a few moments before she spoke.

I didn't plan to say anything, but as this will probably be the last time Harry's family and so many of his friends and colleagues will be together like this, I thought I'd like to thank you all for coming and showing how much you thought about him. I appreciate it and I'm sure Harry would have done too . . . She looked down at the coffin and patted the polished lid. And while I'm on my feet, perhaps I could say a bit about Harry's life just to add to what the vicar's already said about him . . . She glanced across at the vicar who smiled in response. I know a lot of you didn't agree with Harry's politics, especially over Russia, but in spite of all the terrible things that happened there, especially under Stalin, it was the example of the Russian revolution that mattered most to Harry, and that's what kept him going. It was a kind of dawn of hope and the promise of a better world. And just because the revolution was betrayed, you don't condemn the ideal, you condemn the people who betrayed it. Just look at the terrible things that have happened in the name of religion. I'm sure the vicar would have left the Church long ago if he thought they were anything to do with the teachings of the Christ that *he* believes in . . . She turned to the vicar a second time and he nodded sagely in agreement. All Harry ever wanted when you get down to it was a just society, and that's not too much to ask for, I'm sure you'll agree. And the battle's not over, not by a long chalk, in spite of what the government and the papers say. We might have lost the strike, although Harry never admitted that. He said that the greatest victory was in the struggle itself. But whether we lost it or not, what we did achieve was to show what you can do when people work together, and the pride that you feel when you're fighting for a cause. And what's happened since, with all the unemployment and that, has started to make people realize that perhaps selfishness and greed are not the answer. Anyway, I'll finish now. I don't want to give a sermon or the vicar will think I'm after his job.

The laughter was so loud that it sounded like the Working Men's Club.

Thank you all again for coming; you've done Harry proud and I can assure you that the family will never forget it.

As Cal stared down at his unfamiliar shoes during the Lord's Prayer, the story line of *It's a Dog's Life*, which had been nagging away at him for days, suddenly resolved itself . . . PROFESSOR KNUTT identifies the *wrong* dog at the stray dog pound, which then fails to change back into TOBY, the boy. By the time PROFESSOR KNUTT realizes his mistake, and tries to phone the dog pound to suspend the killing of any more stray dogs, a violent electric storm brings down the power lines and he can't get through. This leads to a climactic dash across town with torrential rain and lightning striking buildings and trees which narrowly miss the car, etc . . . Brilliant! The rest of the script wrote itself.

Cal came back to the service as the vicar was reading the Committal, then suddenly it was all over and the coffin was being lifted off the stand. Cal briefly caught Christine's eye as he escorted his mother back up the aisle, then they were outside again, blinking in the brilliant, unreal sunlight.

As they stood by the open grave and the vicar intoned the last rites, Cal looked across the graveyard and realized why this place held such significance for his mother. This was where her parents were buried, over there, by the beech tree. And this was where she used to meet Bernardo, over there, by the lychgate, where he would be sitting on the wall, waiting for her to come cycling up the hill. And sometimes they would have sat together on the bench outside the church, where she had sat with him, fifty years later, when she had told him about her first son, Gerald. And now her husband was being buried here, and in time she would lie beside him. And somehow, who knows, perhaps Geraldo would learn about his mother and come to find her and stand before her grave. Then, as the coffin was lowered into the earth, and his mother stopped being brave and cried openly, Cal hoped that perhaps one day his own daughter Becky would learn about her father and come and find him, and the two of them would stand together at her grandparents' grave.

Cal visited his mother for the last time before driving to the airport. She was sprinkling fishfood into the aquarium and playfully chiding the cat as it sat on the back of the armchair gnashing its teeth at the fish. The bed had been removed from the room and the furniture rearranged. Cal noticed that the 'Evils of Capitalism' statuette was back in its original position on the sideboard.

Are you sure you'll be all right on your own? I can stay a bit longer if you like.

No. You must be wanting to get back now. You've no need to worry. The neighbours keep popping in and our Joe'll come over regularly to see me.

Cal watched the fish darting around, gulping the sinking particles of food.

Can you remember when I arrived, and my dad asked me when I was going to write something that mattered?

Maisie laughed. You weren't very pleased, were you?

Pleased! He was about to add, *I could have killed him*, but managed to restrain himself in time.

Well, I think I might be able to now.

I hope you do. There's nothing he would have liked better.

Maisie sat down in the armchair and the cat jumped down from the back on to her knee. Cal scratched it between the ears and made it purr.

Have you got a name for her yet?

Yes . . . *Rosa*.

That's nice. After Rosa Luxemburg, I suppose? My dad would have approved of that.

Maisie smiled, then turned away and gazed into the fire . . . *Soffice* . . . Soft. *Soffice come una rosa*. Cal glanced at his watch. It was time to leave. He was looking forward to going home now. The first leaves would be falling from the plane trees in the village square where the men played boules, and bales of straw would be lying in the golden fields of stubble. He was looking forward to seeing Bruno again and taking him for long walks up the mountain. But most of all, he was looking forward to settling down to his new novel. He already had the opening sentences in his head:

> The houses had been demolished. A peeling hoarding advertised FACTORY UNITS TO LET, but Karl remembered the people who used to live there.